'It was surely another tragic accident; the man had taken a mistaken step in the swirling mist that had shrouded the path.'

ISBN: 978-0-9956589-3-6

First Print Edition 2017

Published by fionamacbain.com

Cover design, illustration & interior formatting:
Mark Thomas / Coverness.com

Glasdrum

One town. Five women. Dark events.

FIONA MacBAIN

Thanks for reading!

Fiona MacBain

Aug 2017

fionamacbain.com

~

For my sons, Robert and Andrew.

~

Prologue

Extract from the Glasdrum Journal, *Thursday, 5 May 2005*

The body of missing hill walker Mr Kenny MacIver, 46, from Glasgow, was found at the bottom of Crofter's Gully at 11pm on Tuesday. The Mountain Rescue Service had been alerted earlier that day when he failed to return to his holiday accommodation. Mrs Margaret Cameron, owner of Loch View Guest House, confirmed Mr MacIver had been staying since the weekend. 'He was a considerate guest. He always left his muddy boots outside,' she said.

Mr MacIver's daughter has been contacted and is being comforted by friends.

Mr Robertson of Glasdrum Mountain Rescue said the team had been saddened and surprised to find Mr MacIver, an experienced mountaineer, at the bottom of the steep-sided gully that ran alongside part of the main path up Ben Calder. 'I'd like to remind those planning to walk in the hills, no matter how competent, to heed weather warnings and leave details of their walk with a responsible person or with the local police. We have seen a recent increase in avoidable deaths.'

Against an average of one death per year on Ben Calder, Mr MacIver was the third fatal accident in eight months. Local people have begun to talk about a 'Mist Murderer'.

Reporter: Catriona MacKinnon

Chapter One
MEGAN

Friday, 6 May 2005, 10.30pm

Megan was drinking beer in the kitchen with a few friends when her collie, Glen, ran through the open back door with a muddy stick in his mouth. When he dropped it at her feet, she stared in disgust. It wasn't a stick; it was a bone, with dried-out flesh faintly discernible beneath the dirt that clung to it.

Revolted, she steeled herself to lift it, grimacing at its cold dampness. She went to the door to hurl it back outside but paused, puzzled. It was a pretty big bone.

With a mix of curiosity and dread, Megan followed the dog across the overgrown garden to the hole where the septic tank had been removed earlier that day. In the meagre light from the kitchen window, she spotted more bones in the dark pit. It looked like a skeleton.

Pushing her dog out of the way when he tried to pull the bone from her, Megan leant into the hole and prodded the earth with it. A glint of gold caught her eye and she bent to pick up the object. It was a man's ring... a familiar ring. Her heart started to thump.

The shock of who this might be and how his remains had come to be there was immense. She must be mistaken. She'd have to take a closer look.

First, her visitors would have to be sent home.

She hurried back into the house. 'I'm sorry,' she said to her small gathering of friends. 'I'm knackered and the boys will be up early. I better get to bed.'

The handful of folk from the Glasdrum Hill Runners Club made a few token grumbles but were mainly relieved. They were people who rose at five in the morning to run up mountains and they'd already had a few drinks at the Taj Mahal on the High Street, celebrating their success in the cross-country district championships. They were out the door in no time.

Megan stared out of the kitchen window towards the back garden. Jim must have unearthed the bones when he'd removed the old tank earlier that day, no doubt too pissed to notice he'd dug up a dead body.

Megan's friend, Vicky, who had been babysitting Megan's three boys while she had been out with the hill runners, came up behind her. 'Are you wondering what Glen found out there?'

'Did you see the bone he had?' Megan asked.

Vicky nodded. 'Deer?'

'I don't think so.'

'What, then?' asked Vicky, putting a hand on Megan's shoulder, giving her a fleeting sense of comfort. Megan sensed Vicky felt protective toward her; people often did. Her diminutive frame and cropped hair made her seem like her sons' older sister rather than their mother. Perhaps it was because Vicky knew how hard it was to raise kids on your own; her own daughter, Louise, was asleep upstairs. Or maybe she sensed Megan's anxiety. When Megan had returned ashen-faced and asked people to leave because she was tired, Vicky had raised her eyebrows in surprise.

'I'm going to take another look,' said Megan.

'Want me to come with you?'

Megan nodded in gratitude. It was stupid to involve Vicky but she couldn't face it on her own. She put on her rain jacket and handed a spare that hung by the back door to Vicky. 'Better put that on. It's still pissing down out there.'

It was close to eleven, and despite low clouds the sky held a faint glow as they picked their way across the sodden garden, hemmed in by trees that hung heavy and damp. Beyond the decrepit fence, a mini digger stood guard over the earthy pit. The new tank, still enveloped in heavy-duty polythene, stood beside it. The upheaval had meant the toilet had been out of use since the old tank had been removed earlier that day, but the boys had found peeing in the garden a hoot and Megan's runner friends were well used to crouching behind bushes halfway up hills.

Vicky grabbed Megan's arm as they approached the grave-like opening. 'I've never seen you looking so scared. What are you expecting to find?'

'It might be better if you don't get involved. I think it's… it's…' Megan tailed off, not able to put into words what she was dreading.

She noticed Vicky hesitate and didn't blame her. Vicky had witnessed the chaos of Megan's life many times. 'You should go back inside. Leave this to me,' Megan said to her.

But Vicky took her hand. 'It's okay, I'll stay.'

Megan felt relieved. Vicky could be trusted with a secret; she reckoned Vicky had a few of her own.

'I should've brought a torch,' said Megan as they peered over the edge. 'Can you see anything down there?' Vicky was leaning over the hole, still holding Megan's hand, when Glen hurtled past their legs, chasing an imagined rabbit. Vicky's foot slipped, loose earth gave way and they both slid forwards. Frantically overcorrecting, they fell onto their backsides in the musty-smelling mud beside the sealed-off septic tank pipe.

'Oh my God,' cried Vicky, scrambling to her feet. Something cracked and she looked down to see a broken bone under her trainer. 'What's that?'

'I think it might be my dad,' said Megan.

Chapter Two
SARAH

Friday, 6 May 2005, 10.30pm

On the road that stretched between the shadowy mountains, the car slammed into the deer at sixty miles an hour. Sarah's body was gripped by the seat belt but her head was jerked forward by the impact. Her skull crashed against the door frame as the car spun sideways then juddered to an abrupt halt in a ditch. She felt dazed, shaken and sore.

'Fuck sake, man, not another one.' Gregor banged his hand on the steering wheel before climbing out of the car. Wind howled through the vehicle as Lewis followed him, and they both made their way onto the road to survey what was left of the beautiful creature.

Sarah's head hurt and her hand shook as she unclipped her belt, pushed her door open and stepped out. The cold, damp air hit her face as her foot plunged into slippery mud which closed around her ankle, causing her to stumble and fall to her knees. Lewis appeared and helped her to her feet.

'Are you all right?' he asked and she nodded as they made their way around the car. Gregor was staring at the animal that lay across the white line in the middle of the road. Its back legs jerked but the beast was in trouble. Sarah caught a glimpse of brown Bambi eyes as it tried to lift its head.

'I'm gonna have tae deal with it,' said Gregor as he returned to the car and lifted the boot. Sarah's thoughts of phoning a vet were interrupted when he reappeared with a rifle. She stifled a scream as Gregor lifted the gun to his shoulder and fired a shot straight through the animal's head. A pool of blood appeared on the road, dissipating in the misty rain. Gregor returned the gun to the car then spoke to Lewis. 'Gie us a hand, like,' he muttered, prompting Lewis to take hold of one of the deer's rear legs and help his friend drag the animal onto the verge. Gregor then crossed the road to survey his car in silence. Sarah jumped out of her skin when he kicked the car and screamed, 'Fuck sake, man, will ya look at the state of ma motor!'

Lewis sensed Sarah's alarm and put his arm round her shoulders as they watched Gregor kick and rant at his car. 'He has moments like this.' Lewis looked apologetically at Sarah. 'He'll calm down in a bit.'

Sarah shivered and leant against Lewis, trying to shield her face from the weather. It was May but the night air was fresh and the chill from the mud soaking her lower legs had seeped upwards until her whole body felt cold. She wished she was back in her flat in London, but she had returned the keys that morning before carting two large suitcases to Euston station and setting off on an adventure to Scotland to start a new life with Lewis; rough-around-the-edges Lewis, who had bowled her over with his intense stare and Scottish accent. It had happened at a fortuitous time; she had just turned thirty, she hated her job, and several of her girlfriends had become mothers and disappeared into their houses, never to be seen again. Sarah had taken Lewis to meet her family and noticed that her stepmother,

Cecilia, had taken an instant dislike to Lewis's forthright and sometimes coarse manner of speaking. It had given Sarah great delight to announce she was leaving with Lewis to start a new life in Scotland.

'Oh, darling, really? Must you?' Cecilia had asked. 'I've enjoyed spending time with you now that Robbie's away at uni.'

That's one of the reasons I want to go, Sarah had thought. Cecilia had been visiting her more often since her half-brother Robbie had left home the previous year. *Too bloody late. You can't make up for ignoring me and wishing I wasn't there when he was a baby.*

Sarah's father had wished her well but, as usual, seemed only vaguely interested in her plans.

However, this was not the start she had envisaged for her new life.

'You'll have to take the wheel, Sarah. We'll try to push the car back onto the road,' said Lewis, after an earnest discussion with Gregor.

With misgivings, she climbed into the car and tried to follow their shouted instructions: *Accelerate! No, not that hard! Take it easy for God's sake. The tyre's spinning, stop, STOP!* Sarah found it stressful. She had driven occasionally since passing her test ten years previously but, having lived in London all her life, had found little need for a car. Her confidence was low driving on a road, never mind out of a ditch. To her relief, with a last push from the boys, the car leapt forward onto the tarmac. Sarah retreated to the back seat of the ancient Fiesta to let the two men in. Relief and misery, in equal measure, enveloped her as they set off again, the dead animal abandoned by the roadside, the two men straight back to their intense and incessant conversation.

'I'll get a good blether with Gregor on the way up the road,' Lewis had said as the train had arrived in Fort William. Sure enough, they had not stopped talking since they'd got into Gregor's car, and Sarah had barely understood a word. They might have been speaking a different language for all she could comprehend. Perhaps it was Gaelic. She had spotted several road signs with long, unpronounceable words written above the English. It was like entering a foreign country. She had become used to Lewis's Scottish accent but the speed of his speech had increased tenfold since crossing the border.

The babble from the front of the car had almost lulled Sarah to sleep before the accident, but now she felt alert and on edge as the road twisted between mountains that disappeared into the mist and around rocky outcrops, eventually reaching the sea, a black expanse beneath the gloomy sky. It was almost eleven by then but the darkness was incomplete despite the low clouds. After the day's surreal and nightmarish events, Sarah's sense of being transported into another world was complete.

As they sped along the coastal road Sarah stared out at the water, dotted with distant hulks she guessed must be islands. They had left London at seven that morning, changing trains in Glasgow, and she felt a long way from home. How much longer was this journey going to take? Why did Gregor have a gun in the boot of his car? He was apparently a school friend of Lewis, but Sarah knew little more than that. None of her school friends owned guns. She also wanted to know more about Lewis's sister and her kids, who they were going to be staying with, something Sarah had only found out about that morning.

'You know I said my mum was staying in the old folks' home for a bit? I forgot to mention that Megan is staying at her house while she's not there.'

'It'll be nice to meet her.'

He had paused for a moment. 'Her three boys will be there too, unfortunately.'

'Oh well, I suppose they'll be glad to see us so they can get back to their own house.'

Lewis sighed. 'Yeah, let's hope so.'

A short while later, before reaching the town, they turned off the main road and bumped along a stretch of potholed single track before stopping outside a large house with peeling, once-white paint, crowded by tall trees. Gregor and Lewis jumped out and pulled Sarah's two heavy suitcases from the boot. 'See ya,' shouted Gregor before he drove off.

Lewis stared at the building for a while. 'This place has gone downhill a bit since I was last here.'

'Five years?' said Sarah.

'Yeah, I cannae believe it.' He glanced at her. 'I hope you're going to find it okay here. It's a bit different to London, like.'

'I was sick of London. We both needed a change.'

'Yeah, I guess. That shift work in the factory was doing my head in.'

'And you wanted to come home,' Sarah reminded him.

'Aye, so I did.'

Lewis picked up one of Sarah's cases and opened one side of the ancient red door before disappearing inside. Sarah heaved the other suitcase over the threadbare gravel towards the door but struggled to get herself and the case through the narrow opening. She battled with it for a few moments, but wasn't strong enough to turn the suitcase and pull it through the door behind her, so she left it wedged in the doorway and followed Lewis, her heart fluttering in anticipation. She crossed a large, unlit hall and stumbled down an unexpected step in the middle of it, twisting her ankle. Suppressing a yelp of pain, she walked toward the room with the light on. Inside the kitchen, Lewis was embracing a young boy, while a woman with dark blonde hair watched them. The three of them looked at her.

'Come and meet my sister,' said Lewis and Sarah smiled at the blonde woman, wondering what she should do. Shake her hand? Hug her? Just keep smiling? But Lewis laughed and put his hand on the blonde woman's shoulder. 'Nah, this is Vicky. She's Megan's pal.' He playfully punched the young boy who, on closer inspection, was, indeed, female, and not as young as she had at first seemed. 'This is my sister. Who managed to forget we were coming today.'

Megan punched him back, harder. 'I didn't forget. You told me you were coming tomorrow.'

'Aye well, we're here now,' said Lewis. 'You gonna make us a cup of tea or something?'

'You know where the kettle is, don't you?' Megan looked over at Sarah apologetically. 'Come in, take a seat. Sorry about the mess.' Megan indicated the floor, which Sarah noticed was covered in mud, not just from the collie that was padding about with earth all over its underside, but from Megan's and Vicky's shoes, too. Sarah pulled a chair out but saw that it, too, was covered in mud.

'Sorry, that was me,' said Megan. She turned around and

showed Sarah her soaked backside. 'Vicky and I went out to...
em... check something in the garden, and we both fell over. It's
a quagmire out there. New septic tank getting put in.'

'A new tank?' asked Lewis. 'Why?'

'Why do you think, you big eejit? The old one was falling
apart. Leaking all over the place.'

'So, who's doing the work?'

Megan ignored him. 'Take a seat, Sarah. Do you want some
tea?'

'Yeah, thanks,' said Sarah, looking at the other chairs to see if
there was a clean one. A deep fatigue came over her, her ankle
throbbed from her stumble in the hall and her head pounded
from the bang in the car. All she wanted to do was sit down. But
first, 'Can I use your loo? It's been a long journey.'

'Sure,' said Lewis. 'It's on the first floor, on the right.'

'Actually, you can't,' said Megan as Sarah set off out of the
kitchen. 'It's out of action just now. The septic tank, you see.
We're waiting for them to install the new one. Sorry.'

'So, there's no toilet?'

'Nope. We've just been peeing in the bushes at the side of
the garden. And if it's, you know... well, there's these.' Megan
pointed to a packet of black dog poo bags on the counter.

'But it's raining,' said Sarah in a quiet, exhausted voice.
Megan went to the hall to get a brolly for Sarah.

'So, em, I just go out the back, in the garden?'

'Yeah, but... well... keep away from the septic tank or you'll
fall into the hole.' Megan pushed the packet of dog poo bags
along the counter. 'Do you need one of these?'

Sarah stared at the little black bags for a moment. She shook her head then went out the back door into the rain.

Chapter Three
VICKY

Friday, 6 May 2005, 11.30pm

'Megan, you could have warned me,' said Lewis, once the door had closed. 'No toilet? She'll think we're a bunch of savages. I should've known it was a bad idea coming back here.'

'You said you were coming *tomorrow*, and the tank is getting installed *tomorrow.*'

'Is it Jim that's putting it in? Looks like his digger out there. I'll give him a hand in the morning,' said Lewis.

'No need,' replied Megan. Vicky could hear the panic in her voice. 'I mean, yes, Jim's doing it, but he's got it all in hand. I think you're going to have your work cut out looking after Sarah tomorrow. She's doesn't seem very happy. Mind you, Glasdrum'd be a shock for anyone.'

Lewis sighed. 'I better go and sort out where we're going to sleep. Don't tell me none of the three rooms are free.' He glanced at Vicky.

'I was watching the boys for Megan earlier this evening when she was out,' said Vicky, 'so Louise and I are staying over. She's already asleep.'

Lewis looked at his sister. 'What about the two attic rooms?'

Megan shook her head. 'No state to sleep in; cobwebs everywhere. Mum hasn't used them for years. I doubt Sarah would want to sleep up there.'

'So where are me and Sarah supposed to sleep?'

'Can't you stay with Gregor?'

'He's living at his gran's just now. His mum kicked him out.'

Vicky felt sorry for Lewis, just home after five years away and being told there was nowhere for him to sleep. Vicky had always had a soft spot for Lewis; quiet and gruff but she'd always sensed he had a decent heart. 'I could wake Louise and take her home, then you could have the room I'm in,' she offered.

'Don't be daft,' said Megan with a sigh. 'It's far too late for you to wake Louise. Me and Rory will squash into the big bed in the middle room with the other two boys, and Lewis and Sarah can have the big bedroom.'

'Cheers, Sis,' said Lewis, opening the back door. 'I'm away out for a pee myself.' Megan and Vicky exchanged a look.

'Don't go down where the tank is,' Megan repeated, pointing at the mud on the floor. 'You'll bring even more of this into the house.'

'I'll take a look at it in the morning. You know what Jim's like; probably pissed.'

'Look,' said Megan. 'Jim's sorted himself out. He'll do a decent job. You can't come back here and start throwing your weight about, Lewis.'

'All right! Just trying to help.' They stared at one another for a moment before Lewis went outside, slamming the door behind him.

Megan turned to Vicky with a look of despair on her face. 'Lewis will be so upset. Do you remember what he was like when Dad went missing? It was awful. I don't know how he'll

cope if he has to face that Dad is buried in the back garden.'
Megan gulped back a sob. 'I can't believe this is happening! I
need time to think. Don't say anything to him about—'

A whoosh of air as the door opened made Megan spin back
around. 'Don't say anything about what?' Sarah asked.

'Never mind,' Megan muttered. 'I'll go and move Rory so
you can have the big bedroom.'

'She'll be fine in the morning,' Vicky said to Sarah, who was
standing, forlorn, just inside the door. 'It's been a long day.'

'Yeah, for me too. I left London at seven this morning,' she
said, but Vicky had already followed Megan out of the room.

Upstairs, Megan carried her youngest, Rory, into the middle
room, tucked him into the king-size bed with his brothers, then
went back out to the hall where Vicky waited.

'I can't let Lewis see those bones,' said Megan.

'Why not? It might not be your dad! It could just be a similar
ring. Bodies take years to decompose and your dad's only been
missing for what… five years?'

'It's got his initials, DMD, Donald MacDonald, engraved on
it. And the bones aren't totally, you know, *clean*. Maybe Dad
never went anywhere that night he went missing.'

Vicky was quiet for a moment. 'You can't keep this a secret,
Megan. That's a dead person out there.'

Megan sat on the stairs leading to the attic, her hand
massaging her forehead. Vicky sat beside her and put her arm
round her shoulders. 'Sorry. I'm being insensitive. You must be
feeling awful.'

'I just feel numb. Dad was dead to me a long time ago.
He was a good-for-nothing, aggressive drunk. It's Lewis I'm

worried about. He was devastated when Dad disappeared. You'll remember the state he got himself into. He gave up his job, stayed in bed for months, started going on long, pointless trips around the Highlands on his motorbike looking for him. Then just when we thought he was getting better, he upped and went off to London. It's good he's back; he might be able to get through to Mum, you know, bring her mind back to us.'

Megan rubbed her temple again, lost in thought, before carrying on. 'Mum went downhill after Dad disappeared, but it was when Lewis went off to London that she really lost her marbles. She kept getting agitated and saying it was her fault Lewis had left.' Megan looked up at Vicky. 'I can't face dredging it all back up again, not yet.'

'This might help,' said Vicky. 'Once everyone knows he's dead, they can move on.'

'But here's the other thing. I've been wondering how he ended up out there. You know... *buried*. He didn't fall into that hole by himself. And I got thinking about the times I heard him shouting at Mum when he'd been drinking. Mostly she ignored him but sometimes she stood up for herself and, well... she'd have a black eye to show for it. I remember thinking that if anyone treated me like that, I would kill them.' Megan stopped, deep in thought and Vicky didn't know what to say. Could it be true? Vicky knew better than most what people were capable of if pushed far enough.

'Did he ever hit you?' asked Vicky.

'Nah, just Mum. I hated him for the way he treated her, but he was okay with us, on the whole. He doted on Lewis. He was a man's man and I was only a girl, so he pretty much ignored me.

Vicky stared at Megan. Could it be possible that Megan's mother had killed her father and buried him at the end of the garden, then told everyone he'd gone off? It sounded implausible but if he'd been hurting her for years...

'I'm worried how Lewis will react if he thinks Mum had anything to do with Dad's death. Oh God, Vicky, imagine she was accused of murder! What's the point of putting her, and Lewis, through all that?'

Vicky had to agree. She had witnessed Murdina's deterioration over the last few years. The woman was a nervous wreck and had been placed in a care home on a temporary basis to undergo some therapy. 'She might be considered too ill to be called to court.'

'I can't risk it. I need time to see how strong Lewis is. Will you keep it to yourself? At least for now?'

Vicky nodded. 'Of course I will. It's your family. I would never meddle in your affairs.'

'Yeah, I trust you, Vicky. Always have done. I can tell you've a few skeletons yourself you're keeping quiet about.'

Vicky was taken aback that Megan might have guessed she had a secret but there was no time for questions as they heard voices coming upstairs: Sarah and Lewis arguing. Megan got to her feet and looked over the bannister. 'Keep it down, you two. The boys are sleeping.' She pointed towards the main bedroom at the end of the hall. 'You can have the big room.'

'Thanks, Sis,' said Lewis, punching Megan on the arm as he passed.

'You fucker, that hurt,' whispered Megan, kicking out at him. Lewis artfully side-stepped and Megan's foot landed on Sarah's shin. She yelped.

'Jesus, I'm so sorry. I meant to get him,' said Megan, glaring at Lewis.

'Sorry, Sarah, she's got no manners,' said Lewis with a grin.

Once Sarah and Lewis had closed the bedroom door, Megan spoke to Vicky in a low voice. 'I've truly blotted my copybook with the sister-in-law now. That'll give Lewis a good reason to comfort her into bed, the charming bastard. Hope they get to sleep soon so I can get back out to the garden.'

'What are you going out there for?'

'I'm going to move the bones.'

Vicky gasped. 'You can't be serious! Moving a dead body is probably a crime, even if it is your own father. I think we should go to the police.'

'No police! At least not yet. But I can't leave them where they are. Jim's going to start digging again tomorrow, and if Lewis sees them…' Megan tailed off and shook her head before continuing. 'Will you help me, please?'

Vicky blanched. 'I… I can't. It's a real dead body, Megan. I can't face it.'

'I just need you to listen at Sarah and Lewis's door in case they wake. Their bedroom faces the back garden.'

Vicky could see the determination on Megan's face. She was going to move those bones whether Vicky helped her or not. She remembered all the times Megan had supported her since she'd arrived in Glasdrum, how Megan accepted her without questioning her background. 'Okay, I'll help.'

They crept forward and listened at Sarah and Lewis's bedroom door. They heard arguing, then Lewis's voice for a while, then some low mumbling, then silence. Minutes ticked past and Vicky was about to give Megan a thumbs up when they heard a moan, then a gasp, then a grunt. Vicky put her hand over her ears. 'I'm going to wait in the bedroom with Louise,' she whispered and left Megan by the door.

She was dozing when Megan shook her awake. 'They're asleep at last,' whispered Megan. 'Are you still willing to listen out for me? I'm scared shitless they'll wake and see me.'

Megan thrust a walkie-talkie into her hands. 'Get me on this if you hear them waking. It's the boys' toy but it works fine.'

'You look like a ninja,' said Vicky, looking at Megan's skinny, boyish frame, head to toe in black, but with yellow marigolds on her hands. Megan did a brief ninja pose and mouthed a *hiii-ya*, causing them both to suppress nervous giggles. It wasn't until Megan had left, and Vicky was standing outside the bedroom door, that she wondered how long this was going to take.

Bloody ages. A heavy tiredness swept over her as she stood in the hall for over an hour, ear pressed to the door, wishing she had never agreed to help, and that she'd never gone out to the garden with Megan in the first place. She sat on the floor with her legs pulled in and laid her head on her knees. This reminded her of when Louise was a baby, bawling in her cot while Vicky waited outside her door for her to drop back to sleep.

As if on cue, 'Muuuum.' A wail from the small bedroom. Vicky scrambled to her feet and darted into the room to get to Louise before she woke everyone.

'Ssshhh. I'm here. Go back to sleep.'

'Bad dream,' mumbled Louise. 'Stay with me.'

Normally Vicky would have got into bed with her and

wrapped herself around Louise, breathing in her scent, glad of a few snatched moments of closeness, something she rarely got when Louise was awake; she liked to keep her mother at arm's length these days. As Vicky sat beside Louise, stroking her hair and wondering if she'd gone back to sleep, she heard the faint noise of a door being opened. She swore under her breath, pelted out of the room, then collided in the hall with Sarah. A shriek escaped Sarah's lips and Vicky dropped the walkie-talkie in fright. They both looked at it.

'What's going on?' asked Sarah.

Vicky picked it up. 'Uh, well, it was making this static noise.' Vicky pressed the talk button on to demonstrate the sound it made, hoping Megan would be listening. 'I didn't want to wake Louise, so… well… I was just putting it somewhere else.'

'Right,' said Sarah, walking towards the stairs.

'Where are you going?'

'Outside for a pee. I've been trying to hold it in for ages but I have to go.'

'I'm sure as a one-off you can pee in the toilet. Just don't try to flush it.' Vicky held the talk button down on the walkie-talkie. *Please be listening, Megan.*

As if on cue, Megan came bounding up the stairs like the hill-runner she was, a skinny, dark silhouette, making Sarah jump again.

'It's chilly out there, all right,' she whispered. 'You got a bad bladder, too, Sarah? Mine's never been the same since I had Rory.' Sarah frowned and looked at the walkie-talkie in Megan's hand.

'Found this in the garden. Bloody kids must have left it

outside.'

'Aha,' said Vicky. 'That'll be why this one was crackling.'

Sarah gave them an odd look before scurrying past to the bathroom. Megan gave Vicky a thumbs up, although she looked hollow-eyed and exhausted. 'Thanks,' she whispered. 'Guess we better get some kip now.'

Vicky wanted to ask Megan what she had done with the bones but was terrified Lewis would overhear. The seriousness of the situation was daunting; it reminded Vicky of the past and she didn't like that feeling at all. She'd speak to Megan again in the morning. Or perhaps she wouldn't ask at all. Some things in life were best kept secret, and Vicky knew that better than most.

Chapter Four
SARAH

Saturday, 7 May 2005, 10am

When Sarah woke, she was alone in the bed. She was shocked at the time: ten o'clock. She never slept in.

There was shouting in the hall and she sat up, alarmed. More yelling; children's voices, and many of them. It sounded as though an entire primary school was rampaging through the house.

There was a crash against her bedroom door. Then an ear-piercing shriek and the door burst open. Two little boys fell into the room and another two charged in behind them, plastic lightsabres in their hands. The youngest wore a faded Spiderman outfit. Megan's collie dashed in behind them, wagging his tail, and they stared at Sarah as she pulled the duvet up to her neck and looked back at them, unsure what to say. Two slightly older girls appeared in the doorway but didn't cross the threshold.

'Who are you?' asked one of the boys.

'Sarah,' she said. The boys looked at one another and giggled.

'Have you got any clothes on?' asked the oldest of the boys, provoking a cacophony of chortles from the other three. The two girls in the doorway also turned to one another and grinned.

Sarah felt paralysed. She didn't know what to do. Laugh? Give them a row? Talking to children was daunting. How did you deal with their random cheekiness and shyness? She hated the feeling of stupidity that overcame her when faced with friends' offspring, asking them how they liked school then being unsure what to do when they stared back blankly, as though they'd never heard of school, or else said, 'Nuh, I hate it.' Then what did she say?

She was saved from dealing with them by a voice bellowing from the hall. 'Kids, I told you to play outside!' With a last glance in Sarah's direction, the boys raced out of the room, roaring at the girls as they passed. The dark-haired girl smiled at Sarah. 'Sorry about them. They're really annoying,' she said, before pulling the door closed. Sarah felt a wave of gratitude. Those were the first kind words she had heard since she left London. Lewis had been quieter than usual on the train with her, then had talked incessantly with Gregor in the car, not forgetting the gun incident, and Lewis's sister, Megan, had been hostile. Or had she? Sarah doubted herself so much these days. She felt her social skills had been eroded by the pressure of her hated sales job and that was partly why a simpler life in a small town in Scotland had been so appealing. She'd been glad to leave London, its time-consuming busyness, its clamour of people, and her stepmother, Cecilia, far behind. So much so that she had thrown her lot in with Lewis after a whirlwind romance. She'd met him at a crowded bus stop during a tube strike and they'd hit it off so much they'd exchanged numbers and were dating within the week, although he was still an enigma, hesitant to say much about his earlier life with his family. Seeing him in his home setting had been unsettling; she hadn't known what to expect and it all seemed so *foreign* somehow. She hoped she hadn't made a terrible mistake.

On further reflection, Sarah was certain Megan and Vicky had been up to something the previous night. There had been an uncomfortable atmosphere. She hoped it was only because of her and Lewis's unexpected arrival and that everything would be fine this morning, but she couldn't shake the feeling of gloom that had taken hold of her. She tried to talk herself out of it: Megan would soon move back to her own house, taking her brood of children with her, and Sarah and Lewis would get on with their new life together, looking after his mother's house until she got out of the care home, then finding their own. Lewis had said she'd be able to get an admin job with the local Council or maybe at the newly opened outreach branch of the Highland College. 'Glasdrum's such a shithole, European money floods in to try to get everyone to stay. First they fund training, then they give out business start-up awards to provide jobs for the people they've trained, then transport and accommodation grants because the locals can't be arsed working and they have to ship a load of Poles in. You'll find a job no problem.'

There was a tap on the door before it opened and Vicky's head appeared. 'Sorry about the kids; they're a nightmare.' Sarah was relieved it wasn't Megan; Vicky seemed more approachable. 'How are you this morning?'

'I'm fine, thanks,' said Sarah automatically. 'I can't believe I've slept this long.'

'A new start is always a strange experience,' said Vicky, and Sarah felt the sting of tears in her eyes at Vicky's perceptiveness.

'It is a bit, I guess.'

'Come on down whenever you're ready. We're all in the

kitchen.'

'All?' Sarah felt a stab of panic.

'Me, Megan, Lewis and Finella. You'll like her.'

'And the kids? There seemed to be a lot of them.'

'Yeah, too many! Only one is mine, Louise. She's eleven. Then there's Finella's three, who I childmind. They're pretty lively, but not as bad as Megan's three boys. They're proper wild.'

'Mu-um!' shouted a voice from below.

'That's Louise, I better go. See you in a bit, Sarah.'

At the sound of children's footsteps thundering on the staircase, Sarah worried they would reappear and leapt out of bed, wincing as her sore ankle took her weight. In addition to twisting it on the unexpected step in the downstairs hall, she had stubbed her little toe on a heavy antique iron that sat in the corner of the stairs when she'd gone upstairs to bed. It was still purple and swollen and the side of her head, too, was tender from the bang in the car; she could feel a lump under her hair.

But there was no time to dwell on her injuries. She grabbed the previous day's clothes and stood with her back to the door, leaning against it to ensure no more little people could come bursting in as she struggled into her jeans. She didn't relish a return visit to the chilly bathroom with the un-flushable toilet but her bladder was bursting and she wasn't going to pee in the garden in the daylight with those little boys racing around. A glance out the window revealed a man working beside the new septic tank; hopefully the toilet would be operational again soon.

She laid her ear against the door to check the young voices had receded before opening it a crack. The hall was empty so she dashed across it, washbag in hand, and locked herself in the bathroom. The smell made her gag as she crouched over the toilet, noting in annoyance there was no toilet paper. She washed her hands, drying them on her jeans rather than the damp grubby towel that lay on the floor beneath the stone-cold towel rail, then brushed her teeth, tied her hair up and put some make-up on her sharp features.

She returned her bag to the bedroom then made her way downstairs, dread in her stomach when she heard the jovial sound of strangers *having a laugh*.

Chapter Five
FINELLA

Saturday, 7 May 2005, 9.30am

Even though it was Saturday, Finella was going to the office for a few hours. 'Such a pain, but it's so good to clear my desk before the hell of Monday morning,' she said, not that anyone was listening. Her husband and children bustled about as though she didn't exist.

But she enjoyed saying it; she felt important. It didn't matter that there would only be a couple of emails and some paperwork that could wait. There would be no children and that was all that mattered to Finella these days.

'Judith, Tom, James! Time to go!' she shouted, for the fifth time. She hoped that, despite the evidence of the past ten years, her children would stop whatever they were doing and troop obediently to the front door, shoes and jackets on, without her having to lose her temper and scream at them or issue threats which she, and they, knew she would never carry out. She wanted to, of course. Sometimes she wanted to carry out the harshest punishments imaginable. To take away their PlayStations and Bratz dolls as they had taken away her career, her freedom… her sanity, even. But that would only provoke a bout of moaning that made Finella want to throw herself off a cliff. Surely it was wrong to feel like this about your own offspring?

It wasn't that she didn't love them. When they were sleeping, she crept into their rooms and watched their angelic faces in quiet repose and sometimes felt moved to tears by their loveliness. And she worried about them. Oh, how she fretted. About their aversion to vegetables, about Judith's playground fall-outs and desire to wear a bra (she was ten!), and about the twins' love of video games and inherent violent streak.

She had done everything by the book; breastfeeding and slaving over home-made baby food, organic of course. Weaning the twins had been the worst experience of her life, trying to find the time to make the blasted stuff and keep an eye on a wandering three-year-old at the same time. Finella shuddered every time she remembered the horror of sleepless nights and stress-filled days of nappy changing and potty training, stuck in the house for days because the effort to get the three of them ready to leave had been too much for her. She had lived in hope that things would be better when the children went to school but the twins were almost finished with primary one and Finella still felt overwhelmed by homework and activities, dinner time battles and bedtime wars. Alex was little help. His dark moods only made things worse and exacerbated her desire to escape; work was the perfect solution.

Finella shouted at Judith and James to stop pushing each other while physically manhandling six-year-old Tom away from his box of Lego by grabbing the back of his T-shirt and dragging him to the door. She crouched down to put his shoes on his feet, muttering under her breath about how she shouldn't be doing this for him. He was six, for God's sake.

'You should make him do it himself,' said Judith. 'I bet I

had to put my own shoes on from when I was, like, three or something. Baby Tom, can't even put his own shoes on,' she sang at her brother.

'I know I should, all right!' snapped Finella, holding onto Tom's ankle as he tried to kick out at his sister.

She eventually got them into the car, jackets thrown into the boot with three different packed lunches. Every evening she vowed she was going to stop pandering to their individual tastes and make them eat the same thing, but numerous ill-fated attempts had put her off. Plus, Vicky was minding them for her today and she didn't want to cause her problems by having the children complain about their lunch.

Finella was terrified Vicky would decide she couldn't cope with the children and then what would she do? Her mother was elderly and found her grandchildren 'quite exhausting', and Glasdrum did not have many childcare options. Having Vicky to look after the kids had saved Finella's life and she wasn't going to do anything to jeopardise it. Thankfully money wasn't an issue; she and Alex could pay Vicky generously. What astonished Finella was that Vicky seemed to enjoy the company of her children. She understood Judith was good company for Vicky's daughter, Louise, but the twins! Vicky said she found them amusing. Whenever Vicky looked after Finella's kids, she recounted anecdotes to Finella of their adventures looking for crabs on the shore or newts near the pond, and Finella felt guilty for her lack of interest; she was pleased they were happy but aside from that she didn't want to know what they'd been doing all day. It was just so terribly dull.

The children leapt out of the car in delight as soon as she

pulled up at Megan's house, the twins especially pleased to spot a man with a small digger in the garden.

'Why is Vicky here today?' they asked.

'I think she was babysitting last night and so she's going to spend the day with Megan, and thought you'd enjoy playing with her boys.'

'Yeah, cool,' said James.

'Make sure you behave,' said Finella, although none of them were listening to her as they raced off into the house. Finella looked at her watch. It was nine forty-five and she'd said she had to be at work by ten but perhaps Vicky and Megan were both around. It would be nice to have a chat if the children were going to disappear and play. 'Yoo-hoo,' she sang as she crossed the hall.

'In here, Finny,' shouted Megan.

Finella smiled to herself. Nobody except Megan shortened her name, and if they had she would most likely have told them it was *Finella*, *thank you very much*. But for some reason, she liked it when Megan called her Finny. It made her feel special. Megan was someone Finella both admired and liked. She had a relaxed manner, was forthright and had no airs and graces. She was an unemployed single mother from a fallen-on-hard-times family and made no attempt to apologise for it. Finella, on the other hand, was forever trying to keep up appearances. It was exhausting. Daughter of the long-standing local GP, she had always felt intense pressure to be... well... everything: clever, attractive, hard-working, a good mother, a cornerstone of the community. She had achieved it, too. Everyone thought well of her. She went to university (sensible), but came back to her local community to work (commendable), married well (lucky girl) and had three healthy children (marvellous). Now all she had to do was bring them up to do the same. What joy Finella experienced to spend time with Megan, to hear her talk about what little shits her kids were. She was the only person with whom Finella could let her guard down and admit that, yes, hers were rotten little brats, too.

'Hello, ladies,' she said, giving first Megan then Vicky a kiss. 'Thank you so much for having them today, Vicky. You're a lifesaver. I've so much to catch up on at the office.'

'It's no problem, Finella. You know the money is handy for me, and Louise loves seeing Judith. She gets fed up if she's stuck with me all day.'

'Come off it, Finny, you and me both know you just want to get away from them little buggers, eh?' Megan grinned at Finella and gave her a wink, although she had a drawn look to her face that Finella had never seen before; as though the weight of the world had suddenly fallen on her shoulders. Perhaps she was coming down with something.

'I don't know what you mean, Megan. You know I love spending time with the little darlings, apples of my eye.' Saying this felt like delicious rebellion. She thought of the years she had spent at toddler groups vying with other mothers about weaning techniques and discipline strategies when all the while there were mothers like Megan who did whatever they felt like and her children grew up strong and healthy, albeit at the far end of the socially acceptable behaviour scale.

Finella sat down, trying to avoid having her hand licked by Glen, and pointed at Thursday's edition of the *Glasdrum Journal* that was lying on the table. 'I see another man has fallen off the Ben path and been found dead in Crofter's Gully. Poor sod.' She lowered her voice. 'Did you notice the article mentions that story going round town that all the deaths in the last few months on the Ben have been because of a Mist Murderer? What nonsense. I can't believe they printed it!'

'Catriona thinks she's a big shot journalist but she's going to get herself sacked before she's been back a year if she keeps writing shit like that,' said Megan.

'I agree. Catriona ought to go back to Edinburgh and stop trying to turn the *Journal* into a low-grade gossip rag. It's becoming a weird Highland version of that new *Heat* magazine.' Finella frowned at the thought of the raven-haired Catriona staring at her husband Alex with her intense blue eyes. The two of them had gone out together for a while back in high school; they had all been around fifteen but while Finella had still been a cossetted and plump adolescent, Catriona had been one of those girls who had matured early. She had intimidated Finella with her knowing eyes and sharp manner. Alex had admitted to Finella he had lost his virginity to Catriona in his granddad's barn, although the relationship had fizzled out when they were around seventeen, shortly before Alex had turned his attentions to Finella, something she had been thrilled about at the time. He had said Catriona had been 'troubled' but had been unwilling to explain when he meant. But Finella knew they had been hill walking together on several occasions since Catriona had returned to Glasdrum the previous summer; Megan had seen them when she'd been running. When Finella had asked Alex about it, he'd had a haunted look on his face and she was certain something was going on even though he'd said it had been coincidence.

'Maybe it's not gossip,' said Vicky, interrupting her thoughts.

'You've heard gossip about Catriona?' asked Finella.

'I mean about the murderer.'

'Oh, yes. That. Of course. Well,' said Finella, trying to shake the dark thoughts from her head, 'if there's a murderer on the loose up the hill, Megan better watch out next time she's up there running. You too, Vicky, now that you've taken up hill walking. Honestly, I don't know what's wrong with you all. What a bunch of exercise freaks.'

'It's only men who've been killed. Or fallen, depending what you want to believe,' said Vicky, as Lewis came into the kitchen.

'Aye, if it's men getting killed, it'll be Megan that's doing it,' he said. 'Megan the Mist Murderer.'

'Better watch yersel then,' said Megan.

'Want a coffee, Finella?' asked Lewis.

'Yes, please. I haven't seen you for years, Lewis. Are you visiting from London?'

'Nope, I've moved back, with my girlfriend, Sarah.'

'And where is she?'

'She's upstairs sleeping. Long journey yesterday.'

Megan chipped in, 'I think arriving here in the dark to a house full of kids and no toilet was a bit of a shock to poor Sarah. In fact, I think I hear the kids rampaging about upstairs. I better check.' Megan leapt to her feet and raced out of the kitchen.

Lewis continued, 'It didn't help that Gregor had to shoot a deer on the way here.'

'Why on earth did he do that?'

'We hit it, ended up in the ditch. Poor beast was in agony. No choice but to put it out of its misery.'

'Dear God,' said Finella. 'What a trauma for the poor girl. She'll think she's left civilisation. We'll have to arrange a night out to show Sarah we're not complete country bumpkins. Would she like that, Lewis?' Lewis looked uncertain but Finella carried on, 'The Stag's Head is having a cocktail night next Friday. We should go. What do you think, Vicky?'

Vicky looked doubtful. 'Can they make cocktails in the Stag's Head?'

'Yes, well, that's something we'd have to find out, but it would be fun, wouldn't it?'

Finella held her breath; a good reason to spend an evening away from the children and Alex. It would be even better than going to work. She practically leapt to her feet and hugged Vicky when she shrugged and said, 'Yeah, why not.'

'I'm not sure Sarah will want to—' said Lewis, but Finella interrupted.

'Nonsense. The girl needs to have some female company. I'm sure she'll be delighted.'

'She'll be delighted at what?' asked Megan, coming back into the room.

'We're going to take Sarah to a cocktail night next Friday,' said Finella.

'In the Stag's Head,' added Vicky, with a grimace.

'I've just chased the kids out of her bedroom,' said Megan. 'She'll need a drink soon, once she finds out what life's like around here. You gonna babysit the kids, Lewis?'

'Am I getting a choice, like?'

Finella clapped her hands. 'This is excellent news. Now, where's my coffee?'

'Thought you had to get to work, Finny,' said Megan.

'It can wait twenty minutes.'

The sound of light footsteps on the stairs preceded Sarah's arrival. When she hesitated in the doorway, Finella got up and hugged her. 'Darling, welcome to Glasdrum! It sounds as though you've had the most dreadful start. I've been hearing all about it; the journey, the dead deer, Gregor... sorry Lewis, I know he's your friend but he's a dreadful boy... arriving here in the dark and no toilet. Then to wake up to all these horrid children! My God, I'd hate that, and three of them are mine!' Finella pulled back and looked at Sarah. The girl had tears in her eyes; Finella had hit a nerve. 'Come and sit down, Sarah. Lewis, pour her a coffee. You do drink coffee, don't you?' Sarah nodded, bewildered by the onslaught of attention from Finella but relieved someone had taken control of the situation for her. 'I know this might sound presumptuous but we've arranged a night out to welcome you.'

'Oh, er, thanks... but I'm not sure...' Sarah's eyes widened.

Finella patted her shoulder, 'We want to show you the modest attractions this town has to offer'—Megan snorted but Finella carried on—'and it's nice to have girlfriends to show you round. Don't rely on men for that, dear.' Finella winked at Lewis.

The children charged into the kitchen like a swarm of locusts. They were everywhere, clattering and chattering and demanding food. Finella's twins, Tom and James, threw themselves at Vicky and hugged her, one on either side, as Glen joined in the general clamour with a round of barking. Their noise and presence reminded Finella why she was here and filled her with a longing to leave.

'Goodness, look at the time, I better dash after all. Lovely to meet you, Sarah. See you on Friday in the Stag's Head.'

'Well, it's just that… I'm not sure…' Sarah threw a pleading glance at Lewis but he either didn't notice or didn't understand her predicament and Sarah was left floundering, weak in the face of Finella's determination for a night out, with Sarah's arrival as the reason.

'Ta, ta,' shouted Finella as she left the kitchen, adding a vague, 'Do behave children,' over her shoulder as she left.

When she got to the car, her hands were shaking. What was wrong with her? One minute she was looking forward to a coffee and a laugh, and merrily arranging a night out, but the second the children arrived, with their noisy demands, stamping about the room touching things with their grubby hands, she felt something akin to panic. Their shrill voices filled her head and made her want to run and never stop. Perhaps that was why Megan liked hill running so much. Finella wondered briefly if she should give it a try but decided there must be a less strenuous means of escape.

She arrived at the deserted office in the local college by ten thirty, replied to an email asking if she wanted to go to Health and Safety training (no, she didn't) then put the kettle on and got her book out. Unlike during the week, there were no phones, no bustle, no distractions. The quiet stillness settled around her like a comforting blanket and she felt the tension slide out of her body.

Chapter Six
VICKY

Friday, 13 May 2005, 8pm

The Stag's Head was crowded. The people of Glasdrum had a greater desire for cocktails than Vicky had expected.

'Yoo-hoo!' Finella's voice was barely audible over the noise in the pub as she waved from the corner, where she'd reserved them a table. Vicky, Sarah and Megan pushed past a group of men at the bar to get to her.

'Hey, gorgeous,' one of the men said to Sarah, the blonde newcomer, immediately recognisable as *not a local*.

'Get tae fuck, Derrick,' said Megan, giving him a shove.

'Cunt,' muttered the man, but Megan pushed on, ignoring him, pulling a startled-looking Sarah along behind her. The man nodded at Vicky, who took up the rear, and she smiled back. She had fitted in well with Glasdrum's locals; it was part of the reason she'd stayed so long. Megan, as she said herself, had been here too long and had high school history with most of them, much of it relating to her on-off, up-down, and currently terminated, relationship with Johnny, the father of her kids.

Finella stood as they arrived and kissed them all, cheek, cheek, cheek, as though she was in a French wine bar, not a grotty Highland bar with faded tartan curtains and its namesake stag's head hanging grimly on the wall. Vicky was often surprised at how Megan tolerated Finella's pretentious habits; if anyone else had tried to kiss her in greeting, Megan would have shrugged them off with an abrupt 'piss off'.

'First drinks are on me, girls,' said Finella. 'Raspberry daiquiris all round?'

'Honestly, no need,' protested Sarah getting her purse out.

'I wouldn't worry,' said Megan. 'Finny's got pots of money.'

Vicky reflected on that as Finella called over a waitress. She was making loads of money looking after Finella's three kids. At first it had only been two days per week then increased day by day until it was sometimes five days, plus Saturday morning. It suited Vicky. Due to her circumstances, she avoided conventional work; the least trace of her the better. She had even managed without state benefits when Louise had been a baby, although it had been hard scraping enough money together to feed them both and heat her run-down cottage through her long first winter in Glasdrum. Finella had been a godsend, not only for the money but for the company her daughter, Judith, gave Louise. Vicky would have been willing to entertain the twins for free for the pleasure it gave Louise to have a friend, almost like a sister, and every time Vicky watched them together, their heads touching as they bent over a book, she was reminded of the family she'd lost and how alone she was in the world. Thank goodness she had Louise.

A hand on her shoulder and a voice in her ear, 'Move up, why don't you?'

Her heart sank; Finella's husband, Alex.

Vicky shuffled along the bench and Alex squeezed in beside her, his leg pressed against hers. An arm snaked around her shoulders in a jovial manner as his voice boomed across the conversation at the table and the general hubbub of the pub, 'Lucky Vicky, getting to cosy up next to me, eh?'

Everyone laughed; Alex was the life and soul of any party. Vicky grimaced and gave her shoulder a subtle shake in the hope he would remove his arm. But as she expected, Alex ignored her and whispered in her ear how nice it was to see her again. Vicky shuddered in revulsion.

When she had first met Alex, he had been attentive and pleasant, always asking after Louise and taking a great interest in Vicky's life before coming to Glasdrum, something Vicky didn't like to talk about. It was as though Alex had sensed her reluctance to talk and he pursued it relentlessly, under the guise of polite interest, and often in front of others, to make Vicky feel as awkward as possible. Waiting outside the school, surrounded by other parents, Alex would remark on what a great job Vicky was doing bringing up such a charming child on her own. 'Can't be easy, Vicky, with no man around to help you.' Alex had covered his mouth in mock alarm. 'Oops, I'm not supposed to say things like that these days, am I? You ladies can manage perfectly well without us menfolk, eh?' Everyone had laughed, because that's what people did when Alex was being engaging. They smiled and commented on what a thoroughly decent man he was, partner in the local firm of solicitors, giver of discounts to the residents of the old folks' home for their wills and provider of new bike sheds for the primary school.

But Vicky knew the darker side of Alex. One night, about six months earlier, not long after Vicky had started minding Alex and Finella's children, she had offered to babysit to allow them to go to a Rotary Club dinner. On their return, Finella was so drunk she had collapsed on the stairs and he had to carry her to bed. Back downstairs Alex cornered Vicky in the kitchen and tried to kiss her. 'I love a mysterious woman,' he slurred as he groped her breasts. He pressed himself against her and Vicky's wave of panic gave her strength she didn't know she had to push him away. A man had forced himself on her a long time ago and she was determined that was never going to happen again. She grabbed a knife from the countertop and held it in front of her.

'Don't come near me.'

'Jesus, Vicky, keep your hair on. It was just a bit of fun. I thought you were interested.'

'You disgust me,' she hissed. 'If you ever even look at me like that again, I'll tell Finella.'

Alex laughed and ran his hand though his foppish hair. 'Finella wouldn't like that. So you would be risking the tidy little income you are making from us.'

Vicky advanced towards Alex, the weapon still in her hand. Every awful experience she had suffered at the hands of men rushed through her mind, condensed into a ball of deep hatred and fear that obliterated every thought in her brain. 'So if I can't tell Finella, I'll just have to stop you myself.'

Vicky took a step closer to Alex, fury obliterating her fear, and forced him to walk backwards until his back was against the wall, the blade an inch from his stomach. His face had blanched at the rage in her voice.

Vicky's hand was shaking with desire to harm Alex when the fog of anger lifted. She tossed the knife aside. A split second longer and Vicky feared she would have done it. She had shocked herself and could see that Alex, too, looked pale, almost cowering against the wall.

'You're fucking crazy,' he whispered as he moved away from her.

'Only with animals like you,' she replied, then ran upstairs to wake Louise. They were supposed to stay the night but Vicky couldn't bear to.

'What's going on, Mum?' wailed Louise as Vicky lifted her sleepy head from the bed.

'I'm sorry, Louise, but we have to go home.'

'I'm sleeping!'

'Get up, Louise, come on. We have to go home.'

'But why?'

'Just because,' said Vicky, trying to force Louise's arms into her jacket and dropping her shoes at her feet.

'But...'

'Look, Louise,' hissed Vicky. 'I'm not going to discuss it. Just get your clothes on and follow me.'

Louise stared at Vicky with a mutinous look but pulled on her shoes and helped Vicky stuff her things back into her bag.

'Why are we—'

'Not now. I'll explain at home.' Vicky hoped she'd be able to think of a reasonable explanation by the time they got home.

Alex was out of sight when they left and marched the two miles out of town in the dark to their cottage, holding hands as they had done when Louise had been younger and still sought comfort from Vicky. But as soon as they arrived home, Louise ran to her bedroom and slammed the door, disappointed that her sleepover at her friend's house had been ruined. It had made

Vicky miserable that yet again a man was impacting negatively on her life. At that moment she had hated Alex.

In the Stag's Head she remembered that incident as Alex hemmed her in behind the busy pub table. She knew he was doing it on purpose, in public, putting her in as uncomfortable a situation as possible. It was her punishment for turning him down and perhaps for scaring the life out of him, too. For that, Vicky was glad. Men like Alex thought they could get away with anything.

'Excuse me,' she said to him. 'I'm going to the loo.'

'Sure.' Alex stood but didn't move, forcing Vicky to squeeze past him. His hand brushed against her bottom as she passed; whether on purpose or by accident, an onlooker would have found it impossible to tell. But Vicky knew.

She battled her way through the now-crowded bar. There was a queue in the toilets, as always, so she hung about for a bit then went back. It had only been an excuse to get away from Alex, now holding forth at the table beside Sarah, who looked bewildered. Glasdrum was a strange place to end up; Vicky knew that better than anyone. Her earliest memories were of being sent to stay there with her grandmother while her parents toured with a theatre group. Even back then the cottage had been dilapidated, but staying with her eccentric granny had been comforting; they had spent hours searching for crabs on the shore or taking picnics through the gorge at the end of the glen to the abandoned settlement where her granny had been brought up and where she was now buried. Glasdrum had been a haven for the young Vicky, a welcome break from her parents' bohemian existence in London and the never-ending circus of people who visited their home. Of course, back then her name had not been Vicky, and nobody had connected her with that lonely child who had stayed now and then during the school holidays with the crazy old lady in the cottage at the end of the beach.

But Vicky's mother had fallen out with her granny, as mothers and daughters do when the mother starts to criticise the daughter's parenting style, and that had been the end of Vicky's extended stays in Glasdrum, leaving her with nothing but the ephemeral memories of a child and a vague sense of warmth snatched away from her. The only consolation to losing her parents in a car crash just before she became pregnant with Louise had been the inheritance of the dilapidated cottage; a life-saving sanctuary when she'd needed it most.

She glanced around the pub and grabbed an unoccupied stool to put down beside Finella. 'Thanks for the drink,' she said, but Finella didn't hear her. She was staring at her husband who was laughing and gesticulating, regaling Sarah with one of his hearty stories.

Finella leant towards Vicky. 'I bet he's telling her about the stag he shot last year. Bastard. He was supposed to be at home tonight but got my dad to babysit.' Finella drained her daiquiri and waved her glass in the air in the hope that a waiter would appear.

'I think they've given up with the waiter service,' said Vicky.

Finella stared murderously at her husband for another few minutes then stood and set off for the bar, muttering to Vicky that she had to get another drink. Vicky considered going with her; it was awful having to sit and watch Alex. Poor Finella –

imagine being married to the man. She hadn't heard Finella speak about him so venomously before but Vicky didn't often speak to Finella on a one-to-one basis about anything other than the children. Vicky would tell her what the twins had been up to that day or about the funny, grown-up things Judith and Louise had said, but she wasn't sure how interested Finella was. She mostly shunned individual conversation, appearing happier to play the jolly old girl role to a larger group; much like her husband.

Before she got a chance to go after Finella, Megan appeared. 'Pissed yet?' she asked.

Vicky shook her head. 'I've only had one. Can't be bothered queuing at the bar.'

Megan held her bag open to show Vicky two Spiderman flasks. 'Cheaper and quicker if you bring your own. Want a splash of voddy?'

Vicky held her glass out. 'Imagine if the boys found that!'

'How do you think I get them to sleep at night?' said Megan, and Vicky wasn't sure if she was joking.

'What do you reckon his game is?' Megan nodded in Alex's direction after swigging from the blue and red flask.

'Boring everyone to death?'

'Sarah doesn't look bored,' said Megan.

Sarah was giggling and staring up at Alex as he fired an imaginary rifle then made a sad face and leant towards Sarah to whisper something in her ear.

'She seems to have forgotten about Lewis,' said Megan, nodding this time in the direction of the bar, where Lewis stood with Gregor and a few other lads. They were laughing and drinking, but Lewis kept glancing at Sarah, looking despondent.

'Maybe he shouldn't be standing at the bar with his mates,' said Vicky.

'You're right there,' said Megan. 'He should be at home watching his nephews like he said he would. But he decided he wanted to come out so I had to pay my pal's teenager a tenner to sit in with the boys. Maybe Lewis knows Sarah's not a girl he should leave to her own devices. Pretty face and an empty head, if you ask me.'

'That's harsh, Megan. It's not her fault. Alex is impossible to get away from. Maybe we should rescue her.'

'She doesn't look like she wants rescuing to me,' said Megan, glaring at Sarah. 'I'm away to speak to Lewis.'

Vicky was left on her own; so much for the girls' night out. Finella had disappeared, Sarah was ensconced with Alex, and Megan was soon holding forth in the centre of the group of men, her chat with Lewis forgotten. She'd been in a strange mood since they'd found the bones the previous week, and Vicky had been too nervous of her answer to ask what she'd done with them, never mind suggest the police again. Surely it couldn't really be Megan's dad; that was too shocking. Vicky had decided to put the matter out of her head; she was never one to meddle in others' affairs.

The rabble-like noise of the bar swirled around Vicky and she tuned it out, sipping the dregs from her glass, wondering whether to get another. She always forgot how much she disliked crowded social occasions; the sharp, false laughter and the smell of cheap perfume, harsh aftershave and spilled beer. She would have gone home to Louise but she was staying at Finella's house with Judith, despite Vicky's misgivings when she thought Alex was going to be babysitting. Louise had made such a fuss when Vicky had suggested she stay with a different friend that Vicky had, cowardly, given in. Louise had become a force to be reckoned with in recent months; Vicky dreaded what she'd be like as a teenager. And for all his unpleasantness with her, Alex had shown no ill intent towards her daughter; Louise seemed to find him entertaining. To Vicky's irritation she often spoke warmly about how Judith's dad was *so funny*. So as much as Vicky didn't want to stay, there was nothing to pull her home and it was easier to sit, isolated in the crowded bar, watching everyone get drunk.

An hour passed and Alex was still regaling Sarah, and others, with stories. The arm that had been resting along the top of the seat behind Sarah's head had fallen onto her shoulder and her head was slightly tilted towards him, her eyes glassy with drink.

Megan had gone to sit in the opposite corner with Lewis and Gregor, all three of them looking the worse for wear. Vicky watched Lewis get up and push his way through the crowds towards the toilets, passing Megan's ex Johnny on the way.

As soon as Lewis was out of sight, Gregor pulled Megan's face towards him and kissed her, his hand disappearing under the table. Megan didn't pull away. In a matter of moments, Johnny had pushed through the throngs and grabbed Gregor by the shirt. A punch-up was imminent but the bouncers were onto them in a flash. They pulled Johnny away and hustled him out the door. Like a cockerel, Gregor gave a brief shake of his shoulders to show everyone what a big man he was, then sat down beside Megan again. By the time Lewis came back, the scene had returned to normal, as though nothing had happened. The three of them carried on drinking, and it was only when Lewis went to the bar to buy another round, seeming to have forgotten about Sarah, that Vicky saw Gregor snake his hand between Megan's legs, making her smile slyly at him.

Vicky was puzzled. Megan never had a good word to say about Gregor so maybe she was trying to make Johnny jealous. But that seemed unlikely; from what she'd said, Megan knew Johnny doted on her and would have her back in a flash. She could be exceptionally contrary at times: speaking warmly of Johnny but pushing him away at every opportunity; criticising men on a regular basis yet willing to have brazen affairs with the most unsavoury characters. Vicky found this difficult to understand. People were so confusing. Perhaps the evening would be more bearable if she, too, got drunk.

She battled through the throngs at the bar and met a handful of people who worked at the new Highland College outreach facility. They were a friendly bunch, enthused about the project to offer courses via videoconferencing, and Vicky stood with them for a while, wondering if she should have applied for one of the three posts that had recently been advertised. Part of her longed to work in an office again, to use her brain, but she'd decided it was too risky; she had managed eight years living off the radar and planned to continue doing so until Louise was at least a teenager, only two years away. It was with a touch of envy that she listened to their tales of setting up the new service, planning courses, and drawing up marketing plans.

'You guys will need some news coverage,' said a deep but feminine voice behind them. Vicky turned to face the piercing blue eyes of Catriona MacKinnon, eerie in their luminosity. Catriona nodded at Vicky and carried on talking to the assembled group. 'I could do a small series, say one article per weekly edition, with interviews, following your progress finding students. What do you think?'

There was much nodding. 'Sounds good. Thanks, Catriona.'

'No problem, that's what I'm here for. All the new local news, the worthy as well as the dramatic.' She flicked her glossy dark hair over her shoulder and glanced smugly at Finella, who was standing a short distance away.

Finella waved her glass in the air, unsteady on her feet, her usual neat bob looking dishevelled. 'Rumours are not news, dear. I thought you'd have learned that while you were busy being a journalist in the big city. Oh, just a minute, I remember now. That didn't work out for you, did it?'

Vicky stared in alarm at Finella. What had got into her? Finella was usually a perfect example of decorum.

'Perhaps you ought to get someone to take you home, Finella,' said Catriona.

'What I do is none of your business,' said Finella taking a step towards Catriona, who bared her teeth in the least sincere smile Vicky had ever seen. Something about it chilled Vicky to the core.

'You're wrong,' said Catriona, 'everything that happens around here is my business now.'

Finella looked about to launch herself at Catriona when Alex appeared between them.

'Finella,' he hissed.

'Oh, my darling husband has arrived to save the day.' Finella broke into hysterical giggles as Alex propelled her towards the door. Vicky was torn. She wanted to help Finella but it wasn't her place. She turned back to Catriona, who had an unreadable expression on her face as she watched Alex manhandle his wife out of the bar.

Vicky felt an overwhelming desire to go home; what a rubbish evening. The alcohol she'd consumed had made her maudlin and the crowds had made her lonely. Everyone seemed to have someone who meant something to them while Vicky battled through life on her own. That thought brought tears to her eyes as she searched for her coat, ignoring the banter from Derrick and the lads at the bar and noticing that Megan and Gregor were no longer in their corner. Lewis sat alone, pint in hand, perilously close to being spilled, his head bowed in a drunken stupor.

Once Vicky had fought her way out of the sweaty heat and harsh noise, the cool damp air was soothing on her skin. She was relieved to be out of the jarring atmosphere as she set off to walk the two miles over the headland to her cottage. Vicky loved to walk and decided that the following day, before she went to collect Louise from Finella's house, she'd take the shortcut through the gorge to visit her granny's grave at the abandoned settlement where her great-grandparents had run a small croft until just after the start of the Second World War. When they'd been forced to move closer to town due to the distance of the meandering access track, the tiny village and its cemetery had fallen into disrepair, but Vicky's granny had retained permission to be buried there in the family lair and Vicky had often visited her there. The sense of peace she felt was immense and she longed to be able to share this small piece of family history with Louise, who still didn't know that Vicky had come to Glasdrum as a child; nobody did. When she'd arrived in Glasdrum, heavily pregnant, eleven years previously, Vicky had let people believe she had bought the cottage by the beach and nobody had associated her with the quiet child called Ginny who had spent the odd summer there many years earlier.

As she headed down the High Street, a slight movement caught her eye. Two people were hunched together in the shadows of the alley between the Woollen Mill and the Cat's Aid charity shop. She caught a flash of a white leg lifted up and the rhythmic movement of sex. With a quiet gasp she realised it was Megan and Gregor. Vicky stared for a moment then lowered her head and carried on, tutting to herself, disapproving of Megan for her inappropriate behaviour. But Megan didn't care what others thought of her; social decorum was of no concern. And deep down, Vicky didn't really disapprove; she admired Megan for her brash ability to do whatever the hell she wanted. Vicky wondered what it would be like to get drunk and have sex in an alley. She never had and probably never would, and especially not with a sleazeball like Gregor... but she nevertheless felt a stab of arousal at the thought of it. She hadn't had sex for years, too nervous to get involved with anyone, and she thought about that all the way home, wondering if it was time for a change of attitude. She touched herself before she went to sleep, wondering if she might ever find someone else to do that for her; if she would find someone who wanted her enough to lift her leg in a dark lane and push himself inside her. Vicky fell asleep feeling dissatisfied; it was so unlikely, given her past history, that she would ever find a man she could trust.

Chapter Seven
CATRIONA

Friday, 13 May 2005, 10.45pm

'What's happened to Finella?' Catriona raised an eyebrow and made an *awkward* face at the three people from the college. 'She used to be so straight-laced. Not the kind to get dragged out of a pub pissed.'

One of the women sniggered and leant towards Catriona. 'All is not well in paradise, know what I mean?'

Catriona hated it when people said *know what I mean* but she smiled back. 'Really? Do tell.'

'Alex has been having yet another affair.'

'Shut up, Pam, that's pure gossip,' said Pamela's colleague, rolling his eyes.

Catriona was losing interest in the conversation. She already knew Alex was having an affair, or at least had been, because she'd had a fling with him not long after she'd returned from Edinburgh the previous summer. It had gone on until around the time her dad had died in October. Alex ditched her pretty fast after that; he was never one for complications.

The affair had been a mistake of course; Alex wasn't the type of man to leave his *pillar of the community* wife and their *darling* children, and Catriona was furious she'd allowed herself to be used by him, yet again. He'd left her for Finella before, way back in high school, and it had been amusing to watch her get manhandled out of the pub, hair in disarray, by the husband Catriona had fucked. And something in Finella's eyes suggested she knew all about it. *Good.* Flawless Finella, with her neat clothes, fancy house and perfect children. Everyone had thought Alex and Finella had been an *ideal match*; him a law student and her the doctor's daughter. Catriona had hated them for it.

However, the brief fling at the end of the previous summer hadn't been without its benefits. Keen to secure Catriona's silence, Alex had helped her get a job running the *Journal's* Glasdrum and Islands outreach edition. The first article she had written for the paper had been popular, about the tragic death of her father. He had been the hero of the local mountain rescue so everyone in the town had been shocked that he'd fallen to his death on Ben Calder, on a treacherous but well-known section of path that ran along the top of a cliff where the mountain fell away steeply into Crofter's Gully, many metres below. For someone so experienced to lose their way in the mist had been a brutal reminder of the ferocity of the mountains in poor weather conditions, although Catriona had admitted privately to some people that her father had been suffering mentally in recent months, one of the reasons she had come home to Glasdrum to keep an eye on him.

She glanced round the bar to see who she could talk to and spotted the blonde Alex had been chatting up. She was plastered, with a bewildered look on her face, and Catriona felt a stab of sympathy. She looked like a lost soul in a strange place, and Catriona knew what that felt like.

'Hey,' she said, squeezing herself onto the bench. 'I haven't seen you in here before. I'm Catriona by the way.'

The girl raised her head and made bleary eye contact. 'I'm Sarah. Just got here last week.'

'Glasdrum's a shock when you first arrive. I was brought up here but it felt weird to come back. Small-town mentality, you know.'

The girl nodded gratefully at Catriona.

'So what's brought you here?'

'My boyfriend, Lewis…' Sarah looked around then pointed at Lewis, who was sitting on a bar stool, staring at the floor, his beer on the verge of being tipped all over his shoes.

'Ah,' said Catriona. 'A new start together?'

Sarah nodded. 'Something like that. Was sick of London.'

'So have you got a job yet? Those folk from the college might be able to help you.'

'You know Alex, Finella's husband?'

'Oh yeah, I know him.'

'He said he might be able to get me a job in his law firm and that I might be able to help out with the local paper as well. He's given the journalist a desk in his office or something.'

Catriona stared at Sarah. That man was unbelievable. 'He said you could do some work for the *Journal*? Without asking me?'

Sarah's head jerked up at the anger in Catriona's voice. 'Have I said the wrong thing? He said he was going to speak to… oh…' Realisation dawned on Sarah's face. 'Catriona… and that's you, isn't it?'

'Yeah, but don't worry about it. Typical Alex,' said Catriona, feeling sorry for Sarah, who looked as though she was going to cry. 'I started doing it last year and it's going well. Circulation is up and I could do with some help. Have you done anything like that before?'

'I've done heaps of admin work. I temped for years when I dropped out of college.' Contemplating what she'd said, Sarah sat up straighter. 'I didn't leave because I'm a slacker or anything. It was just... well...'

'Life, eh?'

'Yeah.' Sarah paused then said, to herself as much as to Catriona, 'My mum died when I was young but it wasn't until I left school that it really hit me. When my dad remarried I realised how alone I was.' A tear plopped out of Sarah's eye and landed on the table. 'God, sorry, what am I telling you this for?' Sarah wiped her eye with the back of her hand, smearing mascara across her face. 'I've had too much to drink, I should go home.'

Catriona put her arm around Sarah's shoulders. 'My mum also died when I was little. And I didn't really get on with my dad. Do you know the number of times I've got pissed and bawled my eyes out about it? Too many, I can tell you.'

Sarah stared in gratitude at Catriona as she went on, 'You and I will get along just fine. I could do with some help and could show you around the place if you like.' Catriona stared into space for a moment. 'Hill walking helped me, you know.'

'What?' Sarah looked confused.

'Helped me get over losing my mum and everything that happened to me. It's taken a while but it's only in the hills I feel free of everything.'

'That sounds nice,' said Sarah, wiping more tears away from under her eyes. 'I've never been up a hill in my life.'

Catriona leant forwards. 'Let me introduce you to them, Sarah. There's nothing like being at one with nature to release you from your troubles. It puts everything in perspective. What are you doing tomorrow?'

'I'm meeting Alex at ten but not sure after that. Lewis might have plans...' They both looked over at Lewis, who appeared to be asleep on the bar counter, his head resting on his arms.

'He's not going to be doing much tomorrow,' said Catriona in a scathing voice. 'How about I pick you up at lunchtime and take you for a walk? You're staying at Lewis's mum's, aren't you?'

'I don't have any walking gear and I'm not that fit. I'd never keep up with you.'

'We could start with an easy walk through Crofter's Gully. It runs round the side of Ben Calder.'

'Yes, but it's just that—'

'Please, Sarah. I'd love some company and if we're going to be working together...'

Catriona smiled and Sarah nodded. 'Sure, why not. Everyone seems to like hill walking around here so I guess I could give it a try.'

'I'll see you at one then. I need to get home and get some rest now.'

Catriona hurried out of the pub feeling pleased to have met Sarah. Although born and brought up in Glasdrum, Catriona had been away for so long she now felt like an outsider and despised the locals she'd known growing up, with their closed circles and narrow lives. She felt certain they talked about her disparagingly, as they did about anyone who had the audacity to leave and make a new life for themselves. It was nice to meet someone from out of town, and getting help with the *Journal* would be handy; Catriona had grand plans for the newspaper, and for a moment she felt happy at the thought of the future.

But as always, this feeling didn't last. As she made her way down the High Street she felt a familiar prickling sensation behind her eyes. Catriona used to pride herself on her ability to keep her emotions in check but recently she'd been falling apart at the drop of a hat; almost anything could trigger an emotional outburst. It was as though someone had opened a tap on years of pent-up sadness and anger. Her conversation with Sarah made her recall losing her own mother when she was ten and even now, at thirty-eight, that memory could fracture Catriona into shards of misery. She had sensed the same unhappiness in Sarah; both of them left motherless at a young age and both feeling like outsiders. Perhaps Sarah would share Catriona's love of the hills and they could purge their demons together. She was so deep in thought she jumped when she heard a male voice close behind her.

'Hey!' he shouted, and a hand closed on her arm. She spun around and tried to pull away but his grip tightened.

'Get off me, Alex.' She glanced around for help but the High Street was deserted.

'You've got to stop!' he hissed.

With a sharp jerk, she freed her arm. 'Leave me alone.'

She started running before he could say anything more. A few months previously she'd have been out of breath, but strenuous hill walks had reaped benefits and Catriona kept up a steady pace all the way home, checking behind her now and again to make sure he wasn't following. It wasn't only the loss of her mother that had been brought to the surface by her return to Glasdrum. She'd been reminded of other long-buried trauma from her youth, and Alex's betrayal featured prominently. She knew she needed to let it go but this was becoming harder, rather than easier, the older she got. Despite knowing it was wrong, her resolve to destroy him strengthened a notch.

Chapter Eight
MEGAN

Saturday, 14 May 2005, 7am

Megan woke early, her head woozy. The morning was light and the birds made a racket in the woods behind her house as she stretched and remembered the events of the night before: Gregor.

'Fuck,' she muttered to herself, her lazy mood broken. Why did she keep doing things like that? And with *Gregor*? She knew he'd always fancied her since they'd been at school together, and he was useful for buying the odd lump of hash from to sell to the mums at the toddler group, but what had possessed her to have sex with him? He was weird. And one of Lewis's best pals…

Megan jumped out of bed. She had to go for a run to clear her head. Not only of the previous night's events but also of the deeper worry that was weighing her down: the bag of bones she had stashed in the garage.

All her life Megan had lurched from one mini disaster to another. From poor attendance and 'not achieving her potential' at school, to bad relationship choices, followed by one unplanned pregnancy after another. She had taken it all on the chin and bounced back with alacrity, always looking forward, but the bones were praying on her mind, dragging her back into the past. She wanted to forget about them and move on. So her dad was dead… so what? Missing or dead, she hadn't wanted to see him again anyway. But now he filled her thoughts, day and night. How had he ended up in that hole?

She tried to focus on all the times he'd come home drunk and hit her mother, but other memories kept creeping into her head: Donald teaching her to ride a bike, taking her up the hill with him and telling her the Gaelic names of all the mountains they could see on a clear day, showing her how to fish for salmon and keep quiet about their lack of fishing permit. Every time she saw Lewis she struggled to stop the words bursting out of her mouth about the bones; fear of his reaction held her back. And in the meantime, Donald's skeleton waited in the garage, tormenting her with its presence.

She pulled on her running kit before creeping down to the kitchen, where she left three bowls, a box of Cheerios and a jug of milk on the table in case the boys woke while she was gone. At least Lewis and Sarah were in the house this morning; normally Megan left the boys for the hour or so it took her to run to the halfway point of Ben Calder. She would have preferred to go to the top and back but that would take her three hours, too long even by Megan's relaxed parenting standards. Vicky had been horrified when she told her.

'Keep yer hair on, Vicky, they'll be fine. Kyle is eleven, same as Louise. You leave her on her own, don't you?'

'Yeah, but Rory's only four. What if he ran off or hurt himself?'

'Then they'd phone you,' said Megan with a grin. 'They all know how to, even Rory. That's why your number is taped to the wall beside the phone.'

Megan crept out of the house with Glen close on her heels. There was every chance the boys wouldn't stir.

The morning air was fresh and damp with a bank of mist low on the hill as she followed the trail through the woods to meet the main path up Ben Calder. Glen bounded ahead; he knew the route. It was so good to be living here again, in the house she'd grown up in, rather than on the street at the top of the hill, in the damp, Council-built shoebox of a house, where rubbish and graffiti were permanent features of the street. She had received a letter telling her it had been brought to the Council's attention that her house had been empty for over two weeks, and unless she reoccupied it, her tenancy would end. Some fucker had dobbed her in, probably that cow Gemma who lived next door. Megan had decided to give the Council house up, except Lewis coming home had complicated things. What if he and Sarah wanted to stay there permanently and her mum got better and came home? There wasn't enough room for them all.

The ground rose and her breathing quickened. It was hard this morning with the previous night's alcohol coursing through her blood but she relished the feeling of exertion that drove other thoughts from her head, leaving only the will to keep pushing up the incline. The path disappeared in places and she bounded through heather, her trainers soaked from the heavy dew and unavoidable bogs as the myrtle filled her nose with its sweet, resinous scent. It was supposed to keep midges at bay, but it wasn't true; nothing could keep those tiny, blood-sucking gnats away.

At the halfway point, Megan paused, tempted to carry on. Above her on the path, heading into the mist, someone was walking fast. It looked like a woman but it was hard to tell. And far below on the filter path that joined the main track, another walker plodded upwards, clad in waterproofs. *Busy hill this morning*, she thought, as she gave one last longing glance towards the cloud-topped summit before descending.

She had a big day ahead; she was going to visit her mother, although she wasn't hopeful of getting much sense out of her. Megan's head spun when she contemplated breaking the news to Lewis about finding Donald's skeleton; maybe a talk with her mum would help her decide what to do.

As she had anticipated, the boys were still asleep when she got back, and she showered. It was almost nine when they appeared and threw themselves at her in a mass of energy and enthusiasm. She felt a little bereft when Johnny came for them half an hour later. 'I'm going to take them fishing this afternoon. Want to come with us?'

Megan was tempted. Recently she'd been wondering why she was so quick to distance herself from Johnny. He'd dumped her when she'd got drunk – again – and he'd caught her snogging his pal, but she knew he wanted her back. The trouble was that Megan seemed hell-bent, for some inexplicable reason, on destroying any chance of happiness that was put in her way. But maybe it was time for a change, to introduce some stability into her life and take Johnny up on his offer to spend the day as a proper family again. But the bones... she had to visit her mother.

'Can't, gotta visit Mum in Fort William.'

'What's happening with her, like?'

'Dunno. She was in a bad way last week but maybe there'll

be some improvement. I was thinking I could look after her if they'd let her come home; I might even get a carer's allowance. I'm going to lose the Council house up the hill soon anyway. That bitch Gemma's been talking to the social, told them I'm not staying there any more.'

'Remember when we moved in there before we had Rory? We were so pleased to get a house together.'

'Aye, well, that was then, this is now. And ain't you seeing Tracy now, that fancy bird who does the secretarial work at the fish farm?'

'Nah, it didn't work out. And now she's giving me a hard time at work, putting me on all the crappy shifts.' He looked miserable, and as he stared at Megan she could see the longing in his eyes. She wanted to reach out to him... but a sickening memory flashed through her head of Gregor pumping himself inside her. Oh God, if Johnny found out about that he'd soon change his mind about wanting her back...

Her thoughts were interrupted as the boys came pelting out of the house and threw themselves at their dad, their faces alight. She fetched their overnight bag and kissed them goodbye.

'Come with us, Mummy!' said four-year-old Rory, his chubby cheeks dimpling as he smiled at her.

'Another time, my wee lad. Mummy's going to visit Granny today. I'll see you tomorrow.'

Megan felt a wave of regret when her boys left. They were irritating but a hoot to be around, always making her laugh. The house was quiet without them.

Vicky arrived shortly afterwards with Louise. 'How's your head this morning?' she asked Megan, giving her a strange look.

Megan hoped Vicky hadn't spotted her leaving the pub with Gregor.

'Felt like shit when I woke but had a run and it fair cheered me up. How about you?'

'I was fine, didn't drink that much really. I got up early and went through the gorge before I picked Louise up from Finella's.'

'Visiting that old graveyard again?'

'It's peaceful; I like it there.'

*

On the way to the station, Megan asked Vicky to make a quick detour to one of the fancier houses on the outskirts of town. For a generous sum she'd promised to deliver to Penelope, who had three children under five, a quarter of hash and a packet of Rizlas, hidden inside a Tommee Tippee cup. 'Penny left this at toddler group and I promised I'd drop it round,' she muttered to Vicky as she dashed out of the car then waited on the step until a dishevelled-looking woman with a baby on her hip and a smaller child clinging to her leg opened the door then took the colourful cup with a nod of thanks.

After that, they drove the short distance to the station to take a train to Fort William; Vicky's car was forever on its last legs and only used for local journeys. When they arrived an hour later it was a short walk from the station to drop Louise at the leisure centre opposite the care home.

'Thanks for coming with me,' Megan said to Vicky. 'You can help me figure out if you think Mum knows what actually happened to Dad. It's hard to get any sense out of her now but she always likes you.' Megan paused for a moment, sadness etched on her face. 'She's mostly angry with me these days.'

A member of staff showed them into a small day room where a tiny woman sat on an enormous armchair. With cropped grey hair and smooth skin, she did not look her sixty-eight years, despite her furrowed brow. 'You again,' she said when Megan approached and gave her mother a peck on the cheek. 'Trouble herself.'

'I've sorted myself out, Mum. I'm bringing the boys up good.'

Murdina frowned and shook her head. Her hands shook as she kneaded them together.

'Hello, Murdina. Nice to see you again,' said Vicky, wondering if she was going to get the same treatment.

'What's your name, then?'

'I'm Vicky.'

'You're not Vicky.'

Vicky froze and Megan touched her arm. 'She's getting muddled.'

Megan sat opposite her mother, took her hand and told her what the boys were up to at school and about Lewis coming home with his new girlfriend. Murdina stopped fidgeting and perked up when she heard his name.

'My boy is back?'

'Yes, just the other day. He's coming to see you on Monday.' Megan paused for a moment. 'He wanted to come with us today but I wanted to speak to you on your own first. About Dad.' Murdina wrung her hands together, her brow furrowed. 'Mum, have you heard from Dad since he disappeared?'

'He's gone and he's never coming back.'

'What makes you think that?' asked Megan gently.

Murdina shook her head. 'Nobody knows where he is.'

'Mum, I think I might have found him in the garden.'

Murdina began a loud keening that brought a nurse into the room. 'What's happening in here, Mrs MacDonald?' She gave Megan and Vicky an enquiring look.

'I asked her about my dad,' said Megan, 'I didn't realise she'd get so upset.' Megan took her mother's hand again. 'It's okay, I won't ask again. Good riddance to him as far as I'm concerned.' But Murdina carried on wailing.

'I think you better go, dear. We'll take her back to her room for a nap. We can give her a sedative if she needs it.' The nurse put her hand on Megan's arm. 'It's hard to see them like this.'

Megan wiped a tear from her eye as she and Vicky left. They went for a coffee beside the swimming pool to wait for Louise.

'Are you all right?' Vicky asked Megan. 'I had no idea how much she'd gone downhill. Your poor mum.'

'I should never have mentioned Dad's disappearance.' Megan looked at Vicky as she realised what she'd said. 'Except he didn't disappear. Someone killed him.'

'Keep your voice down!' Vicky whispered, looking around the café. 'When are you going to tell Lewis?'

'I don't know…'

'Are you still thinking it could have been…' Vicky couldn't bring herself to say it. It seemed so wrong to accuse a frail old woman of murder.

Megan seemed to read her mind. 'I know it's hard to imagine. But you didn't see what she went through with him. And she could be pretty feisty when she was younger. Maybe they fought and she just, you know… lost it.'

Vicky nodded. 'It's surprising what people will do when they're pushed into a corner. How do you think Lewis will react?'

'That's what I'm not sure of. He went off the rails when he thought Dad had disappeared but finding out he's in the garden is so much worse.'

'Five years is a long time. He seems settled with Sarah now.'

'If he keeps getting pissed and leaving her on her own in the Stag's Head, he's not going to have her for much longer. Did you see how Alex was all over her?'

'Yeah, Finella noticed, too.'

'I reckon Finny hates Alex anyway. Doesn't seem like much of a marriage to me. She told me she thinks Alex is having an affair with Catriona, that journalist. Wouldn't surprise me; I've seen them up the hill together several times. I actually saw a couple of folk up the hill this morning that could have been them, although they weren't actually together. It's hard to tell in the mist.'

Vicky nodded. 'Alex isn't a nice man; I know that for sure. But although Finella might not love him she wouldn't want the shame of him having an affair. Pillars of the community that they both are.'

'Yeah, everyone's fucked up all right,' muttered Megan. 'I can only hope Lewis doesn't freak out too much when I tell him about Dad. I don't know what he'll be like with Mum if he thinks, you know…'

'I just don't see your mum killing anyone, Megan. That's ridiculous.'

'Who else could it have been?'

'When did Donald disappear? Wasn't it on New Year's Eve?'

'Yeah, Hogmanay 1999. The whole village was out partying. That's why nobody noticed for ages. We didn't report him missing until the second of January, just presumed he'd got pissed and conked out at someone's house.'

'So you need to find out who he was with that night.'

'God, you're right, Vicky. I'm jumping to conclusions. We need to investigate this further.'

'I'm not sure that's a good idea...' Vicky looked alarmed but Megan got up and hugged her.

'Of course we should! I fucking love you, Vicky. You're such a good pal.'

The train home was quiet and so were they, lost in their reflections. Megan could hear a faint metallic beat from Louise's headphones and was surprised Vicky didn't issue her usual warning about ear damage. Vicky fussed so much about Louise, no wonder the girl was grumpy with her. Maybe that's what happened when you only had one child.

Megan's thoughts turned to Lewis and how she would break the news to him about their father's remains. How would he react? Every conversation she had with Lewis ended in a shouting match and she wasn't sure why that happened. She loved him but he was annoying. He meddled where he shouldn't, then backed off when he was needed. He made himself out to be a tough guy but underneath he was as soft as Play-Doh. He was the life and soul of the party one minute, then contradictory and difficult to understand the next. Megan resolved to deliver the news kindly to him, not wanting to disrupt his equilibrium. Finny had given her some advice about handing out bad news:

if you're too blunt with people, they'll blame you for the bad news.
Speaking your mind isn't always in your best interests.

By the time the train pulled into the station, Megan had decided to go home, sit Lewis down and explain calmly and quietly about the bones, but not reveal her suspicions about their mum.

*

'What were you thinking, you dirty little slut?' Lewis shouted at her the minute she walked into the kitchen, Vicky and Louise trailing behind her.

'Lewis!' said Vicky. She turned to Louise. 'Go upstairs to the boys' room and wait for me there.'

'But, Mum, you said I could—'

'Go, Louise. Don't argue with me. The boys are at their dad's. Find Kyle's Nintendo or something.' She pushed her out the door and closed it.

Lewis seemed not to notice this exchange and that Vicky was still in the room as he advanced on Megan, pointing his finger at her. 'When I came to in the pub last night, I went to get some fresh air and saw you humping Gregor in the lane. Disgusting.'

Megan knocked his hand away as he approached her. 'Who do you think you are? Lord of decency all of a sudden? It's none of your bloody business what I do.'

Lewis stood over Megan, his fists clenched at his sides, his face red, his eye bulging. 'It is my business, all right! It's my business because I'm your brother. And... and... so is he.'

The silence that followed was broken by footsteps and a knock on the door. 'Mum! Can I—'

Vicky pulled the door open and hissed at Louise in her furious-don't-mess-with-your-mother voice. 'Look, we're having an adult conversation. Go upstairs and wait for me there.'

'But—'

'NOW!' Vicky shut the door again.

Lewis had sat down and Megan was standing over him. Her head was reeling. 'What the hell are you on about?' she demanded.

'Just what I said. He's your half-brother.'

'My half-brother? Gregor? How can that be?'

'Dad had an affair.'

Megan went pale and put her hand out towards Vicky as though to steady herself. Vicky pulled a chair out and lowered Megan into it as though she was an old woman. 'But I… I… last night.' Megan covered her mouth with her hand. 'What have I done?'

'I tried to warn you away from him,' said Lewis.

'You could have told me he was *my brother*. Jesus Christ. That might have focused my mind a bit more than your vague warnings that he was a bit of a loser. I mean, come on, look at my relationship history. Bad choices of men all over the place.' Megan spluttered on her words as questions exploded in her mind. 'How long have you know about this? Does Mum know? Does'—Megan gulped and steeled herself—'does *Gregor* know?'

'He does.'

Megan leapt to her feet. 'He knows? That shit knows I'm related to him and he still…' Megan turned away with her head in her hands. 'I can't take this. It's too much.' She looked at Vicky. 'What am I going to do?'

'*I'm* going to kill him,' said Lewis.

The girls exchanged a glance. Lewis sounded serious. 'Don't be silly,' said Vicky. 'You can't—'

Megan interrupted her. 'How long have you known, Lewis? Tell me.'

Lewis sagged and put his head in his hands. 'Since the night Dad disappeared.'

'What the fuck...?' Megan stared at him in dismay. 'How could you keep this from me all this time? Well, I've got something to tell you, too. Dad didn't disappear.'

'Megan!' said Vicky. 'Now's not the time.'

'I don't care. No more secrets.' She turned to her brother. 'Dad's not missing. He's dead. And his bones are in the garage.'

It was Lewis's turn to blanche.

Chapter Nine
SARAH

Saturday, 14 May 2005, 9am

Sarah felt ill when she woke on Saturday to the sound of Megan's children rampaging about the house yet again. She sensed Lewis stirring beside her.

'Did you have a good time talking to Alex in the pub last night?' he muttered as he heaved himself upright.

Through the fog of her hangover, Sarah retorted, 'You were with your friends all evening! What was I supposed to do? Finella and Vicky ignored me, then Vicky sat staring into space and Finella disappeared. The last time I saw her was when Alex had to take her home. She looked like she was about to have a fight with Catriona from the newspaper. She must have been really drunk, same as your sister. She got plastered and went off with that awful pal of yours.'

'That bastard is no friend of mine.'

'You seemed pretty friendly with him when you talked to him all the way from Fort William on that awful journey last week.' Sarah was unable to keep the resentment from her voice.

'Well, things have changed.' Lewis sighed. 'I'm going to have to speak to Megan today. Family stuff, you know? Probably best if I get her on her own. If that's okay with you?'

The last thing Sarah wanted to do was spend any more time

with Megan. 'It's fine. Last night Alex was talking to me about doing some admin work for him and to help Catriona with the local paper so I'm meeting him at ten. Then Catriona invited me to go on a walk with her in the afternoon.'

Lewis swung his legs out of bed then pulled his jeans on. 'I didn't know you were into walking.'

'I'm not. It's just that she asked and I didn't know how to get out of it, especially since I'll be working for her.' Lewis nodded vaguely but his mind was far away as he grabbed his towel and left the room.

Sarah lay a while longer, her head pounding and her mouth dry, contemplating her new life. It had only been eight days since she'd arrived but it felt longer, and already the people and their strange habits were becoming familiar.

Except for Lewis, who was becoming harder to fathom. He'd changed since they'd left London. Back then he'd been gregarious and attentive, besotted with her and unable to keep his hands off her. He had promised so much from this fresh start but now he was distant and uncommunicative.

'What's wrong with you these days?' she'd asked him a couple of days previously.

'Nothin'.'

'You seem down since we got here.'

'Aye, well, coming home ain't the craic I thought it would be.'

'The craic?'

'It just means, like, having a good time. What's the craic?' he gave her a smile.

'So,' Sarah had said in her most posh English accent, 'I could ask you, *Hey Lewis, what's the craic, man*?'

He grinned. 'Aye, sometimes the craic's no bad. No bad at all.' He'd leant over to kiss her and she'd felt happy she'd cheered him up. But it hadn't lasted; he had soon become morose again. Maybe it was because he hadn't found a job yet; he'd earned well in the Heinz factory in north London even though he'd hated the shifts. Hopefully something would come up for him soon.

She edged her way out of bed, trying not to move her head too fast, and heard a car and voices at the front of the house. Outside, Megan was giving a holdall to a scruffy guy in double denim. The boys ran out of the house and threw themselves at the man. *Must be their father*, thought Sarah, as the boys clambered into the car and left with him. Megan stared after the vehicle, long after it had disappeared, and Sarah wondered if she was wishing she'd gone too. She was about to turn away, worried Megan would look up and see her watching, when Vicky pulled up in her ancient car. Megan jumped in and they left together. *Oh well*, thought Sarah, *Lewis would have to speak to Megan about their 'family stuff' later.*

Sarah showered, left her blonde hair loose over her shoulders and made her face up carefully. She pulled on tights, planning to wear a skirt, then changed her mind and put her pale grey trouser suit on instead; she wanted to look business-like. Working for a newspaper would be amazing, even if it was only part-time for a tiny local rag.

When she went downstairs Lewis pretended to wolf-whistle before giving her a lift to the High Street in his mother's old car. It had been locked in the run-down garage for over two years but a few days previously Gregor had helped Lewis get the engine turning over again. Sarah worried about getting her best suit dirty as she lowered herself into the grubby passenger seat. 'You and Gregor had a great laugh together this week when you were fixing the car. When did you fall out?'

Lewis gritted his teeth. 'I saw something I'm not happy about last night.' He gripped the wheel then banged his hand on it, making Sarah jump. 'Just wait till I get my hands on that bastard.'

'Lewis…' Sarah started, but wasn't sure what to say. She was beginning to feel she didn't know him at all.

The short journey over, Lewis parked at the end of the High Street, near the ferry terminal to the islands. 'Don't worry, it's just a blokes' fallout. We have them too, you know.' He tried to raise a smile but it didn't reach his eyes. 'I'm going to see if there's a job going on the ferries for the summer. I worked there years ago. It'll give me time to find something else before winter.'

'Okay… Good luck. Thanks for the lift.' Sarah got out and set off up the street to the offices of Campbell & Co.

The misty rain was barely noticeable yet her hair was damp by the time she reached the offices; she could feel it curling with every second that passed and wished she'd brought a brolly. She would have to get one of those colourful waterproof coats everyone wore around here, and no wonder – it had been drizzly since her arrival and she'd hardly had a glimpse of the famous mountains everyone raved about. Nothing but heavy cloud reflected in the grey sea that stretched into the distance, to the islands dotted along the horizon.

Sarah waited outside Alex's office feeling chilled; it didn't feel like May. She turned and stepped backwards as she sensed a figure striding towards her. The man was close before he undid the tie beneath his chin and lowered the hood.

'It's you,' she said, relieved. People looked so sinister with their heads covered.

'Who were you expecting?' Alex asked with an irritated look on his face that made Sarah wonder if he regretted arranging to meet her on a Saturday morning. 'Let's get out of this rain,' he said, unlocking the office door. 'How are you today anyway?'

'A little tired after last night. How about you?'

'Me? Fresh as a daisy as always. I woke at six and have been up Ben Calder already.'

Sarah was impressed. 'In this weather?'

'It's refreshing.'

'I plan to give hill walking a try. I've never been to the top of a mountain before.'

'You should get your boyfriend's sister to take you. She's always up the hill. I saw her this morning, in fact.'

'Really?' Sarah had no idea Megan had been out that morning.

'Don't spoil that pretty face with a frown,' said Alex, reaching to take a damp ringlet in his hand and tuck it behind her ear. 'I see our Highland mist agrees with you.' It was an intimate gesture that made Sarah draw in breath, but it was over in moments and she almost felt as though she'd imagined it.

After showing her around the office briefly, Alex took her to the café next door, explaining that he and Catriona had made a deal. The *Glasdrum Journal* had no funds for admin support for their outreach offices so Alex had agreed his firm would provide some assistance in return for free advertising. 'You'd do some reception and secretarial work for me, and a few hours a week for the paper. If you're any good at writing, you might get the chance to submit the odd article. I'm sure a clever girl like you could string a few words together about local ceilidhs and whatnot. I've known Catriona since our school days, that's why I agreed to help her. What do you think?'

'It sounds perfect. Thank you.'

'It's ideal for me too,' said Alex, putting his hand over his heart, 'to have a beautiful woman like you working for me.'

Flustered by his intense stare and uncomfortable with his words, Sarah felt awkward and tongue-tied. She was saved from replying when the waitress arrived to take their order.

Alex resumed normal conversation as they drank coffee and ate scones. Sarah picked at hers, nerves having taken away her appetite, but after a while she relaxed, answering Alex's questions about her life in London and laughing at his stories of small-town life. By the time she left she was looking forward to starting the new job.

After arranging with Alex to start on Monday, Sarah wandered along the High Street trying to phone Lewis on her mobile, but the signal was so poor it rarely worked and she had no option but to walk home in her heels, the bottoms of her trouser legs soaking up the puddles. The overhanging trees dripped onto her head as she trudged along the mile of single track, and her hair was plastered against her head by the time she arrived at the deserted house. She stripped off her suit and hung it to dry over a chair, then went for a shower to warm herself. It was futile; the water was lukewarm. Now thoroughly chilled, Sarah pulled on a jumper and made some hot chocolate, wishing she'd thought to get Catriona's phone number. She didn't feel like going back out in this weather but as she'd agreed to be picked up, Sarah found a waterproof coat of Lewis's and waited till she heard the crunch of gravel outside the house.

'Thanks for collecting me,' she said as she climbed into Catriona's bright blue Lupo.

'Pleasure's all mine, Sarah. I already had a big walk up the hill this morning so a gentle stroll will do me fine just now. It'll be fun to show someone new around.'

Sarah was bemused that here was yet another person who had been up the hill that morning. First Megan, then Alex, and Catriona too; what was it with these people?

They parked at the start of the main path up Ben Calder but followed a lower path that curved round the foot of the mountain, rising more slowly. Sarah felt dwarfed by the solid hulk of mountain, its upper half disappearing in the mist, the lower slopes green with early shoots of bracken, still tightly curled, as she trotted along beside Catriona, who was striding out at some pace.

The light rain had stopped but clouds hung low as they followed the track along the base of an increasingly steep slope that became a rocky cliff face about fifty metres above them. There was now little greenery in the passage that twisted between the hills, deprived of sunlight for much of the day. Catriona pointed upwards. 'The main Ben Calder path is above us, running along the edge of that cliff, and this lower bit is called Crofter's Gully. My dad fell to his death here last year.'

Sarah looked at Catriona in alarm. 'He fell right here?'

'Nearby anyway,' Catriona said, carrying on.

'I'm so sorry,' said Sarah in a soft voice although the words sounded loud and inadequate as they echoed in the silence between the mountains. Greyness surrounded them; the sheer face of the cliff, the boulders strewn beside the path, fallen from above hundreds or even thousands of years earlier, and the mist that hung, eerie and still, as they trudged onwards into the bleak landscape. Sarah wondered how far they were going and from time to time glanced upwards, fearful a rock would come crashing down on them. She tried not to stumble on the stony path in her soaked converses while keeping up with Catriona's confident steps in her well-worn walking boots.

Suddenly Catriona stopped and pointed at a splash of bright blue on the ground to the right, at the bottom of the cliff. 'What is that?'

Sarah stepped past her and walked towards what looked like a waterproof coat lying beneath the cliff. As she got closer she saw dark trousers and boots. A sickening dread came over her and she could hardly bear to go any nearer. Surely it couldn't be…?

She glanced at Catriona, who was rooted to the spot with her hand covering her mouth, then back at the figure, now only twenty metres from her. She could see it was a person lying immobile on the loose scree at the bottom of the cliff. Sarah raised her eyes to the rock face that towered above them. Had this person been walking on this lower path and collapsed, or had they fallen from above? Or… Sarah remembered the article in the *Journal* which had mentioned the Mist Murderer. She craned her neck, half expecting to see someone at the top of the cliff, before shaking her head; that was ridiculous.

Catriona caught up with her and grabbed her arm. She was

distressed and breathing hard. 'Go and see if he's still alive. It might not be too late,' she said. 'I can't bear to go any closer.'

Not wishing Catriona to be reminded of her father's fatal accident, Sarah steeled herself and walked cautiously towards the motionless shape. 'Please let him still be alive,' she muttered, looking at the man lying face down with his hood over his head. She felt paralysed with dread for a moment before gingerly touching him. When he didn't move she clutched his coat and pulled him onto his back, gasping and recoiling when dead eyes stared unseeing from his battered, blood-splattered face. With a muffled cry she ran back to Catriona, tears in her eyes.

'Dead?' asked Catriona and Sarah nodded, unable to speak, a sob in her throat.

To Sarah's astonishment, Catriona pulled out a camera and took a few snaps of the body from a distance. When she saw the look on Sarah's face she lowered the camera. 'Sorry, I know it's insensitive but Sarah, don't forget, we're the local journalists and we have just happened upon a dead body, very possibly a murder victim.'

Their eyes flicked upwards before they checked themselves. 'Do you really think it's possible?' Sarah asked, looking around, fearful as she took in their remote location and the poor visibility.

'That's too many falls to be a coincidence. Something's going on.'

'Shit, this is awful. We have to get help.'

Catriona checked her Nokia. 'There's no signal here. Let's go.'

They hurried back as fast as they could, Sarah stumbling along behind Catriona, tripping over rocks and splashing heedlessly through puddles, desperate to get back to civilisation as quickly as possible. With still no phone reception at the car park, they drove to Megan's mum's house to call the police and alert the Mountain Rescue Service. It was after four by the time Catriona headed off to the police station to give a statement about their discovery. Feeling drained, Sarah was relieved when Catriona offered to go alone, leaving her to creep upstairs to lie down and try to shake the vision of the man's pulverised face out of her head. The shock that she'd potentially discovered the victim of a serial killer was immense and she kept telling herself it simply wasn't possible. It was another tragic accident; the man had taken a mistaken step in the swirling mist that had shrouded the path like a malevolent spirit. The image wouldn't shift from her head, and every time she closed her eyes she imagined the sensation of falling so keenly she found herself gripping the sides of her bed.

Around five Lewis arrived home, his mood little better than it had been in the morning. 'I'm so glad you're home,' she said, joining him in the kitchen. 'You'll never guess what happened to me today...'

'What's that then?' he asked, though he didn't look up from the kettle.

'I found a dead body. Another man has fallen into Crofter's Gully.'

Lewis turned to look at her. 'Shit. That's bad. You found him?'

'Yeah, with Catriona. He was just lying there... and I'm worried it might have been...' Sarah's lip wobbled at the memory and couldn't bring herself to voice her fears about a killer. It sounded so implausible and yet...

Lewis got up and held her. 'I'm so sorry, Sarah,' he murmured in her ear. 'What a terrible experience. Everything about coming back here has been awful.' Lewis clung onto her for so long she wondered who was comforting who.

She pulled away from him and held his hands. 'What's wrong, Lewis? You've not been yourself since we arrived.'

Lewis sat at the kitchen table and put his head in his hands. 'I'm sorry, Sarah. I've things on my mind, that's all. Family stuff wi' Megan I need to sort out. I'll be right as rain again soon.'

'What is the family stuff you keeping talking about?'

At the sound of a car pulling up, Lewis jumped to his feet. 'That'll be Megan. I really need to speak to her on her own. About… about our mum. Do you mind?'

She felt let down that her traumatic afternoon was being pushed aside but didn't feel in a position to say anything as Lewis hustled her out of the room. She went upstairs with a heavy heart. What was she doing in this godforsaken town? But the thought of going back to London was not appealing either; back to the job she hated, the long commute, the friends with their husbands and babies, to overbearing Cecilia and her distant father. Anyway, her flat would have different occupants, her job was filled, and Glasdrum still held the promise of a new life. Hopefully Lewis would soon be back to his previous jovial self, and this unfortunate spate of accidents – because that's all they were – on the mountain would come to an end.

As she sat on her bed contemplating her life, she heard the kitchen door slam, some angry shouting, then the crash of the front door. After a while she went back downstairs and found Lewis on his own at the kitchen table, a picture of despair.

'Hey, what's up?'

He looked close to tears. 'I'm sorry about all this. I should have thought about my insane family before we came here. How could I have forgotten what a nightmare they all are? None of them normal, not one of them!'

'You're normal.'

Lewis slammed his hand on the table, startling her. 'But I'm not. You don't know how fucked up I am, Sarah. I thought I was better after... everything that happened when my dad, you know... disappeared, but I'm not. Coming home has brought it all back. And the situation is much worse than I expected.'

Sarah sat down. She didn't know what he meant, and after everything that had happened today she didn't feel she had the energy to deal with this despairing, troubled man. She wanted easy-going, attentive Lewis back. She wanted someone to look after *her*, not the other way round. 'What did you fall out with Megan about?' she asked.

Lewis slapped himself on the head and made a groaning noise that reminded Sarah of his pal Gregor when he'd hit the deer that night. 'I'm going to have to go and visit my mum,' he said.

'I'd like to meet her too. When are you going to go?'

'I need to go now but I don't think you should come this time. I need to talk to her on my own about, you know...'

'The private family stuff?'

'I'm sorry, Sarah, it's complicated,' Lewis said miserably. He held his hand out, as though reaching for hers, but she turned her back and ran upstairs to their bedroom, her heart hammering so hard it was painful in her chest. She hated being shut out. It was no doubt a kickback from her childhood; losing her mother and never feeling a proper part of her father's new life with Cecilia and the baby. But this was different; she was an adult, Lewis was her boyfriend, and despite his awkward behaviour since coming home, she loved him and wanted their new life together to work out. Maybe she wasn't being supportive enough? He was clearly having some kind of crisis. She racked her brain to think what it might be about, and there was an obvious answer: the house and who lived in it. Sarah had complained so often about how noisy the children were; cheeky, too (downright rude at times). Perhaps Lewis had told Megan to move back to her own house and that was why they'd fallen out, and why Lewis was going to see his mum. It seemed so obvious. Megan had made several barely veiled comments about how nice it was for her boys to be living in the family home and not in the Council-built henhouse up the hill. Poor Lewis must have felt a right piggy-in-the-middle. Sarah decided to reassure him he didn't have to worry his mother with it. Megan had the right to live here. She and Lewis would find their own place as soon as they both got jobs.

Sarah heard Lewis leaving, and she grabbed her bag and jacket. She'd go with him, meet his mother and stop any worries arising about the house. It was almost six o'clock. They could grab some dinner in Fort William afterwards.

She pelted downstairs, out the door, and hauled open the passenger door just as Lewis started the engine.

'Sarah! I'm just leaving.'

'I know,' she said and jumped in, slamming the door. 'I'm coming too.'

'But I need to speak to my mum.'

'Yes, and I know why.'

'You do?' Lewis looked uncertain.

'About Megan's situation.'

Lewis looked aghast. 'You know about Gregor?'

It was Sarah's turn to look confused. 'Gregor?'

'So you don't know about Gregor?'

'What's he got to do with anything?'

'I've got to get going. The home will only let me visit Mum before half seven.'

'So let's go.' Sarah smiled at him. 'I'm coming with you whether you like it or not.' The look of annoyance that passed across Lewis's face made her confidence falter but it was too late for her to get back out as he accelerated away from the house with such severity the car's tyres left deep grooves in the gravel.

Sarah attempted conversation a couple of times but got nothing back except monosyllabic replies, even when she tried to tell him more about her and Catriona's gruesome discovery earlier. Had that only been today? It had already taken on a dream-like, or nightmarish, quality. Lewis's lack of interest started to annoy her but rather than risk a confrontation she stared out of the window and rehearsed in her head what she'd like to say to him. By the time the road veered away from the coast and inland through the hills, she had a withering speech fully formed. But she knew she'd never voice it. *Story of my life*, she thought with a touch of bitterness, *always keeping my mouth shut*. Her thoughts turned to her new job and Alex. He was a charming man at times but something about him made her nervous. Then she felt irritated with herself; everyone made her jumpy these days. Maybe it was time she started asserting herself a bit more.

*

Fort William looked bleak when they arrived and drove along the concrete bypass, grey loch on one side and the drab backside of the High Street buildings on the other. Various people in outdoor jackets, hoods up, wandered on the pavement as the cars flashed past them along the side of Loch Linnhe ignoring the forty mile per hour speed limit.

At the care home, they were shown to Murdina's room. Her face lit up when she saw her son, and Sarah noticed a tear in Lewis's eye as he embraced his mother.

'This is Sarah, Mum. She's from London.' Sarah stepped forwards feeling anxious. What should she do? Shake hands? Hug her like Lewis had done? She took Murdina's outstretched hand briefly, smiled and, when no return smile was forthcoming, sat down in the furthest chair. Lewis sat beside his mother and told her a bit about London and what had happened since they'd come back. 'We're living at yours, Mum, with Megan and the boys.'

Sarah listened. Would Lewis ask his mother about who should be living in her house? Having now met Murdina, Sarah could see the woman was seriously ill. Her mind came and went, sometimes lucid, other times barely following what Lewis was saying.

'Is your father still at the house?' Murdina asked.

Lewis glanced at Sarah. 'Mum, that's what I wanted to speak

to you about. Megan told me she'd been talking to you about Dad and you got upset. And… well… you need to understand that Dad's gone. We should all stop worrying about him.'

'But Megan knows where he is—'

'Mum…'

Murdina leant forward and whispered, 'She said she found him in the garden.'

Sarah's eyes flitted back and forth between Murdina and Lewis, confused, and Lewis swore softly.

'Now, dear, that kind of language isn't…' Murdina paused mid-sentence and stared at Sarah. 'I can't find my tights. Where did you put them?' She became agitated and moaned softly.

'Mum,' said Lewis, taking her hand, but she pulled it away and started banging it on her chair. 'Mum, stop it,' said Lewis and he tried to grab her hand again. She screamed.

'I'll get someone,' said Sarah, relieved to escape the oppressive atmosphere.

A nurse settled Murdina and advised Lewis to come back in the morning when she tended to be less prone to outbursts.

*

Back in the car, Lewis sat immobile in the driver's seat, gripping the steering wheel, his jaw clenched, making no attempt to start the engine. She reached across and laid her arm on his shoulder gently, stroking the back of his neck as tears rolled silently down his face.

They sat like that for some time, until Lewis turned towards her and they embraced. 'Thank you for being there for me,' he said, his voice muffled against her hair. 'I'm glad you're here; I couldn't face all this on my own.'

'Face what on your own?' she asked. 'Your mum's illness?'

'It's worse than that,' he said. 'It's some fucking story, let me tell you.'

Lewis started the engine and set off on the road back to Glasdrum, the unspoken conversation hanging heavy in the air.

Eventually Sarah couldn't bear it. 'What did your mum mean about Megan finding your dad in the garden?' Lewis glanced at her anxiously and she waited until he eventually spoke. 'What Mum said is true. Megan found Dad's bones last week when they moved the old septic tank, so she gathered them up and put them in the garage.'

'*What?*' Sarah covered her mouth in horror. 'So... that means...'

'Yeah, my dad's dead. Someone must have killed him and buried him in the garden. And I want you to know the truth – Megan thinks it might have been Mum. That's why she doesn't want to go to the police.'

'Oh my God, Lewis, how awful. And surely that can't be true...'

He shrugged. 'It's insane.'

'So who could have done it?' asked Sarah in a hushed voice as she realised she was, yet again, contemplating a possible murder in Glasdrum.

Lewis shook his head. 'I've no idea. And I'm sorry but I just can't talk about it any more.' Lewis looked close to tears and Sarah felt her heart burst in sympathy. She knew exactly how he felt: today was proving too much for her, too.

By then the road had reached the sea, the bleak, dark expanse that merged in the distance into the low cloud. Sarah couldn't believe only eight days had passed since she'd made the journey with Gregor and Lewis, and this time her sensation of being transported into another world was even more acute; over the hills and along the coast to the world of rain and death.

Chapter Ten
FINELLA

Saturday, 14 May 2005, 5.50pm

'Where have you been?' Finella asked Alex, in the nagging voice that made her hate herself. She'd had a pounding head all day after the cocktails the previous evening, and the twins had been a nightmare, begging for longer and longer on their PlayStation, then arguing about what game to play. She knew she shouldn't give in, that she'd be setting a precedent, but actually, she had long ago established the principle that if her children moaned for long enough, she'd crumble. She knew it, and they knew it. Their whining voices caused something akin to a panic attack.

'Up the Ben, then I popped into the office for a bit. I thought you were going into work, too?'

'Vicky couldn't have the kids today. She's going to Fort William to visit Megan's mother, which is odd. Why would she do that?' said Finella, half to herself. She often found herself voicing random thoughts to Alex, even though she knew it bored him.

'Thankfully I'm not privy to Vicky's social diary. There's something strange about that girl.'

'For goodness sake, don't start that again. It's a godsend she looks after the kids. If you dare jeopardise that…' Finella glared at her husband.

'I don't trust her and don't like her looking after the kids.'

'So why don't you look after them for a change? You didn't even stay in with them last night like you were supposed to.'

'Your dad was happy to come over. He said I deserved a night out.'

'It was supposed to be a girls' night out.'

'Don't blame me for your ruined evening. You abandoned that poor girl Sarah even though she seems a very nice young woman. Not so sure about your other friends. I don't know what you've got in common with that little tramp Megan. And as for Vicky, well… Do you know what your dad told me about her?'

'What?' Finella asked, though she didn't really want to know. Since his retirement as a GP her dad had become increasingly indiscreet, and Finella wanted Alex to leave her alone; speaking to him frayed her nerves even more than conversing with the children.

'He always thought it odd Vicky never had any proper identification. She had Louise at home, with a midwife in attendance, but in the days afterwards, even though your dad visited her and asked repeatedly for some ID for the documentation that there had been a home birth, she never provided any. He thinks she might have had a false name.'

Finella stopped tidying and faced Alex. 'Dad shouldn't be talking to you about things like that. He was her GP! Honestly, you men go to that Rotary Club and turn into a bunch of gossiping fishwives.'

'I'm his son-in-law. He can trust me. And admit it, that's odd.'

'Hmmm.' Finella tried to imagine why anyone would give birth at home. She'd gone to hospital at the first sign of a contraction. And Vicky was such a cautious person. She had to admit it was difficult to understand. 'Dad's probably remembering wrong.'

'No, he was certain. He said he's always wondered if he did the right thing.'

'What did he do, exactly?'

'He gave up asking for ID and issued the documentation she needed, with the name she said was hers. But I think she was lying. And is this the kind of person we want looking after our kids? Think about that, Finella.'

Alex walked off to the living room to play the jovial Dad for half an hour before tea time. It was so easy for men, she thought, they could wander in and out of their children's lives when it suited them. *I'm off to work; I'm off to the golf club lunch; I'm working this evening, try to keep them quiet if you can.* Finella had once overheard Alex telling his colleague he was going to babysit his children that night. It had caused an almighty row. 'When it's your own kids, it's called responsibility, not bloody babysitting.'

'You sound so sexy when you swear, Finella.' Alex had leered at her and she had turned away from him in disgust.

Sometimes, and increasingly, she dreamt of leaving him. She thought about all the single mother problems and wondered if she'd cope. Of course she would. All the difficult scenarios involved being poor; they had very little to do with being single. But still. What would her parents say? And not just them; everyone in town would be horrified. Finella and Alex were the indomitable couple of Glasdrum's social elite; solicitor and daughter of the long-standing and much loved GP. Irksome to be forever known as 'daughter of' but Finella was practical enough to realise that 'GP's daughter' was a much snappier description than 'third-year social anthropology degree dropout and reluctant mother to disobedient twins and a withdrawn pre-teen'.

She turned on Highland FM and started dinner. 'Is This the Way to Amarillo?' came on and Finella sang along with Peter Kay as she chopped vegetables for a stir-fry, despite knowing the kids would refuse to eat it.

The song faded out for the six o'clock news bulletin. Yet more about Tony Blair being elected for a historic third term, followed by, *And now, in local news, emergency services were called to Ben Calder when the body of a mountaineer was discovered in Crofter's Gully, beneath the main Ben path, around two this afternoon. The forty-year-old man was transferred by air to Belford Hospital in Fort William but was pronounced dead on arrival. He was believed to have been walking alone this morning when he fell. His identity is not being released until his family has been contacted. The police have asked anyone who was in the area this morning to contact them.*

'Alex. Alex!' called Finella. 'This is important. Come through.'

To the protests of the twins, Alex returned to the kitchen with a frown on his face. 'What is it now? One minute you're complaining I don't spend enough time with the kids, the next you're—'

'You were up the hill this morning, weren't you?'

'Yes.'

'The Mist Murderer has struck again. You'll have to go to the police. You might have walked right past him. Did you see anyone while you were up there?'

'Nobody but that boyish pal of yours who's always up there running. Maybe it's her.' Alex laughed.

'It's not funny! People are dying. It can't be another accident. And if the police want to speak to people who were up the hill, they must be getting suspicious too.'

'Calm down, Finella. People have accidents all the time up there.'

'You should go to the police.'

'This Mist Murderer business is nonsense. The Ben is a dangerous place and people go up there unequipped. I'll go in the morning if it'll keep you happy.'

'You should go now. Someone might have seen you and think it's you.'

'Waste of time,' he said, but went to fetch his jacket. Tom spotted him and started crying. 'Da-ad. You said you'd play on the PlayStation with me.'

'Sorry, son, your mum needs me to pop out for a bit. Maybe after dinner?'

Alex went out the back door and left Finella with two wailing six-year-olds.

She stared at them in despair. 'I'm sorry, boys...' She wanted to explain, but how could she? *There's a killer pushing people off mountains.* It sounded ridiculous but what if it was true? That wasn't going to help James sleep through the night. Her brain too befuddled to come up with a different reason for their father's absence, she shrugged and turned back to her preparations.

'What's for dinner, Mum?'

'Stir-fry with—'

'I hate stir-fry,' yelled Tom. 'I'm not eating it.'

Judith walked into the kitchen and looked with horror at the sliced onions and peppers. 'I only want plain noodles.'

'That's not a proper dinner.' Finella sighed.

'I can't eat any of *that*,' said Judith pointing at the veg and the bottle of teriyaki sauce. 'Sorry, Mum, but it's disgusting.'

'Yeah, it's like puke,' said the twins, making gagging noises.

Finella stared at her children. She chased them out of the kitchen, boiled the noodles, added a dob of butter and threw it onto three plates. 'Dinner's ready,' she shouted, then poured herself a glass of wine and went upstairs to her bedroom, no longer caring if they ate it or not.

Her mobile rang: Alex.

'It's me. I had a chat with Bob at the station, told him I was up the hill and didn't see anyone except that friend of yours.'

'At least you told them. Dinner is—'

'Look, I hope you haven't gone to much trouble with dinner, but the boys at the station are off to the Stag's Head. Old Murdoch is retiring. I'm going to pop along, and there's a buffet laid on so that'll do me for supper.'

Finella was on the one hand relieved she wouldn't have to bother finishing the dinner yet annoyed she was being left to deal with the children on her own, again. She was about to reply when Alex carried on. 'Better get going. See you later.'

'Mu-um!' a voice bellowed from downstairs. 'We're still hungry. Can we have Cheerios?'

Finella lay on the bed and put her hand to her forehead.

'Mum! Can we?' The voice had an impatient tone to it. Like a servant responding to its master, Finella heaved herself to her feet. It felt like an effort due to the extra two stone she carried around her midriff. How had that crept up on her? She used to be so slim. Yet another thing she had lost control of.

'MUM!'

'All right, I'm coming!' She made her way downstairs. 'Right kids, Daddy's had to go back to work, and Mummy isn't feeling too well, so you can have some Cheerios and, as a special treat, you can play these PlayStation games.' Finella retrieved the bag of banned games from their hiding place and gave them to the twins. Cheerios and infinite PlayStation; their perfect Saturday night.

'Thanks, Mum, you're the best,' said Tom, giving her a quick hug, which cheered her immeasurably.

'Can I watch a DVD in my room and phone Louise?' asked Judith.

'Yes, darling, of course you can.' Finella watched Judith run upstairs to her room. She spent so much time in there these days. *Mind you*, thought Finella, as she watched the boys wrestling with one another to open the bag of games, *with those two around, who could blame her?*

Relieved the kids were settled, Finella, too, retreated to her bedroom with a second glass of wine, which she drank, rather quickly, sitting on the edge of her bed. On a whim, she phoned Megan's mobile.

'Hi Finny.'

'You're there!'

'Yeah, I keep the phone loaded when the boys are with Johnny. Mind that time a couple of years ago when Ross broke his arm and Johnny couldn't get hold of me for ages?'

'He phoned me and I drove around until I found you.'

'Yeah, you're a star, Finny. So, what's up?'

'Just wondered if you were busy at the moment. Erm…' Finella hesitated, unsure how to ask for what she wanted. 'You remember that stuff you gave me a few weeks ago?'

'Oh yeah, I get what you mean. Say no more. I'm at Vicky's but was heading off anyway. It's been a pig of a day, and I could do with some relaxation myself. Want me to stop by?'

'That would be perfect, Megan, thank you.'

'See you in a bit.'

The twins were engrossed in their game and Judith still ensconced in her room when Megan arrived, soaked after walking the two miles from Vicky's house in a downpour.

'Let me get you dry clothes,' said Finella as they made their way upstairs to her bedroom. They both giggled when they saw how the clothes drowned Megan's tiny frame. 'I should have got you some of Judith's clothes. You're the same size as her.'

Megan stood in front of the mirror and did an impression of Finella. 'Now children, have you eaten your greens?'

'God, is that what I sound like? No wonder they hate me.' Finella started laughing but it turned into quiet sobs.

'Hey, what's up? I don't look so ridiculous in your clothes that you need to cry about it.'

'Sorry, it's everything. Alex, the kids… I'm not coping.' Finella took a deep breath and got herself back under control. 'Please don't tell anyone. It would be so embarrassing. I mean, other people survive their children's demands. You manage brilliantly with yours and—'

'Yeah… I've no money or bloke.'

'Well, yes, you know what I mean. I'm a spoilt brat. I know it. My dad used to tell me that and he was right.'

'You take things too seriously, Finny. You need to lighten up and I've just the thing to help you.' Megan pulled a plastic-wrapped bundle from the pocket of her jacket, which was dripping water all over Finella's polished wood flooring. 'We both need to get stoned, I reckon.' Megan rolled a joint while Finella opened the window and pulled two chairs over to it.

'Blow the smoke out the window so Alex doesn't smell it,' said Finella. 'He saw you up the hill this morning, by the way. You're keen after last night.'

'Needed to clear my head.'

'Did you hear there's been another murder? Well, another climber has "fallen"'— Finella made the inverted commas with her fingers—'off the Ben. You'll need to watch yourself going up there on your own. Anyone who was up the hill this morning is supposed to go to the police.'

Megan lifted the joint in the air and pointed at it with her other hand. 'Me and the police don't see eye to eye, you know. And anyway, it'll just be an accident. Although hang on, you said Alex was up there? It's not him, is it?' Megan chuckled.

'He's an arrogant bastard but not a killer,' said Finella.

'Here's a laugh for you, if you think you've got troubles.' Megan lit the joint, took a deep drag and passed it to Finella. 'Turns out I shagged my brother last night.'

Finella choked on the smoke. 'What?' she spluttered.

'Yeah, my life just gets better and better. Getting pushed off the Ben by a deranged hiker is the least of my worries.'

Finella stared with horror on her face. 'You slept with…

Lewis?'

'No! Oh my God, no. It was Gregor.'

'Gregor the deer-killer?'

'Yep. Turns out my dad had an affair and he's the result. Lewis has known for ages but didn't get around to telling me until after I'd had it off with him last night. Don't look at me like that, Finny. I know I shouldn't be doing stuff like that at my age. I'm joking about it but I feel sick to my stomach. I've gotta get my life sorted out.'

'What are you going to do?' Finella was curious. The problems in Megan's life certainly put her worries into perspective. She looked closely at Megan. Behind the laughter was something she hadn't seen on her face before: anxiety.

'I'll ruin that fucker's life if I get the chance. He knew, you see. And he still...' Megan tailed off and gnawed on her nails. She looked dejected.

Finella took a long draw on the spliff. 'Do you think your dad knew about Gregor?'

'If he'd been at it with Gregor's mum he must have had an idea. Me and Vicky are going to go and ask her about it tomorrow.'

'I wonder if Donald will ever come back to Glasdrum.'

'No chance of that. He's dead.'

'What makes you think that?'

'I dug him up last weekend in the back garden.'

Finella choked and spluttered on the joint again.

Chapter Eleven
VICKY

Sunday, 15 May 2005, 1pm

Vicky picked Megan up around one and they set off to Gregor's mother's house to ask about her affair with Donald.

'I told Finny about the bones,' said Megan.

'Was that a good idea? I would have thought she'd want you to go to the police.'

'Nah, Finny's not as straight-laced as you'd think. We got stoned together last night.'

'Finella was smoking drugs? Are you serious?'

'Yeah, she's a bag of nerves. Hates her husband, can't cope with her kids, wishes she'd done more with her life. You know… all that middle-class shit.'

Vicky was taken aback; she hadn't noticed and she was distracted by Megan's talk of drugs. After Vicky's awful experience when she'd found out Louise's dad had been a drug dealer, she wanted to steer well clear of any involvement in drug taking or distributing. 'You know what?' Megan continued. 'I reckon Finny's not even at work on some of the days she gets you to look after her kids. She just needs a break from them. She's a woman on the edge.'

'I had no idea.'

'Just so you know, she also told me Alex keeps going on about you. He apparently thinks you've a false name and he wants to find out who you really are.' Megan held her hands in the air at Vicky's horrified face. 'Just passing on the message. You know I don't give a shit myself. And neither does Finny. She's furious her old bugger of a dad can't keep his mouth shut.'

Vicky felt her stomach somersault. Tears pricked her eyes and she felt at a loss to know what to say. After all these years, she'd thought she was safe.

'Look, Vicky, don't worry. Finella is angry with Alex for ferreting about. She thinks you are marvellous and isn't interested in whatever happened in the past. She said she'd speak to her dad and remind him about confidentiality.'

'I don't want anyone to be discussing me! Why can't people leave me alone?' Vicky asked miserably.

'The world is full of meddlesome bastards.'

'I appreciate you telling me and, you know, not asking me about… well… about any of it.'

'No problemo, amigo.' Megan punched her gently on the shoulder. 'Anyway, look what you've done for me. Helping me that night when I got Dad's bones out of the ground'—Megan shuddered as she spoke—'coming to Mum's care home with me, and now driving me to Morag's house. God, I hope Gregor isn't there. I swear I'll kill him if I see him.'

*

Morag opened the door of her run-down house with a suspicious look on her mottled face. She looked from Megan to Vicky and back again. 'He's no here, if it's Gregor you're looking for. He's staying wi' his gran the now.'

'I wanted to have a word with you, Morag, if that's okay.'

'You're Donald's kid, ain't you?'

'Yeah.'

'That bastard showed up yet? Pretty good at running out on his responsibilities, ain't he? Mind you, he ain't the only one. Never found out where that Callum buggered off tae either. Fuckin' men.'

'That's who I wanted to speak to you about.'

'Callum?'

'No, Donald. My dad.'

'Aye well, come in, but I ain't got nothin' good tae say about him.'

Megan grimaced at Vicky as they followed Morag past a kitchen cluttered with dirty dishes and into a squalid living room, where empty bottles and overflowing ashtrays fought for space on the coffee table.

Megan wasted no time. 'I've just found out Gregor is Donald's son. He's my half-brother.'

'Aye? Lucky you, eh? Ignorance was bliss, I bet.'

'Can you remember when Gregor found out?'

'I wisnae going tae tell him. What's the point? That fucker Donald's never going tae care about him, while he's living it up with his own family in that big house of Murdina's. But I got a bit pissed one Hogmanay, it was that big one when they had the fireworks an' all that in the town, and it just kinda slipped out, know what I mean?'

'How did he take it?' Megan asked, and Vicky was bemused by her cool manner. She would have made a good police officer, which was ironic for someone who skirted around the fringes of the law. Vicky often wondered why Megan didn't do more with her life. She was clever and bounced through life with barely a care, yet she had a self-destructive side that ruined anything good that ever happened to her. Any job she got, she fell out with a co-worker and walked out. Any time she got back with Johnny, who was a bit rough but had regular work at the fish farm and adored Megan and his boys, she would get drunk and snog someone else. And Megan was taking such a risk selling cannabis to stressed-out mothers at the weekly baby and toddler group in the Community Centre; Vicky had urged her not to trust the mums but her warnings had fallen on deaf ears. 'They're the best customers; they never want too much, so it keeps me below the radar, and they're so terrified of being caught they'll never breathe a word.'

Morag cackled at Megan's question. 'How d'ya think he took it? He was fucking raging. Mind, it didnae help that Callum was still around then and wound Gregor right up about it. Callum started mouthing off about Donald and how he shoulda given us some cash when Gregor was growing up.'

'Who's Callum?' asked Vicky.

'Ach, he was just one a' the many arseholes who passed through ma life. He buggered off that night an' all. Ah sometimes wondered if he an' Donald pissed off together. Story a' ma life that is.' Morag's face closed in bitterness. 'You better go now, ah cannae be arsed with all these questions. Got stuff tae do.'

'But what did Gregor do after he found out?'

'Fuck sake, ah cannae remember. It was years ago.'

Megan took a joint out of her pocket and handed it to Morag. 'Maybe this will jog your memory.'

Morag grasped the spliff eagerly. 'Aye, right enough, Gregor was in a stinker of a mood and went off into town wi' Callum. Said he was going tae speak tae Lewis, tae break the news he was his brother.'

'Did he see my dad as well?'

'How the fuck would ah know? Ah wisnae there!' Morag lit the joint and sat back in the chair with a contented look on her face. 'This is proper grass, in't it? Cheers.'

They got nothing more out of Morag and returned to Vicky's car, but she didn't start up the engine. She was in no hurry to go to her gardening job at the Church so she turned to face Megan. 'I guess that doesn't help you much. What a state Morag is, eh?'

'Yeah, no wonder Gregor's such a loser. Poor bastard with a mum like that, ignored by his real dad and one tosser of a step-dad after another. At least now I know it was that Hogmanay that Gregor found out about Donald being his dad and that he went off to confront Lewis about it. I wonder if he met Donald that night? Think about it, Vicky. Gregor was drunk and pissed off. Not a good combination.'

'The eve of 2000; everyone was drunk that night. Didn't you say Johnny was in a bad mood that night too?'

Yeah, he was, but that was later. After me and him, you know, got back together again.' Megan smiled at Vicky. 'That was the night wee Rory was conceived.'

'Really? I thought you fell out with Johnny that night.' Vicky was bamboozled by Megan's love life.

'Me and Johnny bumped into each other and were having a good laugh, you know? We'd both had a bit to drink and the boys were playing with their pals on the green up the hill, where everyone had gathered to watch the fireworks. Look, I know it was bad, but we sneaked into someone's garden shed and did the business. And that's how I ended up with Rory. We were only away for twenty minutes tops, but Ross and Kyle had disappeared. Took us ages to find the little blighters.'

'Where were they?'

'They'd gone up to the park and were drinking a can of cider! They were only six and four. Johnny was pure raging with them. They said Grandad Donald had given it to them so then Johnny went off on one with my dad. You know how he hated him anyway.'

'But Donald didn't give it to them. They stole it. I saw them!'

'You saw them?'

'Yeah, I was up on the green that night, too, with Louise. I saw Donald and Lewis. They were shouting at each other, and Kyle and Ross ran up and nicked the can of cider that Donald had put down on the grass.'

'You never told me this before!'

'I didn't know it mattered. I remember it coz I thought about telling Donald or chasing the boys but, well…'

'I wasn't very approachable. Pissed and loud-mouthed, eh?'

'I didn't want to get involved. Thought the can was probably empty anyway.' Vicky shrugged apologetically. 'What else do you remember about that night?'

'It's a bit of a blur.' Megan rubbed her forehead and closed her eyes. 'Me, Lewis, Mum and Dad had set off from the house with Kyle and Ross. I was back living there with the boys coz me and Johnny had split. It was supposed to be a family outing. Dad kept saying the millennium would be a new start for us all.

Crap like that; forgotten as soon as he got a drink inside him.'
Vicky raised her eyebrows at Megan. 'Yeah, okay, like father like
daughter. Is that what you're thinking, Vicky?'

'No! Now, what else happened?'

'Soon enough Dad was pissed and getting grouchy so Mum
decided to leave. She knew the signs; everything she said would
have annoyed him so she went home to avoid it. And then Dad
lost his rag. He started ranting about how pathetic we were, how
we had no sense of family spirit. He told me I was a cheap little
tart and Lewis was a loser, still living at home, no girlfriend.'
Megan sighed. 'We'd heard it all before.'

Vicky thought about what an influence Donald must have
been on Megan's family. It was no wonder she had such a low
opinion of herself. Vicky felt a rush of affection for her. She
reminded Vicky of her sister, another spirited but troubled
woman who had been defeated by circumstances. Vicky hadn't
been able to help her sister, but she was determined to help
Megan piece together what had happened to her father. If
Murdina had not killed Donald, Vicky wanted to do whatever
she could to help Megan find out who did. And the first thing
they needed was to get a clear idea of exactly what had happened
on that Hogmanay night. 'Keep going, Megan. What happened
after that?'

'Mum went home and Dad walked off to get more drink.
Lewis and I had a row because he said I wasn't looking after
the boys properly, and I told him he was a crap son because he
never did anything to protect his mum. It was horrible and I got
really upset. Then I bumped into Johnny and he comforted me.'

'In the shed?' said Vicky, with a flicker of a smile.

'Sexual healing, like the song.' Megan sang a few lines, grinning and swaying from side to side, bewildering and amusing Vicky with her ability to switch emotions from one minute to the next. She stopped singing and continued, 'After we found the boys, Johnny went mad about my dad letting the boys have the cider and went off to try and find him. And I met Finella, who invited me and the boys back to her house. At that time I didn't know her that well and I think she only invited me to annoy Alex.'

'So when did you go home?'

'Me and the boys walked home about three in the morning; they'd had a great time playing with Judith at Finella's but they were knackered; it was a long walk. When we got there, Mum was still up and she said Lewis had come home just before me and crashed out, but she was waiting up for Dad. Which is weird. Why would she wait up? That's kind of why I was thinking Dad might have gone home and they'd had a row and he'd got violent again and she'd, you know, overreacted...'

'Come on, Megan. Your mum is tiny. How could she have killed him, never mind drag his body out to the garden? It's quite a long way to the end of your garden, and Donald was a big man. And why did you go home anyway? Couldn't you have stayed at Finella's with the boys?'

'Alex came home and I could tell I wasn't welcome.'

'He made you walk home with the boys at that time in the morning?'

'The boys are used to walking and Alex wasn't in any state to be driving. Finella was pretty much passed out by then, too.'

'What do you think of Alex?' Vicky asked, wondering

whether to share what had happened the night she'd babysat.

'Toffee-nosed bag of shite?'

Vicky smiled at Megan's description. 'You hit the nail on the head. He tried it on with me one night.'

'That doesn't surprise me. What did you do?'

'I threatened him with a knife.'

Megan sat up, impressed. 'Jesus Christ, did you really? Bloody well done. Bet that put him right back in his place.'

'I don't think he's ever forgiven me. That'll be why he's trying to find out about Louise. He wants to make trouble for me.' Vicky had been hoping Megan would tell her not to be so silly and melodramatic; she had been wondering if she was making more of it than it warranted.

'You're right to be wary of him. He's a creep.' She smiled at Vicky. 'Want me to push him off the Ben next time I get the chance? Finny says he goes up there all the time. I could pretend to be the Mist Murderer!' She winked at Vicky. 'Don't look so shocked. I'm joking. I've already got one dead body to deal with.' Megan grimaced when she spoke and Vicky saw a flash of intense worry cross her face.

Before Vicky could say anything else, Megan opened the car door. 'I've got something to do before I go home, need to teach someone a lesson. I'll make my own way back. Thanks for coming with me.' She jumped out of the car and was gone before Vicky could ask her where she was going. Maybe it was better not to know.

Vicky reflected on the day's revelations as she drove to the deserted church, nestled at the foot of the Ben, not far from Megan's house. It was almost three and all churchgoers had left. She shivered slightly at the thought she was alone. What if there really was a killer on the prowl? She shook that thought from her head, retrieved her gardening gloves from the boot and made her way to unlock the shed at the back of the graveyard. She had flirted with God briefly when Louise had been younger, when she'd been feeling lost and alone, struggling with a toddler, no money and a constant nagging fear of the unknown. The minister at the time had offered Vicky cash to tidy up the graveyard every Sunday afternoon; mainly weeding and litter removal. Reverend MacPherson had taken the time to talk to Vicky and had let Louise play in the church while Vicky worked. She had missed him when he'd died; he had been a comfort. The new minister was a much younger man with more modern ideas but less time to spend on one-to-one chats. Vicky had carried on with the weekly gardening but didn't feel that God was with her after all. And after a few years, neither was Louise. From around age nine, Louise had sat in the car with her arms folded while Vicky gardened. 'I'm bored. Why do we have to do this every week?'

'It's my work, Louise. I'm getting paid.'

'Why can't you get a normal job when I'm at school, like everyone else's parents?'

And now that Louise was eleven, Vicky left her at home. It was a lot easier than dealing with her questions.

She was crouching down below the level of the wall, scraping moss off a flat tombstone, when she heard voices in the car park. She peeked over to see who it was: Alex and Sarah, standing beside Alex's car. They spoke earnestly then Alex bent his head to kiss her. He backed her up against the car and lifted her bottom onto the bonnet, his mouth latched onto hers, his hand fumbling inside her open coat.

Vicky was astonished; first at Sarah, who had only recently arrived in Glasdrum to start a new life with Lewis, then at Alex for betraying Finella so openly, then again at Sarah for being attracted to such a creep. Didn't her instincts tell her what a horror Alex was? Or did she realise but not care?

Vicky raised her hand to swat away a cloud of midges from her head and the movement must have caught Alex's eye. He stopped kissing Sarah, lifted his head and stared over at Vicky. She ducked down behind the wall and carried on with her gardening. Why had she looked? She didn't want to get involved! She prodded away at the moss with her long-handled wire brush for a while before taking a peek over the wall to see if they'd gone.

Sarah was heading out of the car park on foot, towards the path that ran through the woods back to Megan's house, and Alex was striding towards the church; towards Vicky. Her heart went into overdrive but she told herself not to be ridiculous. What could he do but warn her to keep quiet? She glanced around; there was nobody else in the tiny graveyard or car park, both hemmed in by dense trees. She felt very alone.

'Well, Vicky, this is a surprise. Spying on me, are you?'

'I'm not interested in what you get up to. Let's agree to ignore one another.'

'Easier said than done when you turn up everywhere I go.'

'That's hardly my fault,' said Vicky, watching him warily as he came through the gate into the walled grounds. She clutched her brush as he approached.

'I see you've another weapon to threaten me with.'

'Leave me alone, Alex.' Vicky felt sick as he stared at her. He looked around before taking a step closer.

'Get away from me!' Vicky brandished the wire brush in front of her but he grabbed it, twisted it out of her hands and threw it aside. He pushed her against the stone wall of the cemetery and pressed himself against her. Vicky could hardly breathe. She felt her throat constrict in fear. She'd vowed never to let a man take advantage of her again.

She put her arms on his chest to push him away but he knocked them aside and put his hands up to take hold of her head. He lowered his lips to hers and pushed his tongue into her mouth. Vicky tried to wrench her head away but it was clamped between his hands. He released her and stepped back, laughing. Vicky leant against the wall, her legs shaking.

Alex walked away but looked back when he got to the gate. 'Don't forget I know you've got a sordid little secret. One day I'll find out who you are and what you're doing here.'

Vicky struggled for breath as a panic gripped her body. Her chest hurt and she sank to her knees on the wet grass, her mouth wide in a silent scream of despair.

She stayed like that for a full five minutes, getting her breathing under control before standing again, battling dizziness. Then… Louise.

What if Alex had found out who Louise's father was?

But even if he had, surely he wouldn't say anything to a child… would he? In her terrified state, Vicky couldn't take that chance. She abandoned the gardening tools and ran to her car.

Chapter Twelve
MEGAN

Sunday, 15 May 2005, 1.45pm

Megan waited outside Morag's house until Vicky had driven away before slipping up the weed-choked path to look in the living room window. As she'd expected, Morag had finished the spliff and was slumped in her armchair with her mouth hanging open.

She opened the front door and listened. Hearing nothing, she crept upstairs, quickly identifying which of the two bedrooms was Gregor's. She was surprised at how neat it was in comparison to the rest of the house; perhaps he wasn't quite such a degenerate as she had imagined. What chance did he have of turning out normal with nobody but Morag to care for him? She would have felt sorry for him if it wasn't for the memory of how he'd taken advantage of her when she was drunk, knowing they were related. Megan felt a wave of nausea every time it went through her mind.

She rifled through Gregor's drawers and looked under his bed and through the paltry selection of clothes that hung in his wardrobe. Perhaps she was wrong and he kept it at his gran's. But that seemed unlikely; Gregor's gran was a nosy old bitch of a woman. Gregor wouldn't risk leaving his stash at her house. She was about to give up when the hatch to the loft, in the hall just outside the bedroom, caught her eye. Dare she chance it?

She crept halfway down the stairs. Morag was still out for the count so she carried a chair from Gregor's room and, standing on it on tiptoes, managed to push open the hatch and feel around with her hand. She felt plastic, grasped it with her fingers and jerked it towards her. The parcel tumbled out of the loft, bounced off Megan's head, hit the bannister and fell with a thud onto the floor in the hall below. She heard a mumble from the living room.

'That you, Gregor?'

Megan got down from the chair and inched down the stairs, peering over the bannister into the living room.

Through the open door, she could see Morag pulling herself out of the chair. 'Gregor? What you doing back here?'

Megan looked at the parcel lying by the door, the brown cannabis resin barely discernible beneath the cellophane. 'Gregor?' bellowed Morag as she made her way into the hall.

Megan made a snap decision and leapt down the last six steps, landing heavily in the hall beside the package. Morag screamed and reversed into the living room, faster than she'd moved for a long time.

'Hi,' said Megan, as she bent to pick up the bundle at her feet. 'It's me again. I, er, didn't want to wake you. I left something here.

Morag opened her mouth to reply but Megan didn't wait to hear what she had to say. She opened the front door and ran the two miles from Morag's house back through town and along the track road to her home. Despite all her hill running, her heart was hammering by the time she arrived, the drugs clutched in her hand.

At home, Megan stopped inside the outer door and studied the packet; she only sold tiny quantities at a time, but this was a huge amount. Megan wondered if she'd been too hasty in taking it. She didn't want any trouble; just to cause Gregor a bit of angst.

'You're back then.' Megan jumped when Lewis opened the inner door to the tiny porch. 'What's that you've got?'

'Nothing,' she said, putting it behind her back.

'Look, I'm sorry about our row yesterday. I said mean things and I didn't mean it, Megs.'

'S'okay, Bro. I'm sorry about telling you about Dad the way I did. Must have been a shock. I know you were hoping he'd come back.'

Lewis shrugged. 'Not really. He wasn't much of a dad, was he? Mind the way he used to treat mum. Why would I have cared about him?'

'But you were so depressed when he disappeared…'

'That wasn't why.'

'Really? I thought you were devastated.'

'Fuck sake, Megan. Why would I be upset about him going away? He brought us nothing but trouble.'

'What was up with you then?'

'Just life and its utter shit-ness, you know?'

Megan nodded. At the time, she hadn't understood how Lewis could have been upset for so long, but with her recent worries playing constantly on her mind, Megan was starting to comprehend how people could be floored by events and lose their will to go on. If it wasn't for her boys, Megan thought she might just up and leave; disappear to some faraway place, leaving her dad's skeleton and her moronic half-brother far behind.

'I'm sorry about everything, Megs.' Lewis shuffled about in front of her.

'What are you on about?' she asked, trying to edge past him into the hall, wondering where she could put the package without Lewis noticing.

'You know, about Gregor and all that. I shoulda told you.'

'Well, yeah, that would have been handy for sure, but what's done is done. Look, I need to go to the loo. I'll be back.' She deftly switched the packet to her front and sped upstairs, leaving Lewis looking miserable by the front door. She hid the drugs on top of the wardrobe in Lewis and Sarah's room, where she hoped the boys wouldn't find them, and returned to the kitchen to find Sarah sitting with Lewis. Megan was irritated; she wanted to ask Lewis about Gregor's movements on the night Donald died.

'Hi,' said Sarah.

'Hi. How're you doing?'

'Fine, you?'

'Good, thanks.'

'I saw you running.'

'I've not been running today.'

Sarah looked confused. 'You just ran past me. I was walking home on the path in the woods and I saw you running on the road.'

'Oh yeah, well I was running 'cause I was in a hurry. I wasn't *running* running.'

'Right.'

A silence stretched out, broken eventually by Lewis.

'Where've you been, Sarah? I've been waiting for you since before lunch. I was getting worried.'

'You said you wanted to talk to Megan about, you know, the bones, so I went for a walk through the woods to the church.' Tears appeared in Sarah's eyes. 'Then I got a bit scared about, you know, *the murderer*.'

'It's just accidents,' said Megan.

Sarah sniffed. 'I'm not sure. That man Catriona and I found… it was horrible. I can't get it out of my head.'

'The hills around here are dangerous in the mist and people don't realise.' Megan rolled her eyes.

'I'm not doing any more walks around here, that's for sure. This bloody town is giving me the creeps. I'm going to get changed.' She went upstairs.

'You *told* her about the bones?' Megan asked.

'She came with me to the care home yesterday and Mum mentioned Dad's bones right in front of her, because you had asked Mum about them. What did you do that for? You must have known she couldn't deal with stuff like that. What if she mentions it to the staff in the home?'

'I wanted to see how she'd react. The staff will think she's talking rubbish.'

'It's insane to think she might have killed our dad. You've got to drop that.'

'I know it's unlikely to have been Mum. But who did?'

'Dad spent most of his last two years getting drunk and pissing folk off. It could have been almost anyone. A drunken row gone wrong, most likely.'

'Vicky said we should work it out methodically. Figure out

where everyone was that night.'

'You told Vicky? Megan, why? For God's sake! Who else have you told?'

'Nobody!' Then, after a pause, 'Finella.'

'Finella? Jesus, Megan. Why don't you take an advert out in the *Journal*?'

'Maybe we should go to the police and leave it with them,' said Megan, although she didn't mean it. She did not want the police nosing about in her life.

'You, her daughter, thought it might have been Mum,' said Lewis. 'What are the police going to think? Who normally murders husbands? We absolutely can't go to the police. Shit, man, this is getting so stressful.' Lewis slapped himself on the forehead, over and over.'

'Stop it, Lewis. Calm down!'

Sarah came back into the room. 'What's going on now? Lewis?'

'He's upset,' said Megan.

'I can see that,' said Sarah and they stared at one another in a mild sister–girlfriend stand-off before Sarah went to lay a hand on Lewis's shoulder.

'I'm fine,' said Lewis, although he didn't sound it. 'It's just that all this is so... so...' He seemed unable to continue.

Megan explained to Sarah, 'Since you already know, we're trying to work out who might've killed Dad. I went to see Gregor's mum today. She told me Gregor found out Donald was his dad the night Donald went missing.'

Before Lewis could reply, Sarah looked at Megan with her jaw hanging open. 'Gregor's your *brother*? Didn't you two, the other night, outside the pub…'

'Yeah we did. Isn't that just super?' replied Megan, giving Sarah a tight-lipped, false smile. 'Obviously I didn't know we were related at the time I let him shag me because dearest Lewis hadn't bothered to tell me.'

Sarah turned to Lewis. 'You didn't *tell* her Gregor was her brother?'

Lewis covered his face with his hands. 'I know I should have, all right! I only found out myself the night Dad went missing and then… well… I don't know what happened to me. And then I went to London and I guess I just kinda forgot that Megan didn't know.'

'You forgot?' Sarah folded her arms.

Lewis shrugged and Megan felt a stab of sympathy; he didn't cope well with adversity. 'Doesn't matter now anyway,' she said. 'Lewis, you saw Gregor that Hogmanay, just after he found out he was our brother. What did he say to you?'

'He was pissed, everyone was. He kept clapping me on the back and calling me *Bro*. Then he told me. Freaked me right out.'

'Then what happened?'

'He got a bit leery and started mouthing off about how Donald had abandoned his mum. He wanted to speak to him about it.'

'And did he?'

'I don't know what happened after that.' Lewis leant back in his chair, his rugged face close to tears.

'When did you last see Gregor that night?'

'Must have been just before midnight, because the fireworks

went off not long after he disappeared.'

'And what did you do?'

'Fuck sake, Megan. I hung about and watched them, same as everyone. What's with all the questions?'

'It's important, Lewis,' said Sarah. 'Your dad is dead, for God's sake.' She stared at him for a moment before turning to Megan and carrying on. 'So, Gregor found out he was Donald's son. He was angry and drunk, and after he spoke to Lewis, he went to your house to confront Donald. Maybe they had a fight and, you know, Gregor hit him or something. He didn't hesitate to shoot that poor animal the night we arrived here. The man is a violent maniac.'

'But our mum was at home,' said Megan.

'Maybe they had their confrontation on the way here. On that quiet single road. And Gregor dragged his body to the garden and buried him behind the tank. Isn't that where you found him?'

'Dad had done an emergency repair to the pipe into the tank just after Christmas that year. It had been damaged by the cold weather. So the ground was still soft. Maybe it just seemed like the easiest place at the time?'

Sarah nodded. 'Yeah, Gregor probably wanted to hide the body quickly before someone came along.'

Megan could see that Sarah was not only convinced but enthused about her premise of Gregor as Donald's killer. It made sense; he had means and motivation. But strangely, this theory upset Megan more than thinking it might have been her mum. Murdina, in Megan's opinion, had ample excuse for bumping off her husband. But Gregor? Yes, he hunted and killed animals;

there were plenty of rumours about his poaching activities. But that wasn't the same as murdering a human being. He was a waster and she was furious with him for having sex with her when he knew they were related, but she'd known Gregor all her life, on and off. He'd never struck her as the type to commit a murder, even by accident, never mind to be capable of burying a body and keeping quiet about it for five years.

'So, what are you going to do?' Sarah addressed them both.

Lewis and Megan exchanged a glance, united for once. 'Nothing,' they said simultaneously.

'You should go to the police.'

'No police!' said Lewis, loud enough to make Megan and Sarah jump. 'They'll suspect Mum, and Megan will be in trouble for moving the body. We'll work it out ourselves.'

Sarah looked from Lewis to Megan and lifted her hands in the air. 'I can't deal with this any more,' she said in a quiet voice and left the room.

Lewis watched her go before speaking to Megan. 'I'm losing her.' He looked desolate. 'I wish she didn't know about all this stuff. I can tell she thinks we're all weird and violent and I'm a miserable bastard.'

Megan shoved his shoulder. 'Come on, Bro, Glasdrum's new to her and she's a long way from home. Maybe you should just give her some attention. Why don't you put this out of your mind and take her out for tea?'

'I've no cash and still haven't found a job. I reckon she's gonna leave me and go back to London soon.'

Megan could see the sadness on his face and felt scared the depression he'd suffered after Donald's disappearance would return. He held his head in his hands and groaned. 'What're we going to do about the remains, Megs?'

'Let's leave it for now. Nothing's going to bring him back. Let's work out how many people might have had reason to, you know...' Megan paused, struggling to face that her dad might have been killed by someone close to them. She leant forward and whispered to Lewis, 'There's Mum but imagine her getting questioned by the police. We can't put her through that. Then there's Johnny...' She raised her hands at Lewis's surprised look. 'He was raging with Dad that night because he thought Dad had given the boys some cider and you know how Johnny hated him. But Johnny's my boys' dad... and he's *nice*. I can't believe it could have been him. Then there's Gregor.' Lewis and Megan shared a look and they both shook their heads. 'Exactly. I can't see it. I mean, I fucking hate him but he's no killer, know what I mean?'

Lewis nodded miserably. 'It could have been someone we haven't even considered.'

'Maybe Mum was having an affair.'

That brought a flicker of a smile to his face. 'Shut up, Megs.' Lewis slowly got to his feet. 'I can't think about this any more. I'll go and speak to Sarah. See you later.'

Megan sat on her own, worrying. She couldn't believe she had reeled off a list of suspects for her dad's murder which comprised her mother, her children's father and her half-brother. She put her head in her hands, also fretting about the drugs she'd hidden upstairs. What had she done that for? It had been a whim of petty revenge and would probably bring a whole heap of trouble with it. When would she learn to think before she acted?

Her thoughts were interrupted by the clatter of her children coming home from their weekend with Johnny. She welcomed the distraction of their shrill voices telling her about their fishing. She grasped them to her, pleased to have them back. They made all the horrible stuff go away.

*

After dinner Megan sat with the boys to watch *Lemony Snicket's A Series of Unfortunate Events* for the umpteenth time. The boys were crazy about it since the previous year when Johnny had taken them to the cinema during their camping trip to Inverness. They had only been gone for a night but it had been a rare treat to go to the city. Thinking about it made Megan sad she was unable to provide a proper holiday for her boys; thank goodness for Johnny. Why did she have this compulsion to manage on her own?

She stared at her boys' faces, intent on the screen, turning to her every now and again to tell her what was about to happen, little Rory pretending to hide his face when Jim Carrey's villainous character appeared on the screen. Three beautiful children; how had that happened? Well, she knew exactly: a combination of drink and Johnny's sexy smile, three more examples of her getting caught in the moment and not thinking ahead. It dawned on her that she needed to start considering the repercussions of her actions in all aspects of her life. If only she'd left the bones where they were, called the police and let them deal with it... then the whole affair wouldn't be resting so heavily on her shoulders. And now it was too late to report it. The police would want to know why she'd moved the body and they might investigate her life. Megan felt sick with worry and it took a huge effort to shift her thoughts away from her problems and focus back on the delight on her boys' faces as they squashed around her on the worn sofa.

Their cosy evening was spoilt when Sarah and Lewis came into the living room. Megan caught Sarah's barely perceptible eye roll at the sight of a kids' film on the TV. 'Don't worry, it's almost finished, then this lot are going to bed.'

'I'm not going to bed!' said Kyle, the oldest.

'When the film's finished, you and Ross can play your consoles for a bit in your room. Little Rory here needs his bed.' Megan kissed half-asleep Rory's cheek and carried him from the living room upstairs to the camp bed in the small room he was sharing with her. The older boys had the middle room, and Sarah and Lewis had the main bedroom. Megan sat beside Rory and stroked his hair as he drifted into a deeper sleep. Not long afterwards the two older boys came racing upstairs and she heard them bickering over Nintendo games as she lay on her bed, her arms folded behind her head, contemplating the state of her life. It irked her that she felt pushed out of the living room by Sarah and Lewis even though she knew they had as much right to be there as she did. There was nothing to stop her going downstairs to sit with them but there was a strained atmosphere that made it uncomfortable to be in their presence.

Her phone interrupted her thoughts and she answered it before it could wake Rory.

'Megan?'

'Who's this?'

'Vicky.'

'Hey! What's up?' It was unusual for Vicky to phone.

'Nothing much. You disappeared once we got out of Morag's house and I guess I wanted to check you were all right.'

'Eh, yeah, I'm fine.' Megan frowned. When had Vicky started worrying about her?

'Oh… well, that's a relief…'

There was a long pause and Megan could hear heavy breathing. 'Vicky, are *you* okay?'

There was a muffled sob and Megan sat up. 'Are you crying?'

'I've had a bad day, that's all. I'm being silly.'

'What happened?'

'It's nothing, really…'

'Come on, tell me.'

'It's Alex. He scared me and I can't stop thinking about it.'

'Look, I'm at a loose end. They boys are settled and Lewis and Sarah have taken over the living room. Will I hop on the bike and come see you?'

'I don't want to drag you out here for nothing.'

'You'd be doing me a favour. Gotta get out of this place. I'll be there in a bit.'

Megan told Kyle and Ross to listen out for their younger brother and to put their light out at nine, then she popped her head around the living room door, causing Sarah and Lewis to break off from an intense conversation. 'Do you guys mind keeping an ear out for the boys while I pop round to Vicky's?' Sarah looked as though she minded quite a bit but Lewis nodded.

'Cheers. Won't be long.' Seeing Sarah open her mouth to ask

a question, Megan hurried away.

It was gusty but dry as Megan pedalled out of town towards Vicky's, panting with effort as the wind caught her bike. The hilly road had several sharp corners as it snaked along the coast to Vicky's compact, whitewashed cottage, which nestled against the hillside at the end of the beach. Thick walls and deep-set windows protected its inhabitants from the gales that blew in from the sea, and although Vicky complained about the draughts and her lack of funds to renovate it, when she lit the open fire in her living room it was the cosiest place in the world. Vicky had confided to Megan how safe she felt, enclosed by the cottage's solid walls and isolated from the world. 'It's a silly notion,' she'd said, but Megan hadn't found it silly at all. She, too, always felt comfortable and safe inside Vicky's home. She thought the stunning views from the cottage over the dazzling white sands of Camusmhor beach were worth all the hardships of a somewhat run-down dwelling. Louise, of course, as she headed towards her teenage years, had begun to hate the cramped house and the long, weather-beaten walk into town, but Vicky was adamant they weren't moving.

Megan careered down a final incline then veered to the right, past an overgrown car park that had been reclaimed from gorse-infested scrubland for visitors to the beach on rare sunny days. Her teeth rattled as she cycled along the rough track that led to Vicky's, where she propped her bike against the wall and tried the door. It was locked, of course; Vicky was security-conscious, unlike Megan, who rarely locked anything.

A blotchy-faced Vicky opened the door. 'Sorry to bring you out here on a night like this,' she started then burst into tears.

Megan was astonished. Calm, composed Vicky was falling apart in front of her. What could possibly have happened? 'Is Louise okay?'

'She's fine.' Vicky wiped beneath her eyes and gave Megan a small smile. 'Come in.'

Vicky bolted the door behind them and led Megan into the living room. The fire wasn't on but three corner lamps created a soothing glow as they sank onto the throw-covered sofa.

Vicky didn't say anything, so Megan prompted her. 'What's that fucker Alex done?'

Vicky looked nervous, then blurted, 'I saw him with Sarah.'

'Yeah, he's given her a job.'

'It was in the church car park this afternoon. They were... kissing.'

Megan couldn't believe it. 'That little bitch,' she whispered, almost to herself. 'Lewis will be devastated.' After another few moments of contemplation, Megan looked at Vicky again; she was a picture of misery. 'Why has this upset you so much?'

Vicky took a deep breath. 'Alex saw me watching them so he sent Sarah away. He threatened me and he...' Vicky gulped and Megan could see she was trying not to break down. 'He pushed me against the wall and grabbed my head and... and... made me kiss him. It was disgusting and I was so scared he wasn't going to stop.' Tears flowed from Vicky's eyes as her words tumbled out.

'Fuck! That bastard's got to be stopped.'

'Don't say anything to him. It's not that simple...'

'He can't get away with it! And he can't have an affair with Sarah. She needs to know what he's like.'

'Maybe she doesn't care. Look, I can't antagonise him. You know he's been digging around in my past and I'm scared. If he thinks I've told you he'll never drop it. You can't tell him, Megan, promise me you won't.' Vicky's voice rose hysterically.

Megan wanted to ask Vicky what she was scared Alex would find but she had decided some time ago to leave it to Vicky to tell her when she felt ready. Megan was a loud-mouth at times but she could sense that whatever Vicky's secret was, it was nothing to be taken lightly. She guessed it must be something to do with Louise's father, who Vicky never talked about. Another bastard just like Alex, no doubt.

Vicky continued, 'Alex hates me because I turned him down. I've met men like him before. Egomaniacs who think they can get away with anything.'

'I'll have a quiet word with Sarah.'

'No! She'll tell him. And he'll know it was me. Oh God, I should never have told you.'

'I won't say anything if you don't want me to. It's just that if Lewis finds out… shit, he'd be gutted.' Megan thought for a few moments. 'I'll follow Sarah until I catch them myself. How about that?'

'I'm scared what Alex will do if he thinks I told anyone he's having an affair with Sarah.'

Megan thought Vicky was becoming quite paranoid about Alex but she kept the thought to herself. 'Poor Finny being married to him. Imagine what that must be like.'

Megan's phone rang and she answered it with a frown. 'Hi… I'm at Vicky's… Just ignore him and he'll go back to sleep… Can't Lewis sit with him? …' Megan gave an exasperated sigh.

'All right, I'll come home.' She ended the call. 'Rory's crying because he's had a bad dream. Lewis has popped out and Sarah *doesn't feel comfortable* on her own with him because he keeps asking for me. Jesus, honey, it ain't that difficult to occupy a four-year-old. What a useless bitch she is. I guess I better get back.'

'Don't say anything to her about Alex. Please, Megan.'

'Yeah, sure. I'll keep my mouth shut.'

Vicky looked sceptical and Megan gave her a hug. 'We'll think of a way to sort Alex out. Let's hope this mythical Mist Murderer takes care of him, eh?'

Vicky managed a brief smile before Megan fetched her bike and set off home in the fading light. She pedalled furiously, wondering how she would manage not to burst into the house and shout at Sarah for jeopardising her relationship with Lewis. And just as she'd been starting to think Sarah was okay after all.

Part of Megan understood what had probably happened; she was no saint herself. She had seen with her own eyes how gruff Lewis had been with Sarah since they'd arrived, preoccupied as he was with his own problems, and she also knew how easy it was to be charmed by a good-looking rogue of a man. She had promised Vicky she wouldn't say anything to Alex or Sarah but she was determined to put a stop to this affair for her brother's sake; she couldn't bear to watch him fall into a pit of despair as he did before. They squabbled a lot, had done since they were kids, but Megan liked having Lewis back in town, and the boys liked having their uncle around. Lewis was her priority, and the one person who would definitely make sure the affair ended was Finella. A quiet word in her ear and fear of a scandal would ensure she brought her husband back under control. And it wasn't as though Finella would be hurt by the revelation; she had already admitted their marriage was devoid of love, a mere social function to be tolerated until the children grew up. Megan decided she'd go and see her the next day. Vicky would never know.

Chapter Thirteen
SARAH

Monday, 16 May 2005, 8am

Trying to ignore her nerves at the daunting prospect of her first day at Campbell & Co, Sarah pulled on her trouser suit, hoping to make a good impression. She was pleased to have found a job so soon but dreaded seeing Alex after what had happened the day before. She'd followed the track through the woods behind their house until it joined the path that went from the churchyard and wound around the bottom of the mountain until it joined the main path up the Ben. Sarah had turned left towards the church but had started to feel anxious after the gruesome find the previous day. She'd kept telling herself it had been an unfortunate accident, a well-known hazard of the mist, and reminded herself of all the times she'd wandered about London and had no doubt been in much greater danger, statistically, than she was on a path in the rural Highlands.

She'd been relieved when she'd come across Alex and he had taken a great interest in her, staring with his intense eyes and asking questions about her life. She'd been flattered by his attention as he'd walked her back to the car park until, by his car... Sarah shuddered at the memory. They'd been chatting when he suddenly bent to kiss her. She'd been so stunned that for a split second she hadn't pulled away, then before she knew what was happening, he'd pushed her against the car. It had taken her a few moments to push him off and extricate herself. 'No! This isn't right...' she'd said, and he'd stepped back from her, looking mortified.

'I'm sorry, Sarah. You're so pretty I got carried away. I promise I will never overstep the mark again.' Alex had looked into the distance then moved aside. 'You better go. I'm going to stay here and recover from my appalling loss of control. Please forgive me.'

He'd looked so angry with himself, Sarah had almost felt sorry for him as she'd hurried towards the road – she had decided not to walk home through the woods. Perhaps she'd been too friendly and had given him the wrong impression; she questioned herself so much these days.

In the bathroom, she continued putting her make-up on and hoped once she got to the office there'd be no further mention of the incident.

A thump on the door made her blink mascara onto her face. 'Damn,' she whispered at the black streak beneath her eye.

'I need to poop,' wailed Rory.

'Okay, I'm coming out,' she said, gathering up her stuff and letting Rory into the room.

'What are you doing?' he asked as he pulled his trousers down and sat on the toilet.

'Getting ready for work.'

'You look pretty.'

'Thank you, Rory, that's a nice thing to say.' She smiled at him; he looked cute sitting there on the toilet swinging his legs. 'You look very handsome, too.'

'I'm finished,' said Rory as Sarah left the room.

She poked her head back around the door. 'Finished what?'

He grinned at her with dimpled cheeks. 'Finished my poop. Someone has to wipe my bum.'

'Can't you do it yourself?'

'Mummy says I make it all smeary.'

'Where's Mummy?'

'She's running up the mountain.'

Sarah rolled her eyes; Megan should warn them if she was going out without the kids. It wasn't how Sarah planned to behave when she was a mother. 'I used to look after my little brother,' she said to Rory, as she helped him. 'Now don't forget to wash your hands.' Sarah felt pleased with her motherly manner and wondered if she and Lewis would have children one day; the thought appealed to her a lot.

Rory flapped his hands briefly under the water then ran away, and Sarah's anxiety about her first day at work came surging back as she returned to the bedroom to find Lewis still asleep. It suited her not to wake him, plagued as she was with guilt about the incident with Alex, so she got dressed without putting the light on or opening the curtains and was hurrying out of the house when she met Megan standing in the front doorway, flushed and sweating from a run. The look of fury on Megan's face made Sarah take a step backwards.

'Off to your new job, are you?' Megan asked. 'Handy you managed to find one so quickly.' Megan cleared her throat then spat onto the ground just outside the door.

'I hadn't realised you were out,' said Sarah. 'Rory needed his bottom wiped so I did it for him.'

'There was no need. He can do it himself.'

Sarah bit back a retort about how Megan hadn't told them she was going out; there was something odd in her expression that made Sarah nervous. 'I better get going. Don't want to be late on my first day.' Sarah tried to get past Megan but she blocked the way.

'Don't worry, I'm sure your new *boss* will let you do whatever you want.' Megan gave a harsh laugh before moving aside.

Sarah was relieved to get away from Megan's pointed tone and aggressive stare. Surely she couldn't know what had happened the previous day? Her anxiety ramped up a notch. The sooner she and Lewis could find their own place the better.

When she arrived at the office, the admin manager, Donna, greeted her in a broad Glaswegian accent, her flowery blouse straining over large breasts. She showed Sarah round the office and introduced her to the junior solicitor, Alex's partner, Hugh, and their shared secretary. They all shook Sarah's hand, asked polite questions about what she thought of Glasdrum compared to London, and commented on the terrible bad luck she'd had with the weather. They all mentioned, in various forms, how lovely it normally was in May.

'This will be your desk, hen. Take a seat. Alex isn't in yet. He's often late because of his hill walking. He says it keeps him sharp,' said Donna with a wink. Sarah didn't understand what the wink meant, and a paranoid voice in her head said, *Maybe she knows about you and Alex kissing… maybe everybody does.*

Donna bustled back and forth to a large metal cupboard, handing things to Sarah. 'Right, hen, this is your induction form. Read through it and sign it once you've completed it.'

Donna paused and peered at the piece of paper. 'It might be a little out of date, truth be told. But never mind, you'll get the gist of it.' She rummaged through the cupboard. 'Pens... Post-Its... stapler. Now, we've run out of staples, can you believe it? It's so annoying. It was Yvonne's job to order them. That's her over there by the window. But she's *too busy* with Hugh's letters so stationery will be your job from now on. I'll show you how you order it. And we definitely need some staples. You could write that down if you like. There on the Post-It, so you don't forget. Oh, here comes Alex now, with Catriona from the *Journal*. You'll like her. She's so friendly, has time for everyone, though maybe a bit too much time for Alex, if ya ken what I mean?' Donna ended with another wink as Sarah stood to greet them.

'Sarah, very nice to see you again.' Alex shook her hand and winked. What was going on with all the winking? Her nerves jangled at the strangeness of the situation.

'This is Catriona but I believe you two have already met,' said Alex. 'On your unfortunate walk on Saturday. Dreadful business.'

'We have indeed,' said Catriona, 'and we've got grand plans for the *Journal*, haven't we, Sarah?'

'Oh, er, sure,' said Sarah, not quite sure at all what her role was going to be and feeling intimidated by the group of people who suddenly surrounded her: Alex, Catriona, Donna and Hugh, the other solicitor, had gathered in a semi-circle in front of her, smiling and nodding. Sarah could sense herself being scrutinised. She tried to think of something to say but was saved by Donna asking Catriona what the roads had been like on her recent trip to Inverness. The assembled group then discussed the traffic on the A82 at length.

Sarah caught sight of something black lying on her foot, beneath the hem of her trousers. She shook her foot a little but it didn't move, so she bent to pull it off and more material appeared. Then more. It was a pair of tights. A memory flashed through her mind of arriving home soaking wet after meeting Alex at the office on Saturday and pulling the tights and trousers off together before hanging them to dry. With crushing dismay she remembered getting dressed in the dark that morning; she'd put the trousers back on without taking the tights out.

With a final pull, Sarah retrieved the tights and straightened up as five pairs of eyes watched her, bemused. She tried to stuff them into her jacket pocket and wondered if a person could actually die of embarrassment.

Donna came to her rescue. 'Oh dear, that sort of thing happens to me all the time! Come on, hen, I'll show you how to do a stationery order.' Sarah brushed away a tear of humiliation and Donna patted her on the back in a motherly fashion, reminding Sarah of the desolation that had haunted her all her life after losing her mother so young.

'I'll nip to the toilet if that's okay,' she said, feeling the painful lump of a sob pushing its way up her throat. They must think she was off her head; pulling a pair of tights out of her trouser leg then bursting into tears. Sarah locked herself into the cubicle and leant her head against the cool, tiled wall, her hands crossed over her stomach. She did it every time she thought about her mother; it was agonising that she could hardly remember her. If she could recall her face, the sound of her voice, her smell, it would be easier, but all Sarah could conjure up were memories of photos, and one tiny film clip of them together on her first birthday.

Come on, Sarah. Get a grip.

She dabbed some water under her eyes and went back to the desk. Donna had left her a catalogue and a list of required stationery so she spent a while going through that and the induction folder. It contained instructions for saving documents with WordPerfect 5.1, which made Sarah smile; it was more than a little out of date.

At lunchtime, Alex appeared at her desk. 'How about a sandwich next door?'

'Oh, no thanks, I'm fine.'

'But I insist! I always buy lunch for a new member of staff on their first day. Don't I, Donna?'

'It's been that long since we took anyone on I can't remember. Maybe you should be buying lunch for your long-suffering staff members, too...'

'Good idea, Donna. We haven't had an office outing for ages. Organise something for next week and I'll pay for it.'

Donna looked delighted as Alex steered Sarah out of the office. They took a corner booth in the neighbouring coffee shop. 'I had to get you alone to talk,' Alex said across the table.

Sarah froze. 'Listen Alex—' she started but he cut her off as the waitress approached the table.

'Let's order first.'

Sarah gulped back her anxiety and ordered a panini, although she felt too on edge to eat anything.

Alex grinned at her when the waitress left. 'I wanted to apologise again for Sunday. It was terribly inappropriate.'

'Please, no need to mention it again.'

'You really are a very pretty girl, Sarah. I got carried away.' He laughed. 'You must have that effect on men all the time.'

'No, not really...' Sarah didn't know what to say. She felt desperate to get away but couldn't think how to excuse herself without sounding rude.

'Obviously it'll be our little secret. My wife wouldn't understand... nor would your boyfriend, I'm sure.'

'Of course,' said Sarah. 'I won't mention it to a soul. It was a mistake.'

'Absolutely,' said Alex, then he leant forward and grinned at her. 'Although there was a moment, wasn't there? I didn't get the impression it was an entirely unwelcome experience.'

'What?' Sarah looked at him in alarm. 'It wasn't welcome at all.'

'There's really no need to be mean about it,' said Alex, and she could feel his eyes on her, watching her as she floundered. She wanted to escape from the awkwardness so much that her heart thumped painfully in her chest. But crippled with anxiety, she stayed put and smiled politely at Alex, defeated in the face of his superior confidence. He eventually smiled. 'I'm teasing you, Sarah. Dreadful of me, I know. I promise that's the end of it.' He lifted the glass of water from the table in front of him. 'It's only water but here's to a good working relationship! Sarah?'

With tears pricking in her eyes, Sarah lifted her glass to meet his; anything to avoid a scene.

Back at the office, Sarah mumbled thanks to Alex for the lunch and went back to her new desk. Her hands shook as she rearranged the bits of stationery Donna had given her. She longed to go home. How had she got herself into this situation? She wasn't even sure what the situation was; only that she wanted to get out of it and back to Lewis. At least she knew where she was with him.

'How are you surviving Day One in the bear's den?' asked a voice beside her. She looked up into Catriona's bright eyes, deep set in a face framed by glossy black hair.

Sarah didn't know how to reply and Catriona went on, 'Alex can be a charming bastard but don't let him get to you. We went out back in high school, before Finella got her claws into him, and he tried it on with me when I came back last year.' Bitterness crept into Catriona's voice. 'I've had enough of men like him, know what I mean? It's time they got their comeuppance.'

Sarah nodded; she knew exactly what Catriona meant about men like Alex. She, too, was tired of being hit on by creeps just because she was pretty. She wished she could be more confident like Catriona, who didn't seem like the kind to keep quiet when an unpleasant man was making her squirm. 'By the way, thanks for going to the police on Saturday on your own. I was exhausted. I still am. Been having nightmares about it.'

'Yeah, it's been keeping me awake too. But it's no problem about the police. It gave me the chance to, you know, butter them up. Any decent journalist needs contacts in the police, know what I mean?' Catriona winked at Sarah. 'I'm working on a story, you see, that would benefit from some discreet police information. I'll tell you about it soon.'

They were distracted by voices at the door. Sarah looked up and saw Finella marching towards her with a furious look on her face. Her heart squeezed in terror as Finella paused beside her desk and stared at her.

'Hello, Finella,' said Catriona.

Finella looked from Sarah to Catriona but didn't smile before carrying on to Alex's office and closing the door behind her.

Catriona gave a nasty laugh. 'Something's got her knickers in a twist. I must dash. Catch you soon, Sarah.' She walked away, leaving Sarah with her nerves jangling.

Chapter Fourteen
FINELLA

Monday, 16 May 2005, 9am

Finella reversed her Range Rover out of the tight space in the school car park. It was a nightmare trying to find a space then queuing to get back to the main road once the bell had rung. Every morning she resolved to walk the children to school but there was always a drama about packed lunches, gym kit, or show-and-tell items. It was a mystery to Finella that she was an organised person in every aspect of her life except this; her inability to get her children ready for school and out the door on time. It surely shouldn't be that difficult. Megan seemed to manage it effortlessly. Finella saw her every morning walking her three boys to school and nursery no matter what the weather, never appearing stressed or even particularly rushed.

Megan had texted her the night before to ask if she could pop round after lunch for a chat. Finella wondered if she'd bring some dope with her, then quickly berated herself for her thoughts. Getting stoned on a Monday afternoon would not do at all, although it made her smile to consider it. Imagine what people would think!

Finella was looking forward to Megan's visit as she didn't work on Mondays and it gave her an excuse to miss the Pilates class she had signed up for. But Megan arrived in a bad mood.

'Got some bad news for you, Finny,' she said.

Finella was gripped with fear someone had found out she'd been buying cannabis and the news was all around the village. She sat down on the seat in the hall. 'Are we in trouble?'

'There's no easy way to break this to you. You know me, diplomacy's not my thing.'

Finella put her hand to her forehead. 'Fuck,' she said. If the Rotary people had found out... or the local Police Inspector, who was one of their friends... or the teachers at the school... Finella felt her world shift on its axis. Life just wouldn't be worth living if everyone knew she'd been smoking hash. She knew what they were like; cannabis or heroin, it wouldn't make any difference. *Drugs.* It simply wasn't the done thing.

'It's about Alex. He's... well... he's having an affair.'

Finella's head snapped up. 'Alex is having an affair?'

'Seems like it.'

'So this isn't about the drugs?'

'What drugs?'

'The cannabis you've been getting me!'

'Why would that have anything to do with it?'

They stared at one another. Megan's words sank into Finella's consciousness and she felt herself sag. 'He swore he wouldn't do this again,' she muttered.

Megan sat down on the stairs. 'Sorry to have to tell you, Finny. I really am.'

'It's better that I know. So I can do something about it.'

'That's partly why I told you.' Finella looked quizzically at Megan. 'It's Sarah.'

'Sarah? But—'

'Yeah, Lewis's girlfriend. That's why it has to be stopped. It'll break Lewis's heart if he finds out.'

'I have a heart too, Megan.'

'God, I know and I'm so sorry. But I reckon it's more humiliating than heartbreaking for you.'

'Well, Megan,' said Finella. 'You're right about diplomacy not being your strong point.'

'You hate Alex and said you would leave him if it wasn't for the kids, and your dad, and all… this.' Megan waved her hand vaguely around Finella's house; the modern architecture, the polished flooring, the Burberry coat hanging beside the door.

'It's one thing for me to say it but another to have to face it.' Finella leant forward and put her head in her hands.

'Let's get some tea,' said Megan, and Finella followed her to the kitchen, where Megan hunted around in her cupboards for mugs and tea bags. Finella was unable to speak; she felt as though she was having an out-of-body experience, looking down at herself and her kitchen. At what point in her life had things started going so wrong? Or perhaps it wasn't her life that was wrong, it was her. Something was not right with her and hadn't been for some time, for years even. Things she should have been able to cope with left her in pieces. Her husband and children, even though they were well-off and healthy, brought her to her knees on a daily basis. And now this! Finella had suspected Alex was having an affair but she'd thought it was a rekindled passion with Catriona. That would have been almost bearable. They had history and it would have been predatory Catriona's fault; Finella had seen her staring at Alex with hungry eyes, and he was too weak to resist. But Sarah… young, pretty, timid Sarah – who had a boyfriend. Alex must have put some effort into seducing her. Finella wished she could cry. She longed to sob and rant and get it all off her chest. But she couldn't; her emotions were locked up inside her, festering and expanding; waiting to be set free. The thought of what would happen when all her feelings were released scared Finella. They might break her into a thousand tiny shards; there would be nothing left of her. It was vital she kept herself together.

'So, Megan, how am I going to deal with this errant husband of mine?'

'Do you think you can get him to back off from Sarah? Without saying how you know?'

'How do *you* know?'

'I saw them together.'

'He's given her a job. That'll be why.'

'They were kissing.'

'Oh.'

'I'm sorry Finella. Men are such a fucking waste of space. I hate them all.'

Finella, as she always did, pulled herself together. 'Don't you worry, my dear. I'll speak to Alex and we'll put a stop to this sordid little affair in no time.'

'Don't tell him it was me who told you. I don't want any trouble from him, you know?'

'Don't worry. Alex will not be told of my source. Now, I really must get on, Megan. Maybe we could have tea another time.'

'Yeah, sure, I'll head off. Give me a ring any time.'

'Yes, yes, of course.' Finella practically shooed Megan out of her house. She could feel panic rising in her chest and urgently wanted to be alone.

She closed the front door behind Megan and turned to lean against it. Her legs subsided and she sank to the floor, her smart skirt rising inelegantly up her legs. *Come on, Finella*, she chivvied herself. *You have to deal with this*. She looked at her watch. Alex would have finished lunch by now so she went to the bathroom to sort her face out – appearance was everything – then got into the Range Rover and drove the short distance to the High Street.

Donna greeted her like a long-lost friend, forcing Finella to swallow back her internal chaos and endure a round of jolly conversation. She broke away from Donna when she spotted Sarah sitting at a desk, Catriona bent over her, whispering something, her hand lying casually on Sarah's shoulder. Finella stormed across the office and stood in front of them, but was left lost for words by Catriona's defiant face and Sarah's timid look. She carried on past them to Alex's office.

He looked up with irritation but replaced it with a smile when he spotted her anger. 'A surprise visit from my wife, how nice.'

Finella stared at his smug expression and her fist clenched.

'Something's upset you, I can tell. Take a seat.' Alex came round from behind his desk, took Finella's elbow and guided her into a chair as though she was a frail ninety-year-old. He perched on his desk and looked down at her. 'What's up?'

Finella hesitated. Once she said it there would be no going back. The gauntlet would be thrown down and the fight would commence. Whether Alex was apologetic, or whether he denied it, or even defended it, life would become unbearable.

There would be an atmosphere, tension, unpleasantness… more stress. If she said nothing, they could jog along as they had been, vaguely disliking one another but able to maintain the pretence of a happy marriage.

'Hmmm?' he prompted. 'Cat got your tongue, has it?' Alex laughed, stood up and returned to the high-backed leather chair on his side of the desk. 'Look, Finella, I don't have time for this. I'll see you later.'

'I know you're having an affair with that girl out there.'

Alex faced her over the desk and she stared defiantly back. 'Which girl would that be?'

'Perhaps several of them but the one I'm talking about is Sarah, the new one.'

'Don't be ridiculous. I've given her a job because we needed a good administrator and she's pretty experienced.'

Finella felt her temper disintegrate. She pointed at him, her hand trembling. 'Don't think you can talk your way out of this. I have a reliable witness who has seen you. Well… let me tell you something… you are not going to get away with this again. Do you understand?'

Alex held his hands up. 'Okay.'

'So you admit it?'

He hesitated and she could see the debate raging in his head. He was wondering if she was bluffing. She sensed she had the upper hand. With unexpected courage Finella leant towards him. 'Are you going to deny it, Alex?'

'We have kissed but that's all.' He held up a hand to silence any interruptions and indicate there was more. 'I admit I was tempted but sense prevailed and it didn't go any further. And that's the truth, I swear.' As Finella opened her mouth to retort, Alex carried on in a rush. 'I realise how stupid I've been and I'm sorry.'

The wind taken out of her sails, Finella nodded at him. 'Good, well, let's leave it at that, then.' She should have felt triumphant but the look in Alex's eyes was cold. Finella knew he'd apologised because he wanted to avoid a scene in the office. He would make her pay for it later. She felt icy fingers of fear tingle down her spine as she backed towards the door. Why had she come? She should have done what she normally did: kept quiet and jogged along. What did she care, really, if Alex screwed every woman in the office?

She got up to leave and was about to open the door when he spoke again. 'Finella.'

Her shoulders tensed. She turned back.

'We'll talk about this properly tonight. Once the children are in bed.'

Finella left the office and hurried back to her car with a dead feeling in her heart.

Chapter Fifteen
VICKY

Monday, 16 May 2005, 2.30pm

Vicky had been worrying all morning about Sunday's events with Alex in the graveyard. She regretted telling Megan; a moment of weakness when she was feeling upset. Megan was impetuous and Vicky hadn't at the time considered that Megan would want to put an end to Alex and Sarah's affair for her brother's sake.

Her thoughts circled back to Alex. She sometimes bumped into him when she was looking after his kids... How could she face him after what he'd done? She'd put their first horrible encounter down to him being drunk but that hadn't been the case yesterday. She sensed he now had it in for her.

With that unsettled feeling plaguing her, Vicky had spent the morning tending to the vegetable patch behind her cottage; over the past eleven years she had become adept at growing, even managing to produce a surplus to sell to neighbours. At lunchtime she made a cheese sandwich and ate it outside on the table she had constructed from a tree trunk that had washed up on the beach after a storm. What a job she'd had dragging it up the hill from the beach to her house then inexpertly sawing at it to create knee space before planting it in the ground by her front door. It looked ridiculous, a pathetic attempt at rustic, but Vicky kept it as a reminder that she was just an actor in this rural life. This wasn't where she belonged. She was a city girl, really, a Londoner like Sarah, with memories of stylish bars, fancy shops and crowded streets. The cottage had been the only thing her parents had left her, and it had come from her grandmother. Vicky suspected her parents just hadn't got around to selling it yet, and thank goodness for that. It had been the remote bolthole Vicky had needed to save herself and newborn Louise when she'd discovered what a dangerous man Louise's father was.

Still, she thought, as she finished off her lunch, distracted from the beautiful sea view by her worries, Louise was growing up. The time was coming for Vicky to tell her the truth. But with every year that had passed, Vicky had felt her secret become safer and she had pushed the past further and further from her mind. And now Alex had made the fear of discovery resurface.

As though on cue, Vicky looked up and was stunned to see Alex sauntering along the track, gazing at the beach as though out for a summer stroll. She was horrified; Megan must have told him after all. *I'll never forgive her for this*, she thought, remembering all she'd done to help Megan when she'd found her dad's skeleton.

She clutched the front of her jumper, a subconscious, comforting gesture as her heart rate quickened. Her mind jumped wildly. What should she do? Go inside and bolt the door? Make a run for it? He was hardly likely to chase her along the beach in his suit. She looked down at her feet in their oversized wellies; she wouldn't be able to run in these. And it was close to three; Louise would be home soon. She had to get rid of Alex. She was going to have to face him.

Vicky remained at the tree trunk table and braced herself for the encounter. Her trowel was within reach and she wouldn't hesitate to use it as her hatred of men came surging back. She mostly supressed it but sometimes her anger threatened to overwhelm her.

He sat down on the bench on the other side of the front door, crossed his legs and pointed toward the beach. 'Nice view you have here.'

Vicky didn't reply, and the silence stretched out. She clasped her hands together to stop them shaking.

'I remember the woman who used to own this place. Georgina Armstrong.'

Vicky's head jerked up at the mention of her grandmother.

'I've been looking into her. She died in 1991 and left the cottage to her daughter, Vivien. And she, in turn, died in a car accident in 1993 and it passed on to *her* daughter, Virginia Moreau.'

Vicky gulped back a tear, recognising her original name. The world around her disappeared and she felt locked in a bubble of fear; paralysed and dizzy. Alex walked over to her. 'Now, *Vicky*, or whatever your name is, I warned you to keep quiet about what you saw on Sunday. But you obviously can't keep your mouth shut and now my wife is trying to tell me what I can and can't do.'

In her head, Vicky cursed Megan again. Just to save her brother from the humiliation of finding out his girlfriend was cheating on him, Megan had gone straight to Alex and destroyed Vicky's life.

He loomed over her and she tried not to show how intimidated she felt. 'You've spoilt my life so now I feel like ruining yours.' He put his fingers on his chin and had a pretend look of puzzlement on his face. 'Gosh, I wonder what else I can find out about Virginia Moreau. It's amazing what you can uncover when you're a respected solicitor. Other lawyers trust you and will reveal all sorts of things they shouldn't.' Alex stared at Vicky. 'Perhaps this *Virginia* lived with someone, had a baby with them, then took the child away from him. Does that sound plausible to you?'

She nodded, understanding the game. He wasn't going to attack her physically. He was going to do much worse.

'Oh, look. Here comes your daughter.'

Vicky turned towards the track where Louise had appeared, then watched, terrified, as Alex approached her. Louise looked from him to her mum and back again, puzzled.

'Hope you had a nice day at school,' said Alex. 'I'm just leaving.' And he carried on past her, back the way he'd come.

'What was Judith's dad doing here?'

Vicky opened her mouth but no sound came out. She shrugged helplessly and Louise rolled her eyes. 'Can I have a snack?'

Vicky nodded and waved towards the house. She listened to Louise banging about in the kitchen before putting her head in her hands. What should she do? Part of her wanted to pack and leave immediately. But that would be ridiculous. Alex hadn't found out anything concrete and didn't appear to have told anyone else. Maybe she still had time. Maybe all was not lost.

She walked to the edge of her garden, where the ground fell

away and a steep slope covered in gorse descended to the tops of the rocks at the edge of the white beach. She thought about her granny and the enthusiastic advice she used to dish out. *Tackle your problems head on!* Vicky was normally resilient but this had shaken her. She recalled the difficulties and fear she'd faced when she came to Glasdrum with a new identity, relieved to have escaped her brutal life with Louise's father, Phil. Alex was threatening all that was precious to her just because she'd spurned his advances.

This thought festered as she went into the house, locked the door, and tried to engage in a conversation with Louise about school.

'I'm watching TV, leave me alone!'

She sat beside Louise as she munched through a packet of crisps, staring at the screen in that after-school, tuned-out manner children have. Every now and then Vicky reached out to stoke her hair, a kick-back to when she had been younger. The first couple of times, Louise twitched her head away from Vicky's hand, but eventually she gave up and snuggled beside her on the sofa. Vicky wished they could have stayed like that forever, locked in their own bubble, the outside world shut away. She could have forgotten about being attacked by Alex, and let down by Megan. Had Megan not realised how important this was to Vicky? Perhaps she didn't realise what Alex was capable of, but Vicky had seen it in his eyes. She'd sensed the coldness in his heart.

After an early dinner, Vicky drove Louise to the church hall for Girl Guides, remembering, as they parked, she'd abandoned her gardening tools on Sunday afternoon in her hurry to get home. But the tools were gone and the shed was locked. Maybe the new minister had put them away, making a mental note about how irresponsible she was, something else she'd have to sort out because of Alex. She didn't want to lose that bit of income, especially as she was going to have to stop minding Alex and Finella's children. She was due to take them home from school the following day but she couldn't bear the thought of coming into contact with Alex. But what could she say to Finella? She didn't want to be the one to tell her about Alex's affair. Thoughts swirled about her head but she struggled to draw them together into a plan.

As she left Louise at the hall, Vicky saw Catriona arrive by car and head up the Ben path. It was late to be setting off but Vicky knew Catriona was a keen walker and her father had been the driving force in the Glasdrum Mountain Rescue for years before his own tragic death on the Ben not that long ago. He'd been something of a local hero and the whole town had turned out for his funeral, with many having to stand outside the small church. As she reversed her car out of its space, along with several other parents who had dropped their girls off, Vicky spotted Alex arrive and park beneath the trees. In a moment of panic at the sight of him she stalled the engine, her fingers slipping on the key as she tried to restart it, aware she was holding up others trying to leave. She battled an urge to duck down beneath the steering wheel as Alex got out of his car and set off on foot up the Ben path, not far behind Catriona. With a grim expression on his face, he appeared oblivious to what was going on around him, and Vicky wondered whether Alex and Catriona were planning to meet up. Maybe he was having an affair with her as well as with Sarah; it wouldn't have surprised her.

She had been planning to go home and phone Finella to tell her she couldn't look after the children the following day but, knowing Alex was out, Vicky decided to stop by their house. Finella had been good to her; the least she could do was to let her down face to face. She'd tell her she had a last-minute interview for a job and that if she got it she'd have to give up child-minding. If Finella asked what the position was she'd say it was confidential until she knew if she'd been successful.

Judith answered the door and her face lit up when she saw Vicky. 'Hi! Is Louise with you?'

'No, I'm sorry. She's at Guides.' Judith shrugged and her usual sad expression returned. She had gone through Brownies with Louise but hadn't wanted to move up to Guides; Judith was increasingly withdrawn and only wanted to socialise with Louise on their own.

'Is your mum in?'

'She's in bed. She's not well.'

'Oh, right, well… em…' Vicky didn't want to bother Finella if she was ill but when she spotted Alex's work shoes on the rack in their porch she had a sudden vision of being at their house, with Louise, and Alex coming home from work and… 'Actually, Judith, it's quite important. Can you please tell her I'm here.'

'Yeah, sure. Do you want to wait in the living room and I'll get her?'

'Thanks.'

It was over ten minutes before Finella appeared in her dressing gown with her arms wrapped around her stomach. Her usually immaculate face was bare and pale, transformed by the absence of make-up. She looked dreadful and the surprise must have shown on Vicky's face.

'I know, I look frightful. I'm not quite myself tonight.' Finella sat down opposite Vicky. She looked miserable. Maybe she did know about the affair. Surely Megan wouldn't have told Finella as well? Vicky was too confused to process her thoughts any further.

They stared at one another, lost for words, until Vicky's came pouring out in a rush. 'I'm sorry, Finella, but I'm not going to be able to pick the kids up tomorrow. I've got an interview, you see. It's a bit last minute and… er… confidential…' She lapsed into silence again. It sounded ridiculous but Finella barely reacted and Vicky wondered if she'd heard. 'So… er… will you be able to get them yourself?'

'Everything's falling apart.'

'Pardon?'

'My life is a shambles, Vicky. I can't do it any more.' Finella bowed her head and sat as still as a statue.

Vicky didn't know what to do. Finella was normally so upbeat. 'Do you want me to phone your mother?'

Finella shook her head. They sat in silence and the minutes ticked by. 'Well… I better go,' said Vicky, afraid Alex would return and find her in his home, talking to his wife.

'Don't go yet,' said Finella.

'I can't stay,' said Vicky, standing up. She felt sorry for Finella, who was clearly suffering, but Vicky had enough of her own problems.

'Is it because of Alex?' asked Finella.

'What makes you say that?' Vicky felt tears pricking at her eyes.

Finella shrugged. 'I'm guessing. He's... well, he's not a very nice man.'

'You're right there.'

'Please tell me what he's done.'

Vicky sat back down but didn't say anything.

'Is it to do with him asking about your past?'

Vicky was floored by Finella's question. The tears that had been gathering in her eyes slid down her face. 'He's trying to ruin me.'

'Maybe I can help. He's crossed a line with me, too.'

'What has he done to you?'

Finella hugged her arms tighter around her body, rubbing her arms with her hands. 'He has affairs. He controls me. He puts me down and makes me feel bad.'

'Emotionally?' Vicky asked, wondering if Finella knew about Sarah, or if she was talking about other women Alex had cheated with.

'Mostly.' Finella had a strange, tight look on her face. 'I've had enough. But I don't know what to do. What's he done to you?'

'He tried it on with me once. It was that night last year when you went to the Rotary Club event. The night you got really drunk and he put you to bed.'

'I remember. You and Louise were supposed to stay over but you were gone in the morning.' Finella frowned for a moment. 'That was quite a while ago. Has something else happened?'

'He's had it in for me since that night. Barbed comments and subtle put-downs in public. And now threats and… well… it's difficult to explain.'

'He's digging around in your past and there's something you don't want anyone to know.' Finella sat down beside Vicky and put her hand on her shoulder.

The small gesture of comfort was enough to break into the emotions Vicky had been supressing for over a decade, and with a strangled sob she couldn't stop the words come tumbling from her mouth. 'I stole money from Louise's dad before I left him and I'm scared he's going to come after me.'

Vicky paused, stunned she'd revealed her long-protected secret. She tried to gauge Finella's reaction but her expression hadn't changed; troubled and concerned.

Finella waited. 'You don't have to explain if you don't want to.'

'I need to tell someone; it's eating me up.' Vicky fought back her tears and grasped Finella's hand before continuing. 'He was a horrible man but I couldn't get away from him.'

'Violent?' asked Finella gently, and Vicky nodded.

'He'd hit me a few times but it was getting worse. He pushed me down some stairs when I was pregnant and I broke my wrist. That's when I decided I had to leave.'

'But he didn't want you to go?'

'He said he'd track me down if I left him… and I believed him. He had some dodgy connections, you see. At the start of the relationship he told me he was a trader in the city but it wasn't true. I found out he was only trading in heroin.'

'Oh dear God, you poor girl. How terrifying. It's good that you left and if he ever turns up you must go straight to the police.'

'I can't.' Vicky swallowed back another sob. 'I did something really stupid before I left. I knew where he kept his cash, so I took a pile of it with me. I wasn't thinking straight; I just grabbed it.'

'How much did you take?'

'It was about £10,000. It's what's allowed me to live here all these years. I've been so careful with it. So I can't go to the police or I'll probably be in trouble for living off drug money. And then they might take Louise away from me...' Vicky tailed off, misery overwhelming her.

'What an awful thing to have gone through, you poor darling.' Finella held her a while before eventually pulling away to make sure Vicky was looking at her. 'Now, listen... You did the right thing. You protected your child. You did what you had to and I admire your bravery. You can rest assured I won't say a word to anyone. And I'll make sure Alex doesn't either.'

'Thank you, Finella.'

Finella stood to look out the window and Vicky glanced at her watch; Alex could return any moment. She contemplated what she'd revealed to Finella and felt panic fluttering in her chest. What had she done? First she'd blurted out what had happened with Alex to Megan, and now she'd revealed her deepest secret to Finella, who she barely knew. She stood up.

'I better go.'

'Yes, in case he comes home. It won't help if he finds you here. But listen...' Finella took hold of her hands. 'Alex is ruining both our lives and it's time we put our heads together and came up with a solution.'

'You won't tell Megan, will you? She knows there's something

I'm not telling but she doesn't know what it is.'

'Good God, no. I love Megan but discretion is not her strongest point.'

'You're right there.'

Finella gave Vicky a hug before she left. 'Don't worry about the kids. I'm going to take a few days off work to get my head together. Try not to worry.'

Vicky's head was spinning as she picked Louise up and went home. She barely slept that night as thoughts about Alex and Finella and Louise swirled like a mist in her mind. Her life was veering out of control and she didn't like it one bit.

The following morning, with bleary eyes and a headache, Vicky dropped Louise at school then drove to the community centre, a decrepit structure with missing ceiling tiles and rusting window frames that hosted jumble sales, a parent and toddler group, dog training classes and a monthly old folks' afternoon tea. Cleaning it every Tuesday was Vicky's other cash-in-hand job; timed for the morning after the dog training, before the baby group began. She'd started the previous year after complaints from the mothers about the mess. The dog hair had been tolerated but when a puddle of puppy pee had been discovered under a table during the toddlers' snack time there had been a stand-off between the mums and the canine owners, which had resulted in the dog group having to cough up ten pounds per week to have the floor cleaned. Megan had volunteered Vicky for the job. She'd been at the group with Rory, not because she felt the need to socialise, or because she wanted to discuss his sleeping and eating habits with other mothers, but because these people were her customers.

The memory of Megan's helpfulness made Vicky sad. She had considered Megan a good friend but to have gone straight to Alex, after Vicky had asked her not to, was unforgiveable. Resentment ate away at her as she pushed the mop half-heartedly around the hall. Was this all she was good for? Scraping a living, doing the pathetic jobs nobody else wanted? And now it looked as though all the sacrifices she had made had been for nothing. Her carefully constructed life was crumbling and there was nothing she could do about it.

'Morning, Victoria.' She turned to the voice at the end of the hall.

'Morning, Mr Ferguson.' She had tried several times to tell him that Vicky wasn't short for Victoria, but he persisted. Not that it mattered, neither of them was her real name. He hobbled towards her, leaning heavily on his stick. She'd heard he was over ninety but wasn't sure if that was true.

'I was hoping to catch you this morning, Victoria. Bad news, I'm afraid.'

'The Council are taking over the centre after all?'

'The management committee fought them for as long as we could but matters have been taken out of our hands. Most others on the committee have resigned.' He banged his stick on the ground. 'We've looked after this place for years and it's being snatched away from us.'

Vicky sighed; she'd known it was coming. The centre wasn't meeting health and safety standards and the geriatric committee had failed to raise funds to renovate the building. Mr Ferguson pulled a twenty pound note from his pocket and pressed it into her hands. 'That's for you, my dear. I'm afraid this will be the last week. The Council are sending their cleaners from now on. Bloody meddling bureaucrats,' he muttered as he turned and limped back out of the hall.

Vicky carried on mopping, trying to stem the tears that threatened to flow. She was being ridiculous. She hated this job and earned a mere pittance from it. But losing it felt like another nail in the coffin of her life in Glasdrum.

'Hey! You found a cardy in here?' A stout woman marched toward her and she realised it was Gregor's mother, Morag. 'Ah left ma cardy at the auld folk's tea thing the other day. You found it, or what?'

'I haven't found anything,' said Vicky.

Morag looked at her more closely. 'You were at ma hoose the other day. Wi that other lassie that looks like a lad. Thieving little bitch.'

'Me?'

'Nah, not you. Yer pal. Ah caught her nicking summat fae Gregor's room. Dunno what but he's fair doing his head in aboot it.' Morag pointed her finger at Vicky. 'You tell her to gie it back.'

So that's where Megan had gone after she and Vicky had left Morag's house on Sunday. She recalled Megan's words: *I need to teach someone a lesson.* Had she taken his drugs in a crazy idea of revenge? 'Why doesn't Gregor go and get it back from her, whatever it is?'

'Ah havenae told him she wis there. He'd only go and blame me, like, for lettin' her in. Ah cannae be doin' wi any trouble.'

Vicky thought for a moment. It wasn't right but there was something attractive about the idea of revenge. The taste of bitterness was strong in her mouth and she couldn't stop herself.

'You should tell him,' she said to Morag.

'Wha?'

'Tell Gregor that Megan stole from him. Then he can go and get his stuff back.'

'He'll go nuts at me.'

'If he doesn't get it back, other people might come to your house looking for him. Bad people. From Glasgow.'

Morag looked worried. 'Can you no tell her for me?'

'Megan and I aren't friends any more.'

Vicky turned away to finish off the floor, battling a compulsion to escape; from Morag, from cleaning and perhaps from Glasdrum altogether. Sod the floor, she thought, and went to put the mop away. Morag followed her.

'So you gonna have a look for ma cardy? It's blue.'

'Find it yourself,' said Vicky. 'I'm leaving.'

Chapter Sixteen
MEGAN

Tuesday, 17 May 2005, 2.30pm

Inside the chill of the garage, Megan stared up at the holdall on the cluttered shelf. What was she going to do with the bones? She wasn't sleeping properly from worrying about them and that wasn't like her. Johnny always joked she slept like she was dead. Megan grimaced. Dead like Donald.

She couldn't leave the remains in the garage but she couldn't go to the police until she had worked out what had happened, until she was certain her mother had nothing to do with it. She'd even thought about reburying them and pretending she'd never found them. But then she would be forever haunted by them, not knowing what had happened. She'd phoned Vicky several times but she wasn't answering, which was odd; Vicky was wedded to her new mobile, always paranoid the school would need to contact her about Louise. In the hope of catching Vicky before she finished cleaning, Megan had gone early to the community centre toddler group with Rory, who was getting far too old for it and found it boring compared to his afternoon nursery session, but Vicky had already left.

She contemplated the bag on the shelf. She had to have a look. Maybe that would help her decide what to do. The step ladder she'd used to put the bag up there was gone and she vaguely remembered Lewis had said he needed it for some work he was doing on Skye. Megan climbed onto the lower shelf and reached up to grasp the bag. She pulled, expecting some resistance – it had been a pig of a job getting it up there – but the bag came away easily and landed with a quiet thump. There was no clattering, no heavy thud.

She jumped down from the shelf and opened the zip. It was empty.

'What the fuck…' she whispered.

At first she stared in disbelief, then hauled herself back up the shelves, knocking old paint cans to the floor, to peer onto the top shelf, in case by some strange quirk of physics the bones had fallen out of a zipped-up bag. But there was nothing up there.

She sat on a crate beside the holdall and tried to calm her nerves. 'Think it through logically,' she muttered but as much as she racked her brains, her mind was blank. She couldn't come up with any theory for what had happened.

Who had known about the bones? Vicky, obviously, and Finella… and Sarah and Lewis. But why would any of them have moved them? And without the bag… Whoever had taken the skeleton must have wanted Megan to think they were still up there. Her head began to hurt.

She looked at her watch and realised she'd have to collect the boys from school and nursery. Something occurred to her as she hurled the holdall back onto the top shelf; maybe one of them had told someone else about Donald. Specifically, maybe Lewis had got drunk and blabbed to Gregor. They used to be pretty good mates after all – brothers, she remembered with a grimace – and Lewis might have convinced himself that Gregor had a right to know. If Gregor had killed Donald, then he'd have reason to move the bones.

It was the most logical explanation, thought Megan, as she made her way back out of the garage. Except it didn't feel right. Lewis was furious with Gregor and was unlikely to have spoken to him about anything recently, and Megan didn't want to face that Gregor had lied to her on two counts; about being her brother when he'd had sex with her and about being Donald's killer. Her mind reeling from thinking about it, she locked the garage door then turned and came face-to-face with Gregor. A small shriek escaped from her lips and she stepped backwards until she felt the door behind her. Gregor advanced towards her, stabbing his finger in her face. 'You thieving little bitch. Why'd you do it? You know what the guys I get it from are like.'

Megan recovered from her fright and fury took hold. She slapped him on the cheek, then pushed him away. 'Because I was pissed off with you, that's why.'

Gregor rubbed his face. 'That fucking hurt.'

'It was supposed to.'

'What the hell have *I* done? You're the one who's put my bloody life in danger by nicking my stuff.'

'What have you done? *What have you done?* Are you completely thick?' She advanced on him, forcing him to back away this time. 'Heeelllooo? Any functioning brain cells in your head at all… *brother*?'

Gregor looked at the ground, ashamed. 'Oh yeah… that,' he mumbled. He continued to back away, looking from side to side, unable to make eye contact. 'Look, yeah, I'm sorry about that. It was, like, *totally*, out of order. I dunno what came over me. I was pissed, I guess, and I've always liked you and it just didn't seem... *real,* you know? Donald doesn't seem like he's my dad – I hardly spoke to him in my life. Let's forget about it, Megs, eh?' He looked at her imploringly.

'Yeah, let's forget about it...' said Megan sarcastically, with bile rising in her throat as she said the words aloud.

'Shit, man, I'm so fucking sorry you wouldn't believe. But look, Megan, you've gotta give me back my gear. The Glaswegians are gonna be after me.'

'How did you even find out it was me who took it?'

'Ma maw told me you'd been round. She met your pal Vicky and she said to tell me. Not much of a friend if you ask me.'

'Vicky told your mum it was me?'

'Guess you musta pissed her off.'

Megan was floored. Why would Vicky have done that? Gregor looked at her kindly. 'Don't be sad, Megs. People are tossers. Everyone lets you down at some point.'

Megan gave him a small smile. He was annoying and rough but she couldn't help but like him, always had done. There was no way Gregor was a killer.

'Gonna gie me ma stuff back?' he asked.

'Yeah, but I'm already late for picking the boys up. I gotta run. I'll drop it round to you later.'

He started to object but Megan interrupted him. 'Do you remember the Hogmanay when my dad disappeared? The big one at the millennium.'

He shrugged. 'Sure, what about it?'

'Did you see Donald that night?'

'Yeah.'

Megan raised her hands in exasperation. 'Well?' she prompted. 'What happened?'

'Jesus, Megan, that was, like, five years ago. Ah cannae remember what I did last week.'

'Think about it! Was that the night you found out Donald was your dad?'

'Oh yeah, right enough.'

'Well?'

'What?'

It was like pulling teeth, thought Megan, aware of time ticking past and the school bell imminent. 'What did you do when you found out?'

Gregor frowned and kicked at the gravel for a few moments. 'I told Lewis about it. Dead chuffed I was, that we were brothers. But he wisnae too happy.'

'And then?'

'I fell out wi Lewis, and I couldnae be bothered with all the partying and it was almost time for the bells, so I wandered up here to speak to Donald. I wanted to tell him what I thought of him, like, abandoning my mum an' all.'

'And Donald was at home?'

'Yeah, he was here and I told him I knew he was ma dad, and he just shrugged like he didnae care.'

'So you were angry with him?'

'Course I was! The bastard.'

'So you had a fight?'

'A fight? Nah. Lewis came back, just as the fireworks were going off in the town, and he told me to get lost.'

Megan frowned. 'Hang on, that doesn't make sense. I got home about three, and Mum said Lewis had come home just before me. Are you saying Lewis came home at midnight?'

'I dunno what time it was, but the fireworks were going off so it must have been.'

Megan looked at her watch. 'Shit, look at the time. I gotta get to the school. You got your car to give me a lift?'

'Nah, it's off the road the now.'

Megan had four minutes before the school bell rang. She started to run. Gregor shouted after her. 'Don't forget to bring my stuff round!'

She sprinted down the track towards the main road, then turned right into the town and up the hill to the school. Her mind whirred. Lewis had said he'd got home about three in the morning that Hogmanay, that he'd watched the fireworks in town, not at their house. But Gregor was saying Lewis had come home when the fireworks were going off. Why would Gregor say that? A voice in her head answered, *Because he wanted an alibi for those three hours…* If people believed Lewis had been at home from midnight, then Gregor couldn't have killed and buried Donald.

It was possible Gregor hadn't been aware of the time and it was other, later fireworks he'd heard. People had been setting them off in their gardens at all hours that night. Maybe Gregor had gone to their house much later, just before Lewis got home… in which case someone else could have killed Donald… Murdina would have been at home on her own from midnight to three… Megan's head pounded in time with her feet. Despite all her hill running, she was perspiring by the time she reached the school perimeter, having missed the bell by a good few minutes. Mothers leaving with their children glanced at her as she panted in through the gate, disapproval in their eyes. She slowed to a walk as she approached the inner entrance to the playgroup and spotted Vicky and Louise coming towards her. Louise smiled but Vicky looked away and crossed the road, and Megan didn't have time to call after her. She saw Ross and Kyle at the gate and waved to them to follow her to the recently built nursery block. Mrs Henderson was waiting outside, holding Rory's hand. 'Here she is at last, Rory.'

'Sorry,' said Megan. 'I, er, had a visitor I couldn't get rid of, then had to run all the way here.'

Mrs Henderson pursed her lips together. 'If I could have a word please, Miss MacDonald.'

'Aww, Jesus. What's he done now?'

Mrs Henderson bent down to Rory's level. 'Would you like to tell Mummy what happened today?' Rory shook his head. 'Shall I tell her?' More shaking. Mrs Henderson straightened up and addressed Megan. 'It was a sharing incident, I'm afraid. He snatched toys from other children and hit a boy with a police car.'

'Simon kicked me first,' said Rory.

'The other child has been spoken to as well.'

'I'm sorry,' said Megan. 'I'll speak to him at home about it. It's because of his brothers. They grab things off each other all the time.'

'I'm sure he'll soon learn not to behave like that at nursery. Isn't that right, Rory?'

Megan took Rory's hand and felt its comforting warmth. 'I'll get it sorted,' she muttered to the teacher, then walked away, feeling like a chastised child herself.

Ross and Kyle, standing a short distance away, started laughing as Mrs Henderson returned to the nursery. 'What's badass Rory done today?'

'Don't encourage him,' snapped Megan, though she, too, was trying not to smile as Rory grinned up at the three of them with his dimpled cheeks. 'You two are setting him a bad example by winding each other up all the time.'

'What? By doing this...' Kyle pretended to slap Rory on the head, provoking Rory to push him. Kyle then pinned Rory's arms behind his back, making him shriek.

'Stop it, you lot! Mrs Henderson will hear you and she'll probably belt me for not keeping you under control.'

They made their way home and Megan listened to their chatter, the crushing weight of worry about the missing bones dispelled, briefly, by their cheeriness. She watched her boys skipping along beside her and wondered what would happen to them if she was arrested for moving and then losing Donald's skeleton. Johnny would have them, of course. Megan tried to tell herself how bad that would be but she couldn't lie; the boys would be fine with Johnny and he'd have them in a flash. They might even be better off with him than they were with her. Megan's mood dipped a little more at that thought.

Back at home, she gave the boys a snack and watched TV with them, her mind elsewhere. She thought about the Glaswegians who might be after Gregor. They didn't mess about. She'd heard what they did to folk who crossed them, and although Gregor was an idiot, Megan didn't want him to suffer. She'd always had a soft spot for him and seemed unable, once she'd had a drink, to stop herself trying to seduce any men she happened to like. Poor Gregor had been terribly drunk and had probably not given any thought to Megan being his half-sister since he'd found out five years earlier. For all they knew, and given Morag's typical behaviour, Donald might not necessarily be Gregor's real dad. Although she realised, with the benefit of hindsight, that Gregor and Lewis did share some physical mannerisms.

Megan was practical. What's done was done and no harm was meant or caused. She decided to return Gregor's hash; taking it had been wrong and she didn't want to make his life any worse than it already was. Her instincts had always told her Gregor was a decent guy battling the odds of life, not least an absent father and a drunken lazy mother.

Shortly after four, she switched the TV off. 'The mist has cleared, boys. There's a glimmer of blue up there. Go and play outside till tea time.' After initial protests, they trooped outside and, knowing it was only a matter of time before one of them, most likely Rory, ended up in tears, either from injury or because his favourite stick had broken, she raced upstairs. Lewis was away working for the week and Sarah wouldn't be home from work until after five; Megan had to retrieve the drugs from the top of the wardrobe in their room.

The chair that used to be beside the cupboard on the opposite wall was now next to the door, Sarah's jeans hanging over its back. Megan carried it across the room and was climbing onto it when she heard a car door slam outside. She went to the window. Sarah was walking to the front door. Damn! What was she doing home so early? There was no time to move the chair back to the other side of the room so Megan pushed it beside the wardrobe and raced out of the room. She almost collided with Sarah on the landing.

'Hi,' she said, in a false cheery voice.

Sarah paused. Her face was drawn. 'Hi.'

'You're home early.'

'Headache. Going to lie down.' Sarah carried on into her bedroom and shut the door. Megan would have to get the drugs another time.

Chapter Seventeen
SARAH

Tuesday, 17 May 2005, 3.50pm

'Type this up, please.' Alex threw a miniature Dictaphone cassette onto Sarah's desk; it was the third that day. He'd also dumped a pile of draft contracts, scattered with red scribbles, into her new in-tray. 'Doesn't have to be today but if you could get those corrected by the end of the week.'

It was a bewildering change from the previous day's charm over lunch, and while she was relieved he no longer seemed interested in her, the anger emanating off him was palpable.

Was it really only her second day? She'd spent Monday worrying about him flirting, and today wondering what she'd done to annoy him. She wondered if it had anything to do with Finella's visit the previous afternoon; that's when he'd changed. There could be any number of reasons why they had fallen out but in her paranoid mind, she feared it was about Alex's attempted kiss on Sunday. She groaned at the memory. She wished she'd never set eyes on him and now she was spending the day listening to his voice playing in her head on the Dictaphone.

'You all right, hen? You're looking awfully pale.' Donna had stopped in front of her desk.

'I feel a bit sick.'

'It's almost four, you get on home. You've had a hard couple of days. Don't mind him too much.' Donna nodded her head in the direction of Alex's office. 'He's a moody one. Thinks he can ride roughshod over folk. I've been here long enough so he knows better than to speak to me the wrong way. I'll tell him I've sent you to the post office.'

Sarah didn't need to be told twice. She locked the work in her desk drawer, grabbed her coat and fled. Although nostalgic for some aspects of her life in London, she didn't miss the long commute; she was home in under ten minutes.

Her head pounding, Sarah hurried upstairs to lie down, hoping to avoid Megan and her noisy children. But she ran into Megan on the landing; it almost seemed as though she'd come out of Sarah and Lewis's bedroom.

'Hi.'

'Hi.'

'You're home early.'

'Headache. Going to lie down,' she muttered, carrying on past Megan. Sarah didn't want to talk to anyone, especially not Megan.

In the bedroom she took off her jacket and went to hang it on the chair. But the chair was over by the wardrobe, whereas Sarah kept it by the door. Lewis had gone to work on the Isle of Skye, so he couldn't have moved it. Had Megan been in her room? There had been something suspicious about her manner in the hall... Sarah shook her head. She was being ridiculous. No doubt one of the boys had moved it. She kicked off her shoes, draped her jacket over the chair and crawled into bed fully clothed. She fell asleep within minutes.

When she woke she lay still, trying to work out where she was and what time it might be. The room was dim and the house still and quiet; it must be late. A movement caught her eye and she lifted her head. Someone was standing beside her wardrobe. She shrieked and shuffled across the bed in the opposite direction.

'God, sorry, it's only me,' said Megan.

'What they hell are you doing?' Sarah sat up. Her head was thumping and her mouth dry. She looked down and saw her work clothes. The events of the day came back to her.

'Sorry. I was just… er… I was checking if you were okay. I mean, you've been up here since you came home from work and that was hours ago.'

'I'm fine.'

'Fine people don't go to bed at half four in their clothes.' Sarah tried to clear the wooziness from her head as Megan continued. 'Want me to get you a glass of water?'

Sarah registered a change in Megan's tone. She'd been hostile before but now sounded concerned. Or was Sarah imagining it? She struggled to understand anyone in this strange town, but she appreciated the sympathy she thought she could detect. 'Thanks, yeah, maybe I'm dehydrated. My head is splitting.'

Megan fetched a glass of water and handed it to Sarah. She sat on the bed. 'So, what's up with you?'

The sharpness was back. Sarah retorted in kind. 'A horrible day at work, new job, rotten boss.' She sighed. 'It must be nice not having to work for a living.'

'Aye, well, when you've got three kids to bring up, then you can tell me I ain't got no work.'

They stared at one another for a moment before Sarah looked away. She wished Megan would leave. She was tired of her jibes.

'What's so awful about your boss?' Megan asked. 'I got the impression you and Alex are *close.*'

'What do you mean by that?'

'Hit a nerve, have I?'

Sarah felt her bottom lip wobble. She couldn't keep this up. Sarky banter wasn't her thing at the best of times, never mind when she had something shameful to hide and was feeling ill, too. There was nothing for it but to face it. 'What do you know?'

'That you're having an affair with Areshole Campbell and you're going to break my brother's heart. Someone saw you snogging.'

Sarah gasped at Megan's bluntness. 'We're not having an affair!'

'Just dry humping on car bonnets.'

Sarah covered her face with her hands. 'It's not what it looked like,' she mumbled. She lowered her hands and looked Megan in the eye. 'He kissed me. He caught me unaware and pushed me onto the car. It was horrible... and... well, I hate him. He's a rotten man.'

'You hate him because you wanted more but he's turned you down because... hmmm... oh yeah... he's *married* and you've *got a boyfriend.* I saw you and Alex having a great chat in the pub on Friday.'

'You've got it wrong! Alex trapped me at the table and kept going on and on. Then on Sunday I went for a walk, mostly because Lewis kept wanting to talk to you in private, then while I was out I got scared about this Mist Murderer and it was a relief to meet Alex on the path. I didn't want to walk home through the woods so he walked me to the church car park and then… then… that's when he tried to kiss me.' Sarah shuddered at the memory. 'I tried to get away but he pushed me onto the car.' Sarah gulped back a tear. 'For a moment I thought he wasn't going to stop.'

'Then what happened?'

'He stopped and said he was sorry, and then I walked home. That was when I saw you running, remember? You had a package or something in your hand? Anyway, on Monday I started work and he was being overly friendly and weird. He made me have lunch with him and I didn't want to make a scene on my first day, so I just kinda put up with it, you know? And then today he's been really angry all day. I don't know what to think.' A tear slipped out of Sarah's eye.

'I'd have told him to go fuck himself,' said Megan.

'But the job…'

'Get a different job.'

Sarah wiped away her tears. 'That's what I'm going to do. Find another job and toughen up. Like you.'

'Jesus, don't try to be like me. My life's a fucking disaster.'

'No, it isn't. You've got great kids and a brilliant attitude.'

'Honestly, my life is not one anybody should aim for.' As Megan spoke, Sarah noticed the dark circles under her eyes. It occurred to her that perhaps Megan didn't take life as light-heartedly as she made out. They looked at one another again. Sarah sensed their relationship had shifted. 'Please don't tell Lewis. I really want things between me and him to get back to how they used to be.'

''Course I won't. And Lewis'll come round in time. He's upset about his dad but he's well taken with you, I can tell.' Megan gave her a brief smile.

'Don't tell Finella either.'

'She already knows.'

'Oh God... how?'

'I told her.'

'Because you saw what happened?'

'Nah, Vicky saw you and told me. She's terrified of Alex for some reason and didn't want me to say anything to him or to you. So I told Finny in the hope she'd get Alex to end the affair. I didn't want Lewis to get hurt.'

'So that must have been why Finella went to see Alex yesterday. And why he's so pissed off with me today.' Sarah shook her head. 'What a mess. She must hate me.'

'Nah, Finny knows what a fleabag Alex is. I doubt you're the first he's tried it on with. If it was me I'd kick him right out of the house but Finny's got some strange ideas about things. She's too worried about what everyone else thinks, if you ask me, not that anyone should be asking me for advice on life.'

'Tomorrow I'm going to tell Alex I can't work for him any more.'

'I know I said you should get another job but don't be hasty. I'm always rushing into things then regretting it. It might all blow over. Alex is a creep but he's not evil. I better get off to bed now.' Megan moved towards the door.

'Megan?'

'Yeah?'

'Thanks for the chat, and for being so understanding about

everything.'

'No problem. See you tomorrow.'

Feeling better after her talk with Megan, Sarah changed into her pyjamas and brushed her teeth before getting back into bed. But she lay awake for a long time, thoughts in turmoil. Now she knew why Megan had been so cool; she had thought Sarah was having an affair with Alex. At least discussing the experience had lightened the burden of Alex's behaviour; perhaps Megan was right and it would all blow over. It was only an attempted kiss, a misunderstanding, and the job was handy. She was due to meet Catriona in the morning to talk about the admin support she'd be able to offer the *Journal* and Sarah liked the idea of working for a newspaper. Who knew where it would lead?

In the morning, although tired from a fractured sleep, she was cheered when she arrived at the office and Donna informed her Alex would be in Inverness all day. 'Hugh's away as well, hen, so we'll have an easy day.'

Sarah was finishing a letter when Catriona appeared. 'I hear the world's most charming man is not in today so I thought we could have a catch-up. We can grab a coffee next door.'

'I better just finish this tape first. Donna said—'

'Never mind about Donna. Let's go.'

Sarah followed her. She liked Catriona but her presumptuous manner reminded her of Alex, *demanding* that she accompany her to the café. As they walked next door, Sarah imagined herself having the confidence to say, 'No, thanks, I don't feel like going to the café. Let's talk here.' Then she realised she was being petty. She fancied a coffee and a break anyway.

Catriona wasted no time. 'I'm going to need you to handle

the advertising. The more local stuff we can get, the better.'

'What does that involve?'

'A mini sales campaign; phone around, maybe take a wander up the High Street, see if anyone wants to advertise.'

'Okay...'

'And there's the What's On section. I can't keep up with it. Who knew there were so many car boot sales and ceilidhs in this miserable backwater?' She leant over the table, her blue eyes shining in her beautiful face. 'Don't look so worried, Sarah. I'll help when I can but I'm working on something more important.' She paused to glance around the café. 'I'm trying to figure out who the Mist Murderer could be.'

Sarah stared at Catriona, shocked. She'd convinced herself the deaths were accidents. Anything else was too horrible to contemplate. Catriona continued, 'When I went to the police on Saturday to report the man we found, I could tell they thought something suspicious was going on. Four deaths since October, all in roughly the same place? Catriona had a gleam in her eye. 'And I think I know who it is.'

'Seriously?' said Sarah, unable to disguise the incredulity in her voice. She shook her head slightly, struggling to process what Catriona had just said. *That she knew who the murderer was...*

'It has to be someone local, right? A regular walker—'

Sarah held her hand up to stop Catriona. She whispered, 'This is insane, Catriona. There can't possibly be a local killer... pushing people off the hill. It's not possible.'

'People have all sorts of reasons to kill,' muttered Catriona darkly.

'You should go to the police if you think you know who it is.'

'I will, but I need more evidence first. I'm not ready.'

'Ready for what?'

'I'm preparing a series of articles for the *Journal* about serial killers. This could be my big break if I end up being the journalist who cracks the case.'

Sarah was unsure what to say. It sounded ridiculous. And yet… an image flashed though her mind of the bashed-up face of the poor soul she'd discovered on Saturday. She shuddered; why would that man have fallen? From his attire he was obviously an experienced hill walker.

'I know it sounds unlikely,' continued Catriona, 'but there's a personal angle, too, because I think my own father might have been the first victim.'

'*What*?'

'Look at this.' Catriona pulled a well-worn notebook out of her pocket. 'See this list of dates? These are the days bodies were discovered in the gully. There have been four since last October, with my dad being possibly the first one. I checked the hill accident reports; prior to October, the last fatality on the Ben was the previous November, almost a year earlier. So I started my investigation with folk who didn't like my dad.' She closed her notebook and carried on. 'At the time, everyone was astonished he'd fallen. He'd been in the mountain rescue for years, since I was a kid. I told people he'd been getting doddery because it was easier, but it wasn't true. I don't think he fell; I think he was pushed.'

'You think your dad was *murdered*? That's…' Sarah tailed off, unable to find an appropriate word. Her mind was reeling. Was

Catriona seriously on the verge of uncovering a serial killer here in Glasdrum? It was a terrifying thought. Sarah imagined the misty path up the Ben… how many more victims could there be? 'You have to tell someone,' she whispered. 'You could be putting yourself in danger if you go up there!'

Catriona looked cagey. 'I will go to the police but give me a few more days to work on it.' The odd look on her face put Sarah off asking more questions; it still seemed so unbelievable that it made Sarah feel uncomfortable.

By the time they'd returned to the office, Sarah had told herself it was probably nothing but a wild goose chase; Catriona was desperate to be a journalist and was clutching at straws.

It was almost four by the time Catriona left Sarah to contemplate the *Journal* paperwork she'd piled on her desk, much of it awaiting action. She'd enjoyed learning from Catriona but felt overwhelmed at the amount of work; there was enough to warrant a full-time job. How would she fit it all in? She stared into space, her thoughts wandering back to the possibility of a killer in their midst. With that and Lewis's taciturn manner, a return to London was increasingly appealing, but funnily enough, it was Catriona and this new job that made her want to stay in Glasdrum. Beautiful, confident Catriona seemed to like Sarah and that was a nice feeling.

Donna gave her a start as she walked up behind her and pointed to the piles of paperwork on her desk. 'Catriona's taking advantage of you with all that. I'd leave it till the morning and speak to Alex. As for now, I wanted to ask you a favour.'

'Sure. What is it?'

'I've a dental appointment in Fort William at five and need

to get away early.' She handed a bulky envelope to Sarah. 'Alex wants these papers this evening so I said I'd pop them up to his house. Would you mind dropping them in for me?' Dismay must have shown on Sarah's face when Donna added, 'He won't be in; he's in Inverness till late. Just put them through his letter box.'

'No problem,' said Sarah. Her stomach lurched at the prospect of going to Alex's but she felt unable to refuse Donna a favour when she'd been so kind. The prospect of bumping into Finella who, according to Megan, suspected Sarah of having an affair with Alex, was horrific. She'd drop the paperwork into the letter box then run.

Except the box turned out to be too small; an antique letter box set at the bottom of an ornate door. Sarah was crouched low, cramming it through the limited space, when the door opened. Finella stared down at her.

'Oh God, I'm so sorry to bother you.' Sarah remained bent over, cowering in shame in front of the wife who thought she was trying to steal her husband. She straightened slowly and wanted to shout that it was just a kiss, that she had regretted it, that it would never happen again. Instead she lamely pointed at the envelope that hung, crushed and broken, halfway through the door. 'I was delivering that.'

Finella grabbed it with both hands and wrenched it out. The envelope ripped and pieces fluttered away in the breeze. 'For Alex, I presume?'

Sarah nodded. 'It's work.'

Finella walked to the side of the house, lifted the wheelie bin lid and dropped the contents of the envelope into it as

Sarah watched, aghast. She took a step backwards when Finella advanced on her.

'Vicky and I are drinking gin,' said Finella. 'I think you should join us.'

Chapter Eighteen
FINELLA

Wednesday, 18 May 2005, 4.30pm

'I don't think I should have a drink.' Sarah looked at her watch. 'I better go... er... back to work.'

'Donna told me she was closing early to go to the dentist.'

'I... I... have to go home then.' Sarah started backing away, slowly, and looked so miserable Finella took pity on her, not least because her expression reminded her of Judith; bewildered and a little sad. It upset Finella every time she looked at her daughter and this was one of the reasons she had told Alex, the previous day, that she wanted a divorce. She felt certain the terrible state of her parents' marriage was contributing to Judith's difficulties but it hadn't been an easy conversation.

'Don't be ridiculous, Finella. You're not divorcing me.'

'Yes, I am.'

'No, you're not.' Alex had moved towards her and it had taken courage to break a habit of twelve years, more if she counted the pre-marriage years, to face him. She had spotted his fist curling and his jaw clenching but she didn't flinch.

'This isn't a pantomime, Alex. And whatever you do to me will be fodder for my solicitor.'

He had turned away and slammed the living room door so hard the walls of the house had reverberated, bringing the children scurrying downstairs, the twins in fascination, Judith with worry etched on her face. It had been the expression on her daughter's face that had reinforced Finella's decision to change her life. He'd still see the children, of course, but she hoped that a divorce would concentrate his attention on their needs more than at present. Recently he'd been terribly distracted.

Her determination faltered when she contemplated the drawn-out legal battles that lay ahead; there was still part of her that wished she'd kept quiet, that she'd let Alex have his sordid affair with this wishy-washy blonde who now stood on her doorstep shaking like a startled doe. What a joke. Little did Sarah know it was she who held the power. Finella was nothing; she was pathetic, a wronged wife, a woman who couldn't keep her man, who couldn't handle her own children… She was a nervous wreck.

'Don't look so worried,' she said to Sarah. 'Alex and I are getting a divorce. I don't care what he does with you.'

'But—'

Finella held up her hand and stood to the side. 'I think you better come in.'

Sarah obediently stepped into the hall. When she hesitated, Finella propelled her, with a hand on her lower back, towards the kitchen. Vicky was sitting at the breakfast bar, dropping a slice of lemon into her drink. She looked up, surprised.

'Take a seat,' said Finella, and Sarah perched on one of the high stools, still wearing her jacket and clutching her handbag to her chest. She glanced from Finella to Vicky and back again.

Finella picked up a tumbler, poured a generous shot of gin into it, and topped it up. 'Ice and lemon?'

'Thanks but I don't want a drink,' said Sarah.

Finella dropped two ice cubes and a slice of lemon into the glass and slid it along to Sarah. She picked up her own half-full glass, drained it, then fixed another. 'I've heard the latest fad is to put cucumber in gin but that won't be happening in my house.'

She took another hefty swig before turning to Sarah. 'Look, you can go if you want. But this isn't what you think. I don't want to chastise you for having an affair with Alex—'

'I'm not having an affair with him!' The words burst out of Sarah. 'I hate him!'

Finella took another large gulp of gin. 'Join the club, my dear.'

Sarah stammered out an explanation of what had happened in the church car park on Sunday and Vicky nodded. 'I saw you trying to push him off you.'

Finella stared at Vicky. 'You were there?'

'I was working in the churchyard. It was because Alex spotted me that he stopped mauling Sarah and sent her away.'

'Why haven't you told me this?' asked Finella.

'I didn't know how to tell you what Alex did to me afterwards.'

Finella became conscious of her heart thudding unpleasantly, almost painfully. 'Spit it out, dear.'

'He pushed me against the wall and forced me to kiss him. I tried to get away but he held my head and…' Vicky shuddered and looked down. She finished in a quiet voice, 'I was very scared. I didn't know if he was going to stop.'

Finella put her glass down. Her hand was shaking. She waited a few moments, trying to calm her emotions, but they were gathering pace, threatening to burst out of her. She was hanging on to her sanity by a thread. 'But he did stop?'

'Yes, but the next afternoon, Monday, he came to my cottage and threatened me. He thought I'd told you about seeing him kissing Sarah. But I didn't tell you. I told Megan and she must have gone straight to Alex.'

'Megan didn't speak to Alex,' said Finella in a flat voice. 'Megan told *me* that Alex was having an affair with Sarah and she wanted *me* to make sure it stopped. She said she had seen them kissing herself.'

'So Megan didn't betray me.' Vicky sounded both relieved and dismayed.

'Not intentionally,' said Finella. 'But her loose tongue is having some repercussions for you, Vicky, and for me. Monday afternoon was truly the end of my marriage. So, here's to my imminent divorce,' said Finella in a brittle but bright voice. 'Come on, ladies, let's raise a glass to ridding our lives of that rotten man. Drink up.' Finella drained her glass and watched keenly as Vicky and Sarah did the same before pouring another round.

Finella was aware that she was, yet again, keeping up appearances. This time her role was the bitter but resigned wife: yes, her husband had been philandering and, golly, wasn't it awful, but she'd jolly well divorce him because that's what strong women did when they caught their husbands cheating. Except... as far as she was concerned, what Alex had done was worse than cheating. So he hadn't had sex with either Vicky or Sarah, and she had no concrete proof he'd had sex with anyone else, but he'd threatened and terrified them. He wasn't a philanderer; he was a monster.

She sipped at her drink and listened to Sarah and Vicky exchange stories about their harrowing encounters with her husband, the father of her children. She smothered the sob that rose painfully in her throat as the life she had built with Alex disintegrated. The only thing that kept her from falling apart altogether was the thought of her children upstairs. She looked at her watch; it was after five. They'd be down any minute, clamouring for food and asking when their dad would be home. A strange noise escaped from her lips making Vicky and Sarah break off their discussion.

'Are you okay, Finella?'

She was far from okay. The room was spinning and she was struggling to breathe. 'The children,' she gasped. As if on cue, there was a thundering of footsteps on the stairs. The twins, followed closely by Judith and Louise, burst into the kitchen.

'What's for dinner?' yelled the boys. 'Can we have pizza?'

'Can Louise stay for tea?' asked Judith, linking her arm through Louise's.

'Can we put the PlayStation on?'

'Can Louise and I watch a DVD?'

Finella felt her brain closing down as Vicky jumped down from the stool. 'Your mum isn't feeling well so I'll make your tea and yes, you can have pizza as long as you go back upstairs and play nicely until it's ready. We've got adult things to talk about. Okay?'

'You're just drinking alcohol,' said Louise with a disdainful look.

'Very observant,' said Vicky, 'but it's none of your business. Now, off you all go.'

To Finella's astonishment the children trooped back out of the room. 'They would never listen to me like that.'

'Kids are always more obedient for someone else. Did you notice my own daughter had the back chat about the gin?' Vicky opened Finella's freezer. 'Yeah, I thought I saw pizzas in here. Go through to the lounge, Finella. Sarah can help me make the kids' tea.'

Sarah nodded and Finella left them bustling about her kitchen. She sank onto her brushed suede sofa feeling weary. Her life was in tatters. She'd long ago realised Alex was a selfish man, cruel at times, but she'd told herself that deep down he cared about people. He was charitable (*because it impressed people*, whispered a voice in her head), he spent time with his children (*because she nagged him about it*), he loved her (*no, he didn't*). How could she have been so stupid! All these years. She was a blind fool. Finella clutched her empty glass tightly and used every shred of will power she had not to hurl it against the marble fireplace. She took a breath and concentrated on placing her glass slowly and precisely onto the coffee table. *Keep it together, Finella.* But her control was slipping; the emotion of the past two days and too much gin in the past two hours.

She lay back and stared at the ceiling in a stupor, vaguely aware of noises from the kitchen drifting down the hall, accompanied by the whiff of pepperoni. She dozed on and off, her mind drifting back to Alex. How bad a person was he really? He was a liar, of that there was no doubt. An adulterer? Probably. A rapist? Both Sarah and Vicky had hinted they thought it possible. How much worse could it get? Maybe he was a murderer too. Perhaps he was the Mist Murderer; Megan had joked about that more than once. Finella gave a bitter chuckle as Sarah and Vicky came back into the room with a plateful of leftover pizza and the bottles of gin and tonic.

'Something funny, Finella?' asked Vicky.

'The comedy of life, my dear,' said Finella, slurring her words. 'I was reflecting on how little I know my husband, and since he seems to be the bad guy of the town, I wondered if he might even be this Mist Murderer everyone is talking about. I mean, he's up that bloody mountain often enough.' Finella broke first into loud, hysterical cackles then shook in silent spasms as tears rolled down her cheeks. She struggled to continue speaking. 'Wouldn't that be the icing on the fucking cake? I only thought it as a joke... but now... I mean he's been up that hill every time there's been a death. I was only teasing him about it the other day...'

Finella stopped laughing. She stared at Sarah and Vicky with dead eyes. 'What do you think, girls? Am I married to a murderer?'

They exchanged a glance then looked away. Sarah pulled at a loose thread on her skirt. Vicky clasped her hands in her lap and looked upwards, as though for divine guidance.

'Don't hold back. I may as well face the worst.'

Finella tried to read their expressions as Sarah and Vicky reflected on the prospect of Alex as a serial killer. Neither of them rushed to tell her she was being ridiculous. 'I need another drink,' she said and poured an enormous gin. There was only a dribble of tonic left, so she took a swig of the almost-neat spirit and grimaced as it burned down her throat.

'Do *you* think it's possible?' asked Vicky.

'Well, I didn't,' replied Finella, 'but you two obviously do.' She took another gulp of alcohol, hoping the pain of the harsh liquid in her mouth would stem the tears that threatened.

'Why would he want to kill anyone?' asked Sarah. Her voice was quiet and shocked.

'Some folk are born evil,' said Vicky, thinking not just of Alex but of Louise's dad and the casual violence he had dished out.

Finella felt a flash of anger. That was her husband she was talking about! Alex, who had promised to love and cherish her, who had stood by her side when her children had been born, who had worked hard and provided for them for all these years. But darker thoughts crowded into her head, too. How he had controlled her, disrespected her, deceived her. His lack of interest in their children, especially in the last year, his occasional outbursts of violence…

'Has he really been up the hill when each of those people have fallen?' Vicky asked Finella, adding, 'If they fell…'

Sarah spoke. 'I've heard the police don't believe they were accidents. There's been, what, four now, including the poor man Catriona and I found at the weekend?' She paused, deep in thought. 'Catriona is convinced there's a Mist Murderer and she thinks she knows who it is. She's been investigating them—'

Vicky interrupted. 'Megan said she'd seen Catriona and Alex up the hill at the same time several times, and I saw them both setting off up the hill on Monday night, one after the other.'

Finella flapped her hand to get their attention. 'They're no doubt having an affair and are meeting up the hill.' She was slurring so badly Vicky and Sarah had to lean forward to catch what she was saying. 'He's not murdering, he's just seducing.'

'Or else Catriona was following him,' said Vicky. 'You've got that pile of *Glasdrum Journals* in the study. The dates of the accidents will be in them. Will I fetch them?'

Finella nodded, her heart heavy. Nothing seemed real any more; this was no longer her life. It couldn't be.

Vicky returned and started flicking through the *Journals*. Sarah helped but kept glancing at Finella, and Finella wondered what she was thinking. Probably considering what kind of woman could be married to a rapist serial killer and not realise it. Finella tried to focus on Sarah's face, to understand what was going through her mind, but she couldn't. Maybe she needed her glasses. She put her hand to her face but she was wearing them so it couldn't be that. The room started to spin then everything blurred. Darkness folded around her and she passed out.

When she woke, Vicky was stretched out on the opposite sofa with her eyes closed. Finella sat up and groaned. Her skull was alive with pain. The memory of the heart-wrenching discoveries of the last few hours caused waves of nausea to sweep through her body. 'I'm going to be sick,' she muttered.

Vicky opened her eyes and sat up. 'God, right, let me get you something.' She staggered to her feet and glanced around before hauling the heavy brass coal bucket from beside the fireplace to Finella, leaving a long black mark on the cream carpet. 'Oh shit. Sorry…'

Finella retched and leant forward. She fell to her knees, clasped the bucket with both hands and spewed into it, spattering the remnants of coal with regurgitated gin and half-digested pizza.

It took a good five minutes before the spasms ceased and

Finella leant against the sofa, exhausted. She wiped her mouth with the back of her hand and left a smear of soot across her face. She then put her blackened palm to her clammy forehead. 'Oh my God, Vicky, I've never felt so bad in my life.'

Vicky sat on the floor beside her and rubbed her back. She tried to wipe away some soot from Finella's face but only made it worse.

'What time is it?' Finella asked.

'Just past midnight. I put the kids to bed and let Louise sleep on the camp bed in Judith's room. Didn't want to leave you alone.'

'Sarah?'

'She went home.'

Finella groaned again. 'Think she'll tell anyone about... what we talked about?'

'I don't think so. She's going to try to get a look at Alex's diary tomorrow in the office. We looked up the dates on which each body was found and she's going to check them against his diary since you said he keeps a note of everything he does.'

'I said that?'

'Yeah.'

Finella looked at Vicky, bleary-eyed with misery. 'Surely you don't actually think he might be the Mist Murderer? I mean... I was getting carried away with the drink when I said that. He's not a nice man, but a *killer*?'

'I'm sorry, Finella, but you've got to admit it's a possibility.'

Finella grabbed the coal bucket and started vomiting again.

Chapter Nineteen
VICKY

Thursday, 19 May 2005, 10am

The mist had cleared and the brilliance of the sun's light hurt Vicky's eyes when she opened the front door. Beneath her cottage the white sands shone and the turquoise sea looked inviting for the first time that year. Perhaps summer was on the way, she thought, searching for sunglasses, her head thumping from the gin she'd drunk the previous evening. She'd woken Louise at seven and they'd come home from Finella's to get ready for school, but Vicky was still worrying about the terrible state Finella had been in. She'd phoned twice without getting a reply, but when she tried again, a timid voice answered. 'Hello?'

'Hi Judith, it's Vicky. You're not at school?'

'No.'

'Are you ill?'

'No, but Mum's in bed. She said we had to get ourselves organised for school or else just stay at home. I tried to get the boys ready but they wouldn't do anything I said so then I thought I better stay at home and help Mum look after them.'

'Isn't your dad there?'

'I think he's still in Inverness. I was going to phone Granny but Mum told me not to. She told me not to answer the phone but I saw it was your number so I guessed that'd be okay.'

Vicky wasn't keen to have a run-in with Alex but felt sorry for Judith and worried about Finella; this was so unlike her. 'Get ready for school. I'll come round in ten minutes and sort the boys out.'

Judith was sitting in the hall in her uniform when Vicky arrived. She looked gaunt. 'Have you had any breakfast?' Vicky asked her.

'Not hungry. I'm too sad. Did you hear about Kylie?'

'Kylie?'

'Kylie Minogue has breast cancer. She's cancelled concerts. Not that I was going to any of them.'

Vicky sat beside her on the stairs. 'I bet Kylie doesn't skip breakfast. I've heard she's a health freak. So I'm going to pretend you are my daughter and *order* you to go and have a piece of toast while I sort out your brothers.'

'I wish I was Louise,' said Judith.

'I'd have said it in a much angrier voice if you were Louise.' The trace of a smile flickered across Judith's face before she slouched off to the kitchen. Vicky watched her, feeling concerned, then went upstairs to see how bad Finella's hangover was.

The room was dark and warm, and smelt of stale drink and vomit.

Vicky pulled the curtains aside to open the window and let some fresh air into the room, drawing a mumble from Finella. 'Leave them closed.'

'I was going to—'

'Just fucking leave them!' Alarmed, Vicky drew the curtains and the room was plunged back into darkness.

Vicky approached the bed, wary of provoking another

outburst from the normally polite Finella. 'Are you okay, Finella?' she asked, then regretted it. Finella was clearly far from okay.

When there was no response, Vicky stood helplessly about a metre from the bed, trying to decide what to do. Was Finella hung-over or was something else wrong with her? She thought about the previous evening's discussion about Alex being the Mist Murderer. In the cold (sober) light of day, it was ridiculous and Vicky regretted voicing it as much as she shuddered at the alcohol she'd drunk. She had to find Sarah to make sure she didn't go snooping in Alex's diary; what an insane idea! It was best if they all dropped it, and if Finella had a good rest, she'd no doubt be back to her normal self in no time. Maybe even the talk of divorce would lead to nothing. Finella and Alex would continue with their lives, and Vicky and Louise would continue with theirs... as though nothing had happened. *Yeah*, thought Vicky, *as if that was possible in life*. Things said and done could not usually be undone. She sensed there was trouble ahead but for now her focus was on ensuring Sarah didn't make things worse by rifling in Alex's office.

'I'll take the kids to school and can pick them up after, if you like. They can come to mine for a bit. We can go to the beach since the sun's out at last.' A pause. 'Finella, is that okay?'

Finella pulled the duvet over her head and lay without responding. Vicky waited briefly, then left.

'Right, boys, where are your uniforms?' She switched off the PlayStation to a cacophony of groans. 'Get upstairs NOW and put them on.'

The boys scampered to their room to change; Vicky had

looked after them often enough for them to realise when she meant business. In less than twenty minutes, Vicky had dropped the kids at the primary school and was on her way to Megan's.

There was no answer when she knocked on Megan's door, but it was unlocked so she went into the hall and shouted hello.

'I'm in here.'

Vicky found Megan sitting at the kitchen table stroking Glen's head. He looked at Vicky and wagged his tail but didn't leave Megan's side. 'Hi,' said Vicky, pulling out a chair for herself. 'How're you doing?'

'Crap,' said Megan. 'What're you doing here anyway? Thought you were pissed off with me.'

'I am annoyed, Megan. I asked you not to tell anyone about Alex and Sarah but you told Finella. So on Monday Finella told Alex she wanted a divorce and he came straight round to threaten me.'

'What do you mean, threaten you? Did he try it on again?'

'Worse.'

'What the fuck is worse than a rape threat? Oh my God, he didn't actually...'

'No, he didn't attack me physically... he is threatening to find out who I really am.' Vicky wrapped her arms around her body. Confiding in Megan had been a mistake in the past but she couldn't help the words come tumbling from her mouth as she explained how she was hiding from Louise's dad and about the drug money she'd stolen.

Megan stared at her when she'd finished. '*Fucking hell,*' she said. 'You're a dark horse.' She put her head in her hands. 'This is all my fault. Jesus, I mess up everything. I'm so sorry, Vicky.'

'It's not your fault, it's just life. It's messy and complicated… I was stupid and I'm still paying for it…' Vicky tailed off. 'Anyway I came round to see if Sarah was here.'

'She's away to work. Looked rough as hell this morning.'

Vicky told Megan about the gin and Finella's ridiculous suggestion that Alex was the Mist Murderer.

Megan snorted. 'He's a bastard for sure but he's not a killer.'

'We got drunk and carried away. And now I need to stop Sarah snooping in Alex's diary. If he catches her and she tells him what she's doing…' Vicky put her head in her hands.

'Fuck me,' said Megan, 'I thought I was the idiot around here. You better phone her.' Megan pushed the phone across the table towards Vicky. 'I've been trying to phone Lewis all morning.'

'Is he still away on Skye?'

'Yeah, renovating an old croft with his pal. No phone signal. Think it's doing Sarah's head in that he's never here.'

Vicky looked up the number for Campbell & Co, dialled it then asked to be put through to Sarah.

'Hi, it's Vicky. How are you this morning?'

'Feeling a bit sick but thought I'd better come in to, you know… *what we talked about.*'

'That's why I'm phoning. Finella was drunk. She didn't mean it about Alex. She was just angry with him because she'd found out about him cheating.'

Sarah's voice quietened so that Vicky could barely hear her. 'I've been awake all night thinking about it. It makes sense. He's a horrible man and he's up to something. I reckon he's the suspect Catriona is investigating.'

'Sarah, it's a ridiculous idea. Please drop it! God knows what he'll do if he catches you.'

'He can't do anything to me, I'm thinking about leaving soon anyway. I may as well see what I can find out.'

'Sarah! I really don't think—'

'Shit, they're here. I better go.' The line went dead.

Vicky looked at Megan. 'This is awful.'

'Life's a bitch all right,' said Megan. 'Want to hear something else that's awful?'

'What?'

'My dad's remains have disappeared.'

'*What?*'

'Someone's moved them and I can only think it must have been Lewis, or someone he's spoken to about it. I can't get Lewis on the phone so I'll have to get the bus up there to speak to him.'

'Want me to get your boys after school for you?'

'Johnny's got them for the rest of the week. I needed some peace to think.'

Vicky had never seen Megan so worried before; she had aged ten years in the two weeks since they'd found the bones. Vicky, too, had been feeling the weight of the discovery hovering beneath her anxiety about Alex and her own secret past. 'What if it wasn't Lewis?'

'Then we're truly fucked.'

'I could drive you to see Lewis,' said Vicky, gripped by an overwhelming urge to find out where the bones had gone. She had helped Megan move them and Vicky did not want the police looking into her life. 'It's almost eleven so there's no time to go there and back before school is finished but we could go after I collect Finella's kids and Louise. There's a ferry at four that would get us to the croft where Lewis is working by five. It's a nice evening for once and the kids will love a trip on the ferry.'

'My boys love going on the ferry. I sometimes take them over and back. It's free if you're on foot. God, I miss them when they're with Johnny. How did all this happen?' Megan looked at Vicky with teary eyes. 'I want everything to go back to the way it was before.'

Vicky patted Megan on the hand. 'You and me both. But it's too late…'

They sat in silence for a few minutes, lost in thought until Vicky spoke. 'Have you got money for the ferry? I can't afford the car fare. I've lost two jobs this week.'

'I'm skint,' replied Megan. 'But I know a woman who isn't. Let's go see if Finny's hangover has abated and get this crap out of her head about Alex being a killer. Those deaths were accidents.'

'There's been four in eight months in roughly the same place…'

'People don't understand how dangerous Scottish mountains are. The mist can descend in minutes and leave you stumbling about in a cloud of whiteness. The path above the gully goes along the edge of a steep drop, and even on a good day I've often thought how easily a tiny slip of the foot could send me over the side. Look what happened to Catriona's dad and he'd been in mountain rescue for years.'

*

At Finella's house, to Vicky's relief, there was no sign of Alex. They let themselves in and crept upstairs to Finella's bedroom.

'I feel as though we're breaking in,' said Vicky as they tapped on Finella's door.

'We're checking she's okay,' said Megan, turning the handle then peering into the still-dark room. 'Hey, Finny!'

There was a movement from the bed and Finella's tousled head appeared from beneath the duvet. She looked at Megan and Vicky, groaned, then pulled the cover back over her head.

Megan threw herself onto the bed beside Finella and pulled back the duvet to peek inside. 'We need your help, Finny.'

'I've enough problems of my own,' mumbled Finella. 'Go away and leave me alone.'

'Can you lend me twenty quid to get the ferry to Skye?'

'There's money in the tin in the kitchen.' Finella yanked the duvet out of Megan's hand and covered her head again.

Megan and Vicky exchanged a look before Megan spoke to Finella's buried head. 'Don't you want to know why we're going to Skye?'

'Not really.'

'Vicky's going to take your kids with us if that's okay.'

Finella looked out of the bed covers at Vicky. 'Thank you,' she said. 'I appreciate it. I don't want them to see me like this.'

'They can stay at mine tonight if they want to,' said Vicky but Finella didn't react. Vicky took a step towards the bed. 'Are you going to be okay, Finella?'

Silence emanated from the inert figure in the bed, prompting Megan to point at the door and mouth a silent, *Let's go.*

'I don't think that's just a hangover,' said Vicky as they left the room and went downstairs to the kitchen to look for Finella's money. 'She's properly depressed.'

'If she thinks her husband is a serial killer, she should be fucking depressed.'

'Don't you believe it?' Vicky asked Megan.

''Course he bloody isn't. Alex is a twat and people are idiots – they fall. Hey, check this out!' Megan pulled a fistful of bank notes out of a circular shortbread tin she found in a kitchen cupboard. She peeled off two twenties before stuffing the money back into the container. 'This'll do us for the ferry.' She hesitated for a second then pulled out another twenty. 'And this will get us a chippy on the way home. Don't look at me like that,' she said to Vicky. 'She won't miss it and it's dinner for her kids after all.'

There was a noise in the hall that made Vicky start but it was only the postman stuffing a catalogue through the low letter box, reminding her how much she didn't want to bump into Alex. She drove Megan back home and agreed to meet her outside the school at three.

*

The four children were keen to go on the trip to Skye despite the squash in the back, with the boys sharing a seatbelt. Judith was delighted to have the evening ahead with Louise, and Finella's boys were excited about the ferry and the prospect of looking for crabs on the shore while Megan spoke to her brother. None of Finella's kids were keen on the alternative, which was to get dropped off at their grandparents' house.

As car passengers had to remain inside their vehicles for the twenty-minute crossing to Skye, Megan took the children onto the ferry as foot passengers and Vicky watched from the car as they climbed the stairs to the viewing platform. The boys raced ahead shouting while the girls walked behind them, giggling, their heads bent together. Megan trailed behind, paying scant attention to the boys who were climbing on the vessel's railing, leaning over the side as the water swirled several metres below them. Vicky wound down the window and tried to shout at them to get down, but the sea breeze whipped her words away. As the boys played, Megan stared out to sea. It was Louise who eventually grabbed the boys' arms and pulled them off the railing.

Vicky took in the view as the ferry chugged across to Skye. The landscape had been transformed by the decent weather. Brilliant blue skies reflected in the sea and stretched into a haze of azure on the horizon, the nearer islands vibrant green, the more distant ones darker hulks of purple and brown. On Skye the Cuillins loomed over the island, topped by patches of stubborn snow. *If only it was always like this*, thought Vicky, *not damp and overcast as it has been of late.* Perhaps this was going to be a good summer, the perpetual hope of locals and tourists alike. Omens were constantly voiced: late frost, early lambs, a cold winter, a mild winter; all were omens of a *good season*.

Filled with optimism by the sun, the bright colours and the happy faces of the children, Vicky tried to picture everything turning out fine. Maybe, as Megan said, there was no Mist Murderer. Alex would stop trying to make Vicky's life difficult and would patch up his marriage to Finella, and Megan would solve the mystery of her father's death and let him rest in peace. She had a sudden memory of her granny's much repeated mantra, *Live for the future, you can't change the past so there's no point thinking about it.* Vicky used to believe that but not any more. Now she knew the past could haunt you for the rest of your life; there was no escape. Maybe she should visit her granny's grave again soon. It seemed to be the only place she was able to cast her worries aside and feel a sense of peace, a connection with a happy memory from the past.

Once off the ferry they drove fifteen miles to the west of the island on single-track road listening to Finella's twins bicker and moan about how far it was. 'What the fuck did we bring them for?' muttered Megan, half under her breath.

'Mum, did Megan just swear?' asked Louise.

'No, you misheard her,' said Vicky, frowning at Megan, who was slumped down in her seat looking morose.

'Sorry,' said Megan. 'I'm just trying to sort things in my head, you know. Can't think straight with them lot. I keep trying to come up with a reason for Lewis to have moved the... *you know what.*'

Vicky whispered, 'Maybe Lewis told Gregor and Gregor moved the *you know what* because it was Gregor who had buried them in the garden in the first place.'

Megan slapped her forehead and her face blanched paler than it had already been. 'Gregor! Fuck.'

The children had gone silent when Vicky had whispered, their kid-radar tuning in when they thought adults were saying something private. When Megan swore, Judith and Louise giggled and the twins starting shouting, 'Fuck, fuck, fuck...'

'That's enough!' Vicky shouted. 'Megan didn't mean to say that and she won't be saying it again, will you Megan?' Vicky glared at her.

Megan was oblivious to the uproar she'd caused. 'I forgot to take Gregor's stash back to him.'

'The stuff you took from his house that day we went to see Morag?'

'Yeah. Oh my God.' Megan put her hand to her head. 'He came to see me because the Glaswegians were after him. I'd hidden it in Sarah and Lewis's room and was trying to get it to return it to him but Sarah came home from work early, then when I tried to get it during the night she woke up. Damn near gave me a heart attack. And then I forgot. How could I have been so stupid?' Megan slapped herself on the forehead then slumped down in her seat, misery etched on her face.

Unsure how to respond, and keen to discourage Megan from saying any more, Vicky drove on in silence. They neared the coast, and the barren landscape was broken by a cluster of yellow vehicles; diggers and dumpers building an extension to the croft where Lewis was working. 'Someone's building a fancy holiday home,' muttered Megan. 'Another rich bastard coming up here to turn someone's house into a barely used summer palace. There'll be nowhere for the locals to live soon. A primary school's already closed because they couldn't get a teacher who could find anywhere to live.'

Vicky pulled over at the entrance to the temporary building site and Megan got out of the car. 'I'll have a word with Lewis and meet you on the shore in a bit.' She set off towards the building, tiny against the mountains, and Vicky carried on another 200 metres to park by the stony beach where she sat on a crumbling dry-stone wall as the boys went to look under seaweed for crabs. Casting aside their pre-teen haughty attitude, the girls joined in and it cheered Vicky to watch Louise have fun outdoors. For all her moaning about small-town life, Vicky appreciated the sanctity it had given her and knew it was a great place to bring up kids; wholesome and beautiful, especially when the mist lifted and the world looked fresh and clean. She stared across the water, beyond the islands and peninsulas, wondering what the future would hold for her and Louise. It felt as though her life was now in Alex's hands. Would he leave her alone or would he keep digging into her past and force her to move away?

How she hated him for his meddling.

'Vicky! Come and help!' shouted Tom, and Vicky pushed aside her troubling thoughts and ran to help the twins lift a rock to see what was living beneath it. They had taken off their shoes and were hobbling about on the slippery stones by the water's edge when Megan reappeared. Vicky felt a moment of resentfulness when she saw her unhappy face – she didn't want to go back to worrying about dead bodies and murderers – but she left the kids and sat beside Megan at the top of the shore.

'I can't bloody believe it! Lewis has reburied dad's bones.'

'Why did he do that?'

'He said he didn't like the idea of Dad's remains lying in the garage. If he was dead, he should be allowed to rest in peace.'

'Where has he put them?'

'Won't tell me. Said it was somewhere peaceful where nobody would disturb him. Jesus.'

'Maybe it's for the best. Put it behind you.'

'But who killed him, Vicky? We still don't know.'

'Nothing's going to bring him back.'

Megan was silent for a while, then, 'Lewis is lying.'

'What about?'

'Gregor said he met Lewis at our house around midnight that Hogmanay in 1999 and he knew that because the fireworks were going off. But when I asked Lewis, he said he didn't get home until about three and he heard me getting home with the boys just after him.'

'Maybe Gregor is lying and *Gregor* was at your house until three.'

'One of them is lying, that's for sure.'

Chapter Twenty
MEGAN

Thursday, 19 May 2005, 5.30pm

Megan was grateful the kids were quieter on the drive back to the ferry, tired out from their play by the shore and keen to earn an ice cream with their silence. Her head pounded, unused to the stress she had been under in recent weeks. Thoughts about her dad, her mum and her brother, both her brothers, tormented her, but she couldn't bring them together into a coherent vision of what had happened that Hogmanay night. She couldn't decide who to believe. Her instincts told her Gregor was telling the truth and Lewis was lying. But that felt like favouring the half-brother she hardly knew over the one she'd grown up with and loved. And it also begged the question: if Gregor left at midnight and Donald had been at home, and Lewis was lying about not getting home until three... what had actually happened during those three hours?

Megan groaned in despair and clutched her stomach.

'Are you going to be sick?' asked Vicky.

'No, I'm okay.'

'Megan's going to spew,' shouted James, followed by a series of gagging noises from the boys.

'Shut up!' shouted Megan. Her vicious tone caused instant quiet. Vicky glanced at her and raised her eyebrows.

Megan was aware she would normally have made a joke at this point, but she couldn't form her mouth into a smile. She stared out of the window, feeling the weight of life crushing her.

Back in Glasdrum they stopped at the chip shop. It was a warm evening and the May sun was still high in the sky as Vicky suggested they eat their fish suppers on the beach in front of her house.

'I thought we were getting an ice cream,' muttered Tom, glancing cautiously at Megan as though expecting another outburst.

'Why not?' said Vicky. 'Ice creams just now and we'll eat the chips at the beach. It'll be a back to front meal with our puddings first.'

The kids beamed as they clutched their whippy ice creams with ninety-nine flakes. 'Don't let any of it melt over my car, please,' said Vicky as the four children squashed back into the rear.

'Have you any change from Finny's money?' Megan asked Vicky.

'Yeah, there's fifteen quid left,' she said, handing it to Megan.

'Back in a mo.' Megan raced to the off-licence on the corner. 'Treat for you and me,' she said to Vicky when she got back and showed her a half bottle of vodka in a brown bag. 'I think I'm going to get into the same state as Finny.'

'I think Finella's having a total life breakdown.'

'Yeah, her and me both.' Megan left the bottle wrapped in the bag but unscrewed it and took a swig, coughing and grimacing. She felt a longing to go home and see her own boys, to allow their cheery faces to soothe her troubles. But they were at

Johnny's and Megan couldn't face going to her own house. She might as well go home with Vicky.

They parked at the end of the track to Vicky's house and went straight to the beach to eat their fish suppers. As soon as they'd finished, the girls took off their shoes and ran to the water's edge, their hair streaming behind them in the evening sun; one dark, the other golden. The boys rolled down the high dunes shrieking. Megan wished her three were there. Something about the last few weeks had made her rethink her life. Motherhood had happened to her by accident and she'd never given it much thought; she'd just got on with it. But the importance of family was dawning on her and the impact of her childhood was playing on her mind; her drunken father, her ineffective mother, her distant brother. She had recently realised she wanted more for her boys, and that they would one day grow up and start analysing her as a mother: a waster, a minor drug dealer with no job and a reputation for getting drunk and sleeping with anyone who'd have her. She decided to turn over a new leaf and, for a brief moment, felt a glimmer of hope. The sun shone on her face, Vicky smiled at her and Megan had a fleeting vision of a happier, more stable life. But the dark cloud returned almost immediately. The missing bones, the drugs that were still hidden in her house, Lewis lying to her, Gregor having sex with her… she knocked back some more neat vodka.

By eight fifteen, the sun was descending, a chill was creeping into the air and the children were tiring. 'Let's go to my house,' said Vicky. 'I'll find my phone and try Finella again. I'll tell her the kids can stay the night with me.'

'Fuck, my phone,' muttered Megan. 'I must have left it in

your car.' She stood up and the world shifted on its axis. She put her hands out like a tightrope walker as though to steady herself.

'How much of that vodka have you had?' asked Vicky, picking up the bottle that was still wrapped in the bag. She looked inside. 'My God, Megan, you've finished it!'

'Sorry. Shoulda left some for you.' Megan starting walking towards Vicky's house, concentrating on staying on her feet as the sand tilted and swayed beneath her.

At the end of the beach, beneath Vicky's cottage, she pulled herself up the narrow path over rocks and between gorse bushes, scratching her arms and legs as, behind her, Vicky shouted at the kids to hurry up. At the top of the incline, standing on the track beside the cottage, looking down at her with his hands on his hips, was Alex.

Megan hauled herself up the last bit of the steep path and stood in front of Alex, her vision blurring. 'It's the dangerous murderer,' she giggled.

Alex ignored her as Vicky emerged from below, the twins right behind her. 'Dad!' they shouted and ran to him. 'We found crabs!'

'We went on a ferry!'

'We had ice cream before dinner!'

'Go to the car, boys, it's time to go home.'

'We're staying at Vicky's tonight. She said we could.' They turned to look at Vicky, who was rooted to the spot, her face pale. 'Vicky, tell him we're staying at yours tonight!'

Vicky turned to look back down the path. 'Louise! Hurry up please. It's time to go inside.'

'Can we stay at yours, Vicky, please?' shouted the boys over and over until Alex grabbed them by the arms.

'Go to the car.' The chill in his voice silenced them and, crestfallen, they wandered towards his car, just visible at the end of the track.

'Does Judith have to come too?' James shouted over his shoulder.

'Yes, she does,' said Alex as Judith and Louise emerged from the beach. Judith followed her brothers without argument.

'You could let the kids stay, for God's sake,' said Megan, drawing a look of alarm from Vicky. 'We promised them.'

'Leave my kids with drunks like you?' sneered Alex. He turned his attention to Vicky. 'I've been phoning you for hours.'

'Sorry, it was in the car. There was no signal on Skye anyway.'

'I was about to phone the police.'

'Finella knew where we were! She was ill this morning so I took them to school and told her I'd pick them up and look after them this evening.'

'You're hardly taking decent care of them. Pissed and out of contact? Playing on the beach at almost nine o'clock on a school night?'

'But I'm not—'

'We won't be requiring your childminding services any more, *Vicky*. You're not who you say you are and I don't trust you one bit.'

He followed his children to the car and Vicky hurried Louise into the cottage, ignoring her protests.

Megan watched them all disappear, the world spinning around her. A longing to be at home gripped her. 'Hey, Vicks, can I borrow your bike?'

'Aren't you a bit drunk for cycling? Come inside.'

'I have to get home. I'll bring the bike back in the morning…'

Vicky glanced down the track. 'Take it if you want, Megan. I can't stand here arguing with you.' She went into the cottage and locked the door. Megan found the hidden key to Vicky's small shed, hauled the bike out of it, then set off on the winding road in the deepening gloom of evening, her head clearing as she sped through the fresh night air. Behind her a car tooted as she wobbled towards the middle of the road and she gave the driver her middle finger as it overtook, muttering 'arsehole' under her breath.

Halfway up the steep hill a mile out from the town, exhaustion overcame her and she got off to push the bike to the top, pausing to admire the twilight view as the lights came on around the harbour and on the boats that were bobbing on the dark sea. Feeling weary, she sat in the grass at the edge of the layby and stared across the sea towards Skye, thinking about Lewis. She wished he would come home. She lay back, admiring the stars in the rare clear sky. It was so beautiful it put her troubles into perspective and strengthened her resolve to be a better mother; she'd get the boys back from Johnny at the weekend and would start anew. Now that Rory was in nursery, she'd get a proper job and stop selling dope to the mothers. She'd *do better*. As she lay there the universe above her spun faster and she put her palms to the ground as though to steady herself. The stars loomed ever closer until they seemed to be dancing before her eyes. Then her eyelids closed and she passed out, spreadeagled on the grass at the top of the hill.

When she woke, a cloud of midges were devouring her face. She leapt to her feet, slapping at her cheeks as she looked at her watch. 'Holy crap,' she exclaimed; she'd slept for almost an hour. Her stomach lurched and she stumbled to the side of the layby where, shaking and sweating, a stream of vomit erupted from her. She had to get home and get to bed. And she absolutely had to stop drinking.

Megan grabbed the bike and set off down the hill, the whoosh of air leaving the midges far behind and relieving her nausea a little.

Instead of carrying on to the junction where the main road joined the single-track road that led to her house, she veered off onto the shortcut that ran through the woods. Darkness closed in on her as she bumped over roots and wobbled around tree stumps and the odd rock. A movement ahead distracted her from the path as she neared home; a silhouetted figure running from the house towards the woods on the other side of the road. As she strained her eyes to recognise who it was, her bike hit a root and she was sent flying through the air. Her helmetless head crashed into a tree and skin was ripped from her cheek as her face scraped across the tree trunk. She landed with a heavy thump on the ground, her arm buckled beneath her, and the world went blank.

When she came to she wasn't sure if she'd been lying there for thirty seconds or thirty minutes. Pain engulfed her wrist as she hauled herself onto unsteady feet and stumbled through the woods towards her house, Vicky's bike abandoned. The side of her face was damp and sore to touch, and another wave of nausea forced her to stop and retch before she reached the front door and paused, trying to gather her thoughts as her vision blurred and her legs threatened to give way.

After fumbling about behind the drainpipe, she located the spare key for the front door and wrestled for a while with the ancient, stiff lock before she realised it was open. *Odd*, she thought, *Sarah is usually so diligent about locking the door, especially when Lewis is away.*

The relief she felt once inside her house was immense and she sat on the lowest step of the stairs, wincing in pain, her head feeling heavy on her neck, trying to decide what to do. She wished someone would come and take care of her... but there was nobody. Her mother had lost her mind, her father was dead, her brother was depressed and uncommunicative, she'd pushed Johnny away and her beautiful boys, her only reason for living, were with him, no doubt being better looked after than if they'd been with her. As sadness engulfed her she decided to sleep in little Rory's camp bed; his familiar scent would be a comfort and by morning she would no longer be drunk, her pain might be gone and she could start over.

She heaved herself up the first few steps in the dark, leaning heavily on the bannister with her good arm. At the sharp turn in the staircase, she tripped and fell onto something large that was blocking the way. A body was sprawled face down across the stairs. Megan gasped; it was Sarah. She threw herself onto her knees to touch her but there was no response. 'Sarah! What the fuck has happened?'

Outside there was a wail of sirens, and blue lights flashed through the windows. Megan jumped up to see what was happening, but when she did the world spun in front of her eyes and she, too, slumped unconscious on the stairs.

Chapter Twenty-One
SARAH

Thursday, 19 May 2005, 11am

Sarah woke feeling terrible after the gin at Finella's house the night before, and sad because she still hadn't heard from Lewis, who had been on Skye since Tuesday. He'd warned her he would be staying in a caravan on a remote building site with no phone signal but she couldn't help thinking he could have got to a phone if he'd wanted to. She didn't know when he'd be home and was fed up being stuck with his erratic sister and those other two, Finella and Vicky; what an odd bunch they were. And what a strange town this was. The only person Sarah liked was Catriona and she wondered why she had come back to Glasdrum; Catriona was scathing about the town and its populace yet seemed disinclined to leave again. Perhaps Glasdrum was the only connection she had to the family she'd lost. Sarah understood that and wished she had something more to help her remember her own mother.

As she dressed, Sarah thought more about Catriona and wondered if it was her work for the *Journal* that was keeping her in town. She'd been animated about the prospect of bringing down a serial killer, and Sarah felt a shiver of fear and anticipation that she might get to help her, ridiculous though it might sound. She was intrigued by everything she'd heard and Catriona's conviction that it might be Alex. Memories of the dead man's battered body still haunted her and she wondered, yet again, if he had fallen or if his last moments had been of terror, alone in the swirling white fog on the hill, seeing an approaching solo figure emerge from the mist. Sarah tried to imagine at what point the innocent hill walker would become aware that something was amiss, and she clutched her hand to her chest envisaging the fear of facing a horrific death falling through the air, frantically grabbing at anything to save yourself before smashing onto the rocks below, perhaps not dying outright but spending your last moments in an agony of broken bones and ripped flesh. The drop from the Ben path into Crofter's Gully was at probably fifty metres, higher in places. It wasn't a fall anyone could survive.

As she ate toast in the kitchen, Sarah fantasised about people's reaction if they discovered she had played a part, through helping Catriona, in bringing down a murderer. She had long harboured dreams of becoming a writer; perhaps investigative journalism would be her thing. *Don't be silly*, she thought, then checked herself; she should stop putting herself down. Why shouldn't she become an investigative journalist? She smiled dreamily as she washed out her coffee cup then set off for work.

The clouds had disappeared for the first time since her arrival and she felt like Dorothy when her house landed over the rainbow. Colour had been restored to the world. Where there had been grey sea, a colourless sky and mist-covered hills, Glasdrum was now awash with bright blue, shimmering gold and vibrant green. Ben Calder and its neighbouring peaks loomed over the town, and beneath the woods beside the road into town, a carpet of bluebells unfurled. As she neared the

High Street, the white and red car-ferry crossed towards Skye while an orange lifeboat and rusting fishing vessels bobbed in the harbour. Sarah couldn't believe how different somewhere could look from one day to the next, and this new vivid vision gave her a sense of purpose. Maybe this was her opportunity to change herself into someone more vibrant; less bland, more confident... more like Catriona.

Later that morning she was working her way through an audio tape when her phone rang.

'Hi, it's Vicky. How are you this morning?'

'Feeling a bit sick but thought I'd better come in to, you know... what we talked about last night.'

'That's why I'm phoning. I don't think you should. Finella was drunk. She didn't mean it about Alex. She was angry with him because she'd found out about him cheating.'

Sarah glanced round the office. There was nobody near her but she lowered her voice anyway. 'I've been awake all night thinking about it. It makes sense. He's a horrible man and he's up to something. I reckon he's the suspect Catriona is investigating.'

'Sarah, it's a ridiculous idea. Please drop it! God knows what he'll do if he catches you.'

'He can't do anything to me, I'm thinking about leaving soon anyway. I may as well see what I can find out.'

'Sarah! I really don't think—'

'Shit, they're here. I better go.' Sarah hung up. She felt proud of herself for making that up to get rid of Vicky. She had decided she'd do what she could to find out if there was any chance Alex could be the Mist Murderer and she wasn't going to let Vicky talk her out of it. Finella might have been drunk when she'd accused Alex, but Vicky had seemed quite convinced and Sarah had experienced for herself Alex's calculating nature. And anyway, it was just a glance in a diary. Not a big deal.

At half past five Donna appeared at her desk. 'We were lucky to get you on board, hen. I appreciate how much work you're doing. It makes my life a lot easier. But I've got to lock up now.'

'I hoped to get this audio tape finished before I go. Would it be okay if I locked up? I could be here first thing to open the door?'

'Aye, why not. Mustn't discourage your good work ethic.'

Donna showed Sarah how to switch on the alarm then hurried away looking relieved she now had someone to help her open and close the office.

Sarah put out the main lights but left her desk lamp on and her work lying about in case Donna came back. Neither Alex nor Catriona had been in all day so she felt fairly safe they wouldn't appear. She'd heard Donna mention Alex had a desk diary and a pocket one – sometimes he got her to cross-reference entries for him – and Sarah felt a thrill of excitement and sense of importance to be playing detective as she went into Alex's office without switching on the lamp. There was no outside window but a little light made it through the glass panels at the side of the door.

The diary was lying on the desk, but as soon as she opened it, she realised the task ahead. Every day had a set of letters against it; his life was tracked in code. She scanned the dates the bodies had been found in the gully but there were similar codes on every day. She thought perhaps he'd noted their meaning elsewhere, and she was leafing through the front and back pages when she heard the front door bang close. There were footsteps, followed by voices. After listening for a moment she recognised them both: Alex and Catriona.

Sarah felt sick. What were they doing here at this time of day? What had been a silly flight of fancy was brought into sharp focus. Even if Alex turned out not to be a murderer, he was still an unpleasant, cheating man who didn't care about anyone but himself. And he wasn't going to be pleased to find her in his office. She bolted into the walk-in cupboard, then immediately regretted it. What an idiot; she should have sauntered out and said she was checking to see if there was another audio tape to be done. Her desk light was on, her bag was under her chair; Alex would know she was in the office. She berated herself as she cowered in the cupboard, barely big enough for one person, hemmed in by heavily laden shelves on all sides.

The door to the Alex's office didn't open but she could hear muffled voices in the open-plan area as Alex and Catriona shouted at one another. When she crouched down and peered through the cupboard keyhole, she made out a person on the other side of the glass panel but couldn't tell who it was. The angry exchange continued until, suddenly, the figure she could see was slammed against the door, as though pushed. Sarah pulled away in fright. By the time she'd got her eye back to the keyhole, terrified of being caught, there was nobody in sight and nothing to hear.

She continued looking through the tiny opening until her eyeball ached. Then she put her ear to the door, trying to hear movement. Had they gone? Sweat broke out under her arms, partly the heat in the tiny cupboard but mostly the fear of discovery. Had Catriona threatened to go to the police and Alex had slammed her against the door panel? Maybe Catriona was lying there unconscious or… dead. Sarah swallowed back a moan of anguish. Was Alex out there right now, dealing with Catriona's body? Perhaps he would take her up the mountain and throw her off the gully cliff; another victim of the Mist Murderer, the only person who knew the truth now dead. But Sarah knew… and if Alex found her… it didn't bear thinking about. Sarah's knees ached from her crouched position in the cupboard but she was too scared to move in case she made a noise or dislodged the paper files that were heaped on the shelves above her.

Minutes ticked by and pain seared through her limbs. She was drenched in perspiration and her legs trembled from the awkward position. She was going to have to move before she fell over. Grasping the door handle with one hand and the edge of a shelf with the other she eased herself upwards. But her muscles had seized up. She fell against the shelves, and her hand sent a heap of files cascading to the ground. For a split second Sarah felt relief that she was again upright but it was immediately replaced with anxiety. Had they heard the files falling? She listened again for movement outside but there was silence. Sarah imagined Alex standing outside the cupboard, waiting for her to come out, with that sardonic look on his face. In her imagination, she could see Catriona's body lying in the office doorway, inert. *I'll get to make it a double tonight*, said Alex's voice in her head. She shook with the unbearable tension. How long had she been in the cupboard? She couldn't see her watch and her phone was on her desk. It was probably only half an hour but felt much, much longer.

Her nerves jangling, she cautiously opened the cupboard door and stuck her head into the office. It was empty and, as she crept forward, she saw that the open-plan area was, too. There were no dead bodies on the floor.

Relief flooded through her, closely followed by doubts. There was no sign anyone had been in the office. Was it possible she had imagined it all?

But no, it had been real. She'd seen them. She'd heard them. She was certain she'd watched Alex slam Catriona against the door.

Sarah wasted no more time. She grabbed her bag, switched off her desk light and rushed out of the office, locking the door behind her.

It was six forty-five and the sun was still high above the horizon, casting a golden glow on the sea as she hurried down the High Street. She thought she saw Vicky's car pulling away from the chip shop at the far end, but it was gone before she could be sure.

She walked out of town and up the road to the house, the evening shadows beneath the trees making her break into a run, uncomfortable in her work clothes. When she reached the house, she threw herself through the front door and slammed it behind her.

'Megan!' she shouted. 'MEGAN!' For once she wished Megan would be home. She needed someone to help her decide whether to go to the police. But there was no reply. She took a quick look around the house but it was empty and she remembered Megan had mentioned the kids were staying at their dad's for most of the week.

Sarah fished her mobile phone out of her bag and tried ringing Megan; no reply and no voicemail option. Where would she be? Sarah had noticed the affinity between Megan and Finella; perhaps she was at her house. And Alex would be going home, too, after he'd disposed of Catriona's body... That sounded ridiculous and yet... Sarah's brain was befuddled as she tried to decide what to do. Phone and warn Finella? But Alex was her husband. Sarah couldn't tell Finella she thought she might have witnessed her husband murdering someone when she had no evidence, and she couldn't go to the police for the same reason. How could she tell anyone she'd been snooping in her boss's diary and had hidden in a cupboard when he'd come into his office? They'd call the men in white coats for her.

Sarah wrestled with her dilemma for a while longer then rang Finella anyway, to hear someone's voice as much as anything, and reassure herself she wasn't losing her mind.

When there was no answer she tried Vicky and left her a message. 'Hi Vicky, it's Sarah. I wanted to speak to you about... eh... well, about what we talked about last night...' Sarah paused, not sure what to say but keen to portray the urgency of the situation. 'Please phone me as soon as you get this. I'm scared.'

Sarah texted all three of them, cursing the terrible phone signal in these parts. *Have to speak to you urgently about A. Ring me asap.*

She checked both doors were locked then went upstairs and sat in bed with the duvet pulled up to her chin. She ignored the hunger making her stomach growl as she looked out the window at the fading light, where only the tips of the distant mountains shimmered pink and gold as the sun sank lower in the sky. She lay down and stared at her phone, willing it to ring, wanting human contact to subdue her fear, to hear them tell her she was being silly, that it wasn't true, that Alex was not a killer… that she was safe.

But the phone was silent.

It occurred to her that one person could allay her fears: Catriona. She thought she didn't have her number but a vague memory came back to her of seeing it on a piece of *Journal* notepaper. She tipped her bag out on the bed and was relieved to find a scrap of paper that she'd written a To Do list on – it had a phone number written in the corner. *Please let it be Catriona's number.*

She dialled anxiously, wondering what she'd say if Alex answered, and was taken aback to hear Catriona's impatient, 'Hello.'

'Oh hi… it's Sarah.' She paused and the silence stretched out. 'I… er… just wanted to check you were okay.'

'Why wouldn't I be?'

'No reason. I was working late and, well, I saw you with Alex and wanted to check everything was all right. You looked like you were fighting.'

There was no response and Sarah cursed herself for phoning. Could she have been mistaken?

'Where did you see us?' Catriona asked.

'In the office. I was leaving and I saw you both going in. I remembered I had forgotten to switch my desk light off and was going to go back but I saw you arguing so I decided not to.'

'What were you there so late for?' asked Catriona, sharply.

'Because of all the work I'd been given, why else?' Sarah felt irked with Catriona for being curt with her. She was only trying to check she hadn't been murdered.

'Well, thanks for your concern, but I'm fine, and I'm busy. Alex and I were just rowing about personal things. I'll see you tomorrow.' The line went dead.

Sarah threw her phone aside and lay down, staring at the ceiling, feeling confused. Catriona was fine. Maybe the fight hadn't been as bad as Sarah had imagined. Fractured thoughts swirled in her head without pattern or organisation; too many incomprehensible things had happened to her in the last week and she couldn't sift out what was real and what was imagined. Numbed by the shock of the evening's events, she fell asleep fully clothed, her last thought to wonder how long it would take her to pack her stuff and get a train back to civilisation.

It was after nine when she woke and heard a scraping noise in the hall.

She sat up. It sounded like furniture being moved.

'Megan?' she shouted, and the noise stopped.

Sarah slipped out of bed, crept to the door and peered around it.

'Megan?' she called again as she made her way through the hall in the gloom; the darkness was rarely complete this far north and this close to summer.

A hooded shadow appeared from the bedroom on the right and Sarah screamed. She took a step backwards. But the figure advanced towards her, arms outstretched. Before she could get a proper look, Sarah turned and ran towards the stairs.

As she pelted towards safety, she tripped and fell forward down the first few steps. She put her hands out in front of her, but with a violent thud her head landed against the heavy antique iron that sat at the spiral of the stairs.

After that, the darkness, for Sarah, was complete.

Chapter Twenty-Two
FINELLA

Thursday, 19 May 2005, 8.45pm

The front door slammed and the boys' shrill voices rang out from downstairs. Finella sat up in bed. She heard Judith's light footsteps padding upstairs and her bedroom door closing, then Alex shouting at the boys to get ready for bed, followed by jostling and shrieking outside her bedroom door. Eventually there was silence and Finella waited, trembling, although she couldn't have said, precisely, what she was scared of. She wasn't sure if she was frightened of Alex or just fearful of how her life was turning out, of the wreck she had become. What had happened to the confident young woman who had gone to university, who had been stylish and ambitious, but who now couldn't even get out of bed to take care of her own children?

The bedroom door opened. 'While you were languishing in bed, I rescued our children from those two appalling women you are friends with. They were cavorting about on the beach at half eight on a school night, both drunk. The one that looks like a boy could hardly stand up she was so pissed.'

Finella stared at Alex, her brain struggling to process his words, consumed with the thought he might be a killer. It was surely ridiculous. He was mean and disloyal but she couldn't believe he was a murderer.

After waiting in vain for a response from Finella, Alex continued, 'I've put the kids to bed but I've a couple of things to take care of. Think you can manage to look after them for an hour?'

She nodded mutely and he added, 'Just so you know, I've started separation proceedings. The children will live with me. You're an incapable mother.' He held his hand up to silence Finella as she spluttered in protest. 'Too late, Finella. You left them, against my wishes, with that woman, Vicky, without doing any background checks on her. You have no idea who she is.'

'I've known her for over ten years!'

'You think you have. I've discovered she isn't who she claims to be. She could be a criminal for all we know!'

'I know about Vicky's past. It's not what you think.'

'I'm sure she's spun you some kind of sob story. And like a fool you fell for it.'

'But—'

'I'm sorry, Finella, I don't have time for this.'

The door opened and Judith's pale face appeared. She opened her mouth to speak but Alex roared at her to get back to her room and she hurried away after a quick glance at her mother.

Finella scrambled out of bed and pointed a finger at Alex. 'Look how scared she is of you. The children will not be living with you.'

'I'm sorry,' Alex rubbed his forehead. 'I shouldn't have shouted at Judith. I'll speak to her tomorrow. But the kids need discipline and you let them run wild. You're no better than your friend Megan whose boys run wild all over the town. And you've no idea the stress I've been under recently. Every fucking thing falls on my shoulders.' Alex looked down, lost momentarily in his own thoughts.

Finella walked towards him. She knew she should keep quiet but the words spilled out of her mouth in fury before she could stop them. 'Is it stressful trying to seduce younger women but having them reject you? Poor Alex has the weight of the world on his shoulders.'

He raised his hand and slapped her. Her head flew sideways and she staggered back towards the bed. Alex advanced on her. 'Don't push me, Finella.' He lifted his arm as though to hit her again but paused, then dropped it again and left the room. She heard the front door slam a couple of minutes later, followed by a crunch of gravel being spat out as Alex's car tore out of the driveway.

Finella curled into a ball on her bed. She thought about her daughter's bewildered face and longed to comfort her but she didn't want Judith to see the red mark on her cheek. She knew she was incapable of putting her brave mask on so it was better to leave Judith to her own devices in case she inadvertently made things worse, something she seemed to specialise in these days. Finella was devastated to be so powerless to help her daughter. Alex was right; she was a pathetic, terrible mother, with a miserable daughter and unruly boys. Finella wished she was dead.

She lay for several hours, her mind numb, her limbs becoming stiff through inactivity. She dreaded Alex returning to the bedroom but he didn't appear; perhaps he'd slept in the spare room.

At some point during the long night, something unfurled in Finella's mind. A spark of anger took hold. How dare he treat her as he did! Especially if he was the monster Vicky and Sarah said he was. Except… despite everything, she didn't believe the murderer theory. What was his motivation to attack middle-aged, hill walking enthusiasts? Those types of men were his friends! As dawn broke, Finella sat up in bed, feeling bleary but determined. Alex wasn't going to take her children from her. She would do whatever was necessary to stop him.

But the thought of leaving the cocoon of her bedroom terrified her. She didn't want to face Alex's anger, Judith's confusion or the boys' incessant clamour for attention. She heard the sounds of them getting up; doors slamming, voices shouting, Alex hurrying them along and asking what they wanted for breakfast. Nobody came to see her and her resolve crumbled. She lay back down on her bed, waiting for them all to leave, thinking about how useless she was.

After a while she glanced at her phone, which had been on silent all of the previous day. Lots of missed calls from Vicky, Megan and Sarah, plus various enigmatic texts imploring her to call them. One from Sarah irked her: *Have to speak to you urgently about A. Ring me asap.*

She threw her phone aside, hating them all. It was a game for them: let's pretend the man who tried to seduce us is a killer and we're the detectives. They didn't care about Finella, whose children would be affected by accusations against him. Overcome with despair and self-pity, Finella threw her head back onto her pillow, her heart fragmenting into a thousand tiny pieces.

She started upright when Alex burst into the room. 'Where are the kids' waterproofs? I'm taking them to school and they've packed to go to my parents in Inverness for the weekend. But I can't find their bloody jackets.'

'You can't take them to Inverness!'

'I've the Highland golf tournament this weekend and I can't cancel it; clients are coming. You're in no fit state to look after them.'

'I'll be fine,' she said scrambling out of bed, her hair a wild bush around her head.

'Finella...' Alex paused and looked at her with a trace of sympathy. 'I don't know what's up with you but I think you should go to the doctor.'

'I've had a virus or something. I'll be fine. Please don't take them away.' How had it come to this? Begging for her own children.

'You've not been yourself for months and, frankly, I can't cope with worrying about you and work and the kids and...' He paused before going on, his mind disengaged, preoccupied. 'The kids are going to my parents for now. We all need a break to... I don't know. To get ourselves back together.' He retreated and shut the door, leaving Finella standing beside her bed, bereft and in shock.

The door opened again. 'The waterproofs?' he asked.

Finella sighed. 'They're in the utility room,' she replied, adding after he'd closed the door again, '...where they always are.'

She sat at the edge of the bed, unable to decide what to do. She heard Alex and the children leaving, then a short while later the doorbell rang. She ignored it but it rang again, followed by the sound of the front door opening then footsteps on the stairs. Her heart sank. What now?

Vicky's face appeared around her bedroom door. 'You're up,' she said.

Finella looked down at her nightdress. 'Not really.'

'Did you get my texts?'

Finella shrugged.

'Where are the kids?'

'Alex took them to school, then they're going to stay with his parents in Inverness. I'm not coping, apparently.'

Vicky sat down beside her and Finella noticed how haggard she looked. 'I've some horrible news. Sarah and Megan are in the community hospital; both were discovered unconscious at home last night. I think Megan came round pretty soon but Sarah was out for a while. But they haven't been transferred to the Belford in Fort William so they must be doing okay.'

'What on earth happened to them?' Finella asked, her stomach lurching at yet more awfulness, even though a tiny part of her thought what bliss it would be to be unconscious, oblivious to the world and its troubles.

'It sounds like they were attacked. You remember the other night when we were drinking I told Sarah to take a look in Alex's diary to check his entries against the deaths on the mountain?'

Finella nodded, her heart constricting painfully, as Vicky continued. 'I phoned her yesterday morning to tell her not to but she hung up on me. Then after work she texted me to say she had something important to tell me about Alex. She kept ringing me, too. But it was a policeman who answered her phone when

I eventually returned her call. He told me they'd found Sarah and Megan at their house after an anonymous tip-off, and they wanted me to go to the station to tell them anything I might know about what could have happened. The officer asked about the *A* in the text message Sarah had sent me but I said I didn't know what she'd meant.'

Finella could see the despair in Vicky's eyes. Alex was right about Vicky having secrets but she was only shielding her child; mothers will do anything to protect their children. Vicky must truly hate Alex for trying to uncover her secret, and Finella didn't blame her one bit. She shook off her thoughts and tried to get to grips with what Vicky was telling her. 'Are you saying someone broke into Megan's house last night and attacked her and Sarah? And you think it might be…' Finella couldn't bring herself to voice Alex's name.

'But didn't Alex bring the kids home after he'd picked them up at mine?'

When Finella nodded, Vicky added, 'So it can't have been him. He was here.'

Finella opened her mouth, but no sounds came out.

'What is it, Finella?'

'Alex went back out again. He brought the kids home, told them to go to bed, then he said he had a couple of things to take care of and he went away in his car. I don't know when he came back because I fell asleep.'

'Maybe he went to threaten Sarah—'

'He wouldn't do that!'

'He would! He's come to my house to threaten me and that was only because I refused to sleep with him. What if Sarah tried to look in Alex's diary and he caught her… maybe that was what her text was about!'

'Stop it, Vicky!' Finella put her hands over her ears like a child. She wanted everything to stop. 'You said Megan was attacked, too. Why would Alex threaten Sarah if Megan was there? It doesn't make any sense!'

'Megan was plastered when she left my house last night. It was around half eight, just after Alex came for the kids. The policeman said they found Sarah and Megan at half nine so God knows where Megan was all that time, but maybe Megan arrived home when Alex was already there. Maybe Megan phoned the police and that's why he turned on her. I don't know. I'm guessing.'

Finella felt light-headed. She clutched Vicky's arm as though to save herself from falling. Physically she didn't move from her seated position on the bed but she felt all the sensations of falling from a great height; her stomach lurched, her mind spun and she heard a muted roaring in her ears.

Her phone rang and without thinking she answered it. 'Finella Campbell.'

'Sorry to bother you, Mrs Campbell. It's Mary Morrison from the school. I was phoning to arrange a date for the next fundraising committee. We were hoping to extend the bike storage areas. So many children are cycling these days despite the terrible weather we've been having.' There was a pause. 'Mrs Campbell?'

Finella's mind was spinning. 'Of course, well, I don't have my diary to hand…'

'We were hoping to hold a meeting next Wednesday at

seven? I could put a note out to parents in the schoolbags today if that suited you.'

Finella stared at Vicky, who was making a throat-cutting gesture. What on earth did she mean? Was she pretending to be Alex?

'Tell her you'll phone back later!' hissed Vicky.

'I'm sorry, Mrs Morrison. I'll be busy next week and I'm afraid I'm going to take a break from fundraising for a while. Perhaps another parent will be able to help you.'

'Oh, well, it's just that we've—'

'I have to go now, goodbye.' Finella snapped her flip-up phone closed. She looked at Vicky. 'I never say no to anyone.'

'You're learning to stand up for yourself.'

'Yes.' Finella's flash of pleasure at getting out of the school fundraising committee receded as she focused on her current situation: her husband was planning to take her children away from her, in addition to being a potential violent killer.

'What are you going to tell the police?' Finella asked Vicky.

'I don't know. The thing is… I can't get involved with the police. They might find out who I am. What if it ended up in the papers? Even a photo of me and Louise's dad sees it.' Vicky's voice rose in agitation. 'I can't risk that happening. I took his money and his child! God knows what he'd do if he found me.' Vicky wiped a tear from her eye and Finella gave her a fleeting look of understanding. Neither of them wanted to speak to the police for the same reason; to protect their children. Vicky needed to protect her secret, and Finella did not want her children to be forever known as the Mist Murderer's children, whether proven or not.

Finella sat up a little straighter. 'Alex is a deplorable man but this nonsense about him being a killer is ridiculous.'

'Whatever he is, I need to get away from here without any more trouble,' said Vicky. 'That's sort of why I came here this morning. I wanted to say goodbye and to thank you for being so kind to me.'

'You're leaving Glasdrum? Because of Alex?' Finella felt as though it was her fault Vicky was leaving. If she hadn't been married to such an awful man... or if she hadn't asked Vicky to look after her children... none of this would have happened. Vicky had been so kind to them; she had shown them love and interest at a time when Finella had been too preoccupied with her own troubles to give them what they needed. For that she would be forever grateful. A slow hatred burned in her heart at the damage Alex was causing everyone.

At the sound of an engine outside, Vicky jumped to her feet and looked out the window. 'It's Alex.'

'I thought he was going to work...'

'I have to go.'

Finella reached out to take Vicky's hand through a blur of tears but Vicky had turned away. Finella heard her running downstairs, trying to escape before Finella's murderous husband returned. Finella felt a wave of hysterical giggles threaten to burst out of her. Was it really only a couple of weeks ago that everything had been normal?

Finella heard the front door open then an angry exchange as Vicky and Alex came face to face with one another in the hall. Finella heaved herself to her feet and walked onto the landing; it was the first time she'd left her bedroom in over thirty-six hours. She crept downstairs, drawn towards the raised voices, yet dreading involvement in the row.

As they came into her line of vision, she saw Vicky push past Alex and run outside.

Alex stepped out the door as though to go after Vicky, and without thinking Finella raced down the last few steps and out of the house to grab his arm.

'Leave her!'

Alex pulled his arm out of Finella's grasp and pushed her away. She stumbled backwards, slipped on the step that was wet after a heavy downpour, and fell, banging her lower back on the doorframe as she hit the ground. She saw Vicky's worried face inside her car as she reversed out of their driveway. The car paused but Finella raised her arm to signal to Vicky to carry on. Finella had a feeling she might not see her again but she wanted to help her get away as Alex loomed over her. Beyond him she saw Vicky's anxious face stare at her for a moment longer, then the car turned and drove away.

Chapter Twenty-Three
VICKY

Friday, 20 May 2005, 9.30am

Vicky stopped reversing for a moment when she saw Finella grab Alex's arm. As the windscreen wipers danced back and forth, she watched as he pushed her away and Finella fell heavily against the doorframe. Vicky wondered if she ought to help. Could she drive off and leave her friend in the clutches of someone she thought could be a killer? That still sounded absurd and Finella herself didn't seem to believe it. But where had he gone the previous night after he'd dropped the kids off, when Megan and Sarah had been attacked?

Indecision crippled her as she watched Finella lying on the ground, Alex standing over her. She was on the verge of getting out of the car when Finella waved at her to go. She felt like a coward but Louise was her priority; she had to get her daughter away from Glasdrum before Alex could reveal her true identity to the police, and there was something Vicky wanted to do before she left. With regret, Finella would have to fend for herself.

Exhaustion washed over Vicky as she drove towards the town; she had been up late packing essential belongings. Louise would be disappointed about leaving without notice but Vicky had decided to tell her they were going on a last-minute break to visit a friend in Glasgow. The thought of Louise's dad tracking her down still terrified her; she couldn't face the stress of staying any longer, waiting to find out what Alex was going to do, and that last encounter with him had helped her to make a final firm decision to get away. She would feel safer in an anonymous city and she had a friend in Glasgow they could stay with while she decided what to do in the longer term.

But first, she felt compelled to make one last visit to her granny's grave. She knew there were other things she should do to prepare for their escape but her heart was breaking at the thought of leaving; she had to say goodbye to her only family before she did. Her granny had been her safety net when she'd been a child, and her passing had provided Vicky with similar security, many years later, when Vicky had needed a bolthole. It wasn't an ideal time to go to the ancient graveyard, with the rain lashing down on the narrow path that led through the treacherous gorge where the river swirled twenty metres below a narrow path, but Vicky found herself driving out of town, and instead of continuing back to her cottage, she turned left after the track that led to Megan's house, onto another single-lane road. She passed the parking area at the start of the main path up Ben Calder, then, after a couple more miles of winding upwards, she came to the small car park where the road ended. In summer it was impossible to find a space, crammed with walkers, from professional climbers laden down with ropes and harnesses off to tackle the higher crags, to day-trippers taking a picnic through the spectacular gorge to photograph the waterfall that cascaded down from a hanging valley.

Vicky locked her car and hurried off along the rocky path.

The rain was getting heavier but she didn't care; she was focused on her destination. She didn't see Alex's car pull into the car park behind her.

Chapter Twenty-Four
MEGAN

Friday, 20 May 2005, 7.30am

Megan wriggled herself into a sitting position in the hospital, wincing as her newly plastered arm banged against the bedrail. She put her good hand up to her face to touch the raw scratches on her cheek; the tree had ripped skin off the side of her face, and her head hurt as though it had been split open. She wasn't sure whether her headache was caused by coming off her bike, the shock of finding Sarah, the awful night she'd spent trying to sleep between the starchy hospital sheets, with bangs and coughs echoing around the wards, or a hangover from the vodka she'd drunk on the beach.

One thing was sure; she was getting out of there as soon as possible. The nurse had said she'd have to stay in until the doctor had done his rounds but Megan had other plans. Johnny was coming round after he'd dropped the boys at school and she intended leaving immediately with him.

Megan's mind had been on overdrive all night, trying to guess what had happened to Sarah and if it had been Lewis she'd seen running from the house. Could he have come home early and fallen out with her, maybe they had a tussle on the stairs that had made him panic when she fell and hit her head? Someone had phoned the police so that made sense to a certain extent. It just seemed so unlikely Lewis would run away and leave Sarah unconscious; as far as Megan could tell he was besotted with her.

Whatever had happened, the police were going to want to question Megan and she was determined to get out of hospital before that happened. She was scared they might be searching her house right now, with Gregor's stash of drugs still on top of the cupboard and Donald's remains wherever Lewis had put them. He said he'd reburied them but what if that was what he was not being truthful about? She was convinced he was lying about something. They could be anywhere... waiting to be found...

What a goddamn mess, she thought, swinging her legs off the bed, her bare feet cold on the floor, despite the room being overheated. She was wearing a hospital gown that showed her arse at the back, so she put on the second one the nurse had left beside the bed, wearing it like a jacket, grateful for the wide sleeves through which her cast could fit. The two gowns came down to her knees, drowning her tiny frame, and she rubbed her head to soothe the pounding and try to remember what had happened to her own clothes.

As soon as she was on her feet the urge to pee became insistent and she hobbled to the loo, every step reverberating through her skull, her arm and face throbbing in agony. On the way back she saw Sarah being wheeled into the ward, having spent the night somewhere else in the small hospital. Megan shuffled towards her bed but a nurse put an arm out to stop her.

'Sorry, keep back for now, please.'

'She's my friend. We were brought in together.'

'You'll have to wait till we get her settled and checked.'

'How is she?'

'As good as can be expected. That was some blow she took to her head. She was out for several hours so she'll be closely monitored. Her vitals are good and she's relatively alert, considering.'

'Considering what?'

The nurse appraised Megan for a few moments before replying. 'How well does she know you?'

'She's my brother's girlfriend. She's from London.'

'Poor girl's a long way from home.' The nurse consulted a clipboard. 'Her boyfriend is Lewis MacDonald? Someone thought he was working on Skye so the police have gone to find him. In the meantime'—she turned her attention back to Megan—'it might be good for Sarah to speak to you. It might jog her memory.'

'She's got amnesia?'

'Short-term memory loss is fairly common with a head injury. She could be a bit fuzzy for a few days. She's also on heavy painkillers, which don't help. There, look,' the nurse pointed at Sarah, who was smiling at Megan. 'She recognises you. That's a good sign.'

'How are you?' Megan asked as the medical staff moved away. Sarah looked terrible against the white hospital pillows; pale and exhausted, with a thick bandage round her head.

'What happened to you?' Sarah said to Megan, who put a hand to her face, remembering that her injuries probably looked worse than Sarah's.

'I fell off my bike in the woods and then I found you lying on the stairs at home.'

'What happened to me?'

'Can't you remember?'

Sarah's brow furrowed. 'They said it would come back in time.'

'You texted to say you wanted to speak to me about…' Megan lowered her voice, '… Alex.'

'Did I?' Sarah frowned again. She whispered, 'I remember Vicky wanted me to check Alex's diary to find out if he was, you know…'

Megan leant in close to Sarah and whispered, 'Who was in the house with you last night?'

Sarah looked at her with wide eyes, dark rings beneath them. 'There was somebody there. I was running away from them… and I fell…' Sarah put her hands to her face. 'I was scared.'

'So it wasn't Lewis?' Megan held her breath. She didn't want it to have been her brother but the more she thought about it, the more convinced she was that the figure she'd seen running through the trees had been Lewis.

'Lewis is on Skye. I remember that.'

'I thought he might have come home early and you'd had a row.'

Tears escaped out of Sarah's eyes and slithered down her face. 'I can't remember who was there. I'm so tired…' Sarah's eyes closed.

'Sarah!' Megan shook her, panic shooting through her. 'Sarah!'

'What's going on?' A nurse spoke behind Megan.

'She's closed her eyes… what's wrong with her? Is she…?'

'She's fine,' said the nurse, moving Megan away from Sarah's bed. 'Her body's in shock and she's sedated so she'll probably sleep for a good while. It's the best thing for her.'

Megan returned to her own bed, disappointed at not having found out who'd been in the house. Surely Lewis wouldn't have pushed Sarah… or killed his father… But, like his father, he has a rare but sharp temper. Megan could hardly bear to keeping pursuing the thought that had been lurking about her subconscious for too long now – what if Lewis and Donald had fought that Hogmanay? If Donald had been drunk and violent to their mother, who knows what Lewis might have done if he'd snapped. Megan felt ill, and the crescendo of pain in her head magnified. She groaned and a passing nurse stopped by her bed.

'Are you all right, dear?'

Megan put both hands to either side of her head. 'My fucking head is killing me.' She looked at the nurse's disapproving face. 'Sorry for swearing. I've never felt pain like it. Can you give me something for it?'

'You can have a dose of codeine if it's really bad.'

'I'll take anything. Cheers.'

Megan swallowed the pill the nurse gave her and lay unmoving on the bed until the agony lessened. She still had half an hour to wait until Johnny would arrive after dropping the boys off. It was the longest thirty minutes of her life.

As nine o'clock approached, Megan hauled herself to her feet and found her clothes in the cupboard beside her bed. She had no chance of getting dressed on her own with the cast but she put her trainers on, and left her jeans and top beside her on the bed. She focused on the entrance to the ward, every cell in her body willing Johnny to appear through it before the police or a doctor, who would delay her with an interminable examination and a ton of questions.

Time crawled along. Eight fifty-five. Johnny would be at the school dropping the kids off. She'd asked him to come straight to the hospital but her phone was out of charge so she couldn't check. Sarah was still asleep and Megan wondered if she'd remember more when she woke.

Nine o'clock came and went. Megan could see nurses and doctors walking about in the corridor between wards. The door opened and Catriona swept in. She looked around then walked towards Sarah's bed.

'She's asleep and not to be woken,' said Megan, intrigued.

'Right,' said Catriona. She looked deliberately at her watch. 'I've plenty of time this morning so I'll sit with her for a bit.'

Megan shrugged, then returned her attention to the door. In preparation for leaving, she tried to gather her clothes onto her knee, but with her right arm out of action she knocked her jeans onto the floor. When she looked up from gathering them back up into a bundle she could carry, Johnny was peering through the glass in the door and she motioned for him to come in.

'God, Megan, what the hell happened? Are you okay?'

Johnny looked close to tears at the sight of her and she remembered how awful she looked. She touched her face. 'The boys'll be impressed, eh?'

'That must have been some tumble.'

Megan shrugged. 'I was pissed and it was dark.' She grinned at him, feeling a surge of pleasure at seeing him. 'Fuckin' tree roots, eh?'

Johnny looked equally pleased to see her, though he pointed at the bed. 'Shouldn't you be lying down?'

'No, I'm leaving.'

'What?'

'I'm ready to go. I've my shoes on and everything. You take my clothes and I'll get changed at home.'

'Megan, are you out of your mind? Get into bed!'

'I have to get home.' Megan glanced around the ward and whispered, 'I nicked Gregor's stash and I've got to get it out of the house in case the police do a search after, you know'—she nodded in Sarah's direction—'what happened to her. I need to speak to Lewis. I thought I saw him running away from the house.'

Johnny whispered back. 'You can't leave dressed like that.'

'It'll take me ages to put my clothes on and we have to leave. I'm not speaking to the police, Johnny. You carry my clothes and let's go.'

Megan started limping towards the door, jumping back when a nurse burst into the room. 'Where are you off to? Doctor's doing his rounds.'

'I'm going to the toilet. My, er, boyfriend is sorting out my clothes for me.'

'Righto,' said the nurse.

Megan waved at Johnny to follow her so he obediently gathered up her clothes and hurried out of the ward after her, then along the corridor and out of the main doors. Megan found the light rain a relief after the stuffy hospital environment and, although a couple of people glanced at her in the double hospital gowns and trainers, they made it to Johnny's car without being stopped.

'I'm not happy about this, Megs. What if there's something wrong with you?' he asked as he drove out of the car park and set off along the front to bypass the town centre.

'Then I'll go back. But I've stuff to do. Holy shit. STOP!'

Johnny slammed on the brakes on the seafront road. 'What is it?'

'Look!' Megan pointed ahead of them where two men were walking. 'It's Lewis and Gregor. And look at them together. Isn't it hard to tell who's who?'

'So?'

'It's 'cause they're brothers.'

'What are you talking about—Hey! Where are you going? Megan!'

Megan had jumped out of the car and was hurrying along the pavement that followed the shoreline, her gowns flapping in the breeze. 'Oi, Lewis!'

Both her brothers turned simultaneously and she was struck again by their matching characteristics. Facially they were dissimilar but their gaits and gestures were almost identical. It dawned on her that it was Gregor she'd seen running from the house the previous evening.

They both stared. 'What the fuck are you wearing, Megan?' asked Lewis. 'And your face...'

She pointed at Gregor. 'What were you doing at my house last night and what did you do to Sarah? She almost died, you know! You're bloody lucky I haven't told the coppers.' Megan advanced on him until he was backed up against the low wall that ran between the pavement and the shore.

'It wisnae ma fault, like! I phoned the ambulance. She'd be dead if it wisnae for me. I was just looking for ma stash 'cause you never gave it back like you said you would. Where the hell is it?'

'What's he talking about? What's wrong with Sarah?' asked Lewis. 'I'm just off the ferry.'

'She's in hospital. Someone'—Megan indicated Gregor—'broke into our house last night and pushed her down the stairs. Everyone's been trying to get in touch with you.'

'I never pushed her, I swear! She got a fright. I was only tryin' to get my hash back. The bloody Weigies are after me, man. I'm gonna be fuckin' dead soon.'

'Why did you take his gear, Megan?' asked Lewis, before turning to Gregor. 'And why have you not told me about Sarah being in hospital?'

Before Gregor had a chance to reply, Megan interrupted, ''Cause he's a lying bastard, that's why. I took his stuff to pay him a lesson for… you know what.'

Lewis and Gregor looked at the ground, a picture of awkwardness as Megan continued. 'While we're at it, which one of you bastards is lying about what happened to our dad? That's what I want to know.'

Lewis looked back and forth along the deserted pavement. The rain was getting heavier. 'I don't think we should do this out here. There's something I have to tell you about Dad. And I need to get up to the hospital to see Sarah. Is she okay?'

'Sarah's okay now,' she spat the words at Lewis. 'She was sleeping when I left. As you'd know if you bothered to keep in touch with her.'

Megan felt herself slipping beyond reason; the pain and discomfort coupled with the stress she'd suffered over the previous few weeks came bubbling to the surface. She was oblivious to the wind and the rain and her paltry, odd attire as she paced about beside the road, stabbing her finger at her brothers while Johnny watched in alarm from the car, concerned but knowing through bitter experience not to mess with Megan when she'd gone off on one.

She addressed both her brothers. 'There's something I want to get straight once and for all about the night Dad went missing. You'—Megan pointed at Gregor—'said Lewis turned up at home at midnight while you and Dad were arguing and that you buggered off. If that's true then Lewis has three hours unaccounted for.' She turned to Lewis. 'But *you* say you didn't get home till three in the morning, which means Gregor could have killed Dad and buried him before you got home.'

'Jesus, Megan!' Gregor grabbed her arm. 'What the hell are you talking about? I didnae kill him. I swear to God I left at midnight when Lewis came home.' He turned to Lewis. 'Tell her, man. It wisnae me. You saw me leaving.'

Lewis put his hand to his head and looked at the ground. He didn't meet either of their eyes.

'Well?' Megan let go of Gregor's arm and stabbed Lewis with her finger.

He brushed her hand away. 'Let's go home. I'm not talking about it out here with you looking like an escapee from a fucking loony bin.' Lewis took Megan's unbroken arm and led her back to the car. He spoke to Johnny. 'Can you drop us both at home, mate? Me and Megs got some things to talk about. Then I'm going to see Sarah.'

Gregor shouted at them that he'd be round that evening to pick up his stuff, then he hurried off towards the town.

There was silence in the car as Johnny drove them home. Megan's arm and head were hurting and she realised she had no painkillers because she hadn't waited to see the doctor. Maybe she'd go back once she'd taken care of what needed to be done at home.

She stared out of the window, dreading the conversation that was imminent. Johnny must have sensed something was up and kept quiet, too.

When they arrived, Megan kissed Johnny. 'You're always there for me. I'm so grateful to you.'

'I'd do anything for you, Megs.'

'I know. The boys are lucky to have you. At least one decent parent.'

'Hey, don't knock yourself.' He touched the unmarked side of her face briefly then got out of the car, ran round to Megan's door and helped her out as Lewis climbed out of the back seat. Johnny looked from Megan to Lewis, then back to Megan. 'I guess you two have something serious to talk about.'

'I've no time for talking. I'm going to get my car and go to the hospital to see Sarah,' said Lewis.

'You're going to answer my bloody questions first,' shrieked Megan.

'Want me to come in with you?' Johnny asked her.

Megan looked at him with affection. 'It's fine, I'll ring you later and speak to the boys if that's okay. God, I miss them. Can't wait to see them tomorrow.'

Johnny looked reluctant but got into his car and drove away with a worried look on his face. Megan watched him go, thinking how much nicer it would have been to go with Johnny, to smoke a spliff and relax for the rest of the day. But instead she turned to Lewis, who was heading through the door into the house.

'Lewis, you've got to tell me what happened to Dad that night. And what you've done with his remains. Jesus, do you realise the police could be here any minute to search the place to find out what happened to Sarah? If they find Dad's bones... Lewis, talk to me!' Megan shrieked at him as he continued across the hall to the stairs, ignoring her.

He turned back. 'Megan, I'm so sorry. I want to tell you but I can't right now. I really want to go and see Sarah. But don't worry about Dad. Nobody will find his remains.'

'You've got to tell me what happened the night he died.'

'Megan, just drop it.'

'I need to know the truth! Gregor said you came home at midnight...'

'That's not true!' Lewis advanced on her. 'I came home at three, all right, like I already told you a million times. Gregor's wrong.'

'You're lying,' said Megan.

'Yes, he is lying,' said a male voice from the kitchen.

Megan gasped. She recognised that voice. But it couldn't be...

A heavy-set figure emerged from the kitchen. Megan stared in shock. Her hand flew up to her mouth and she took a step backwards. 'Dad...'

Chapter Twenty-Five
SARAH

Friday, 20 May 2005, 8am

It had been a long night for Sarah, under observation in a curtained cubicle in the cramped A&E department. She longed to sleep but every time she closed her eyes, a blurry image of a figure coming towards her loomed in her mind; she felt fear and an urge to run. She wished it was a dream, but it had happened. And she couldn't recall anything else properly, just the same endless vision of someone walking towards her in the dark, playing on a loop in her head.

The curtains were pulled aside and two nurses bustled around her bed. 'We're taking you to the ward now and someone there will keep an eye on you.'

Sarah looked up at the women. It was an unusual sensation to be lying on your back, helpless like a baby in a cot, while people bent over you. Her bed started to move and she watched the ceiling lights flash past above her. The movement made her feel as though on a fairground ride; she squeezed her eyes shut until she came to a stop. The staff were talking to her but she struggled to focus on what they were saying, and their words washed over her like white noise.

When the nurses moved away, Megan appeared and asked her how she was. Sarah's initial pleasure at recognising a familiar face was replaced by shock. Megan looked like someone from a horror film. Part of her face was missing. 'What happened to you?' Sarah asked.

'I fell off my bike in the woods and then I found you lying on the stairs at home.'

'What happened to me?'

'Can't you remember?'

Sarah's brow furrowed and she shook her head. 'They said it would probably come back to me in time.'

Megan started talking about a text Sarah had sent her about Alex, and panic fluttered in Sarah's chest. She wanted her to stop. There was something about Alex she needed to remember but she couldn't focus; her brain was full of fog. But Megan kept pressing her. Then she asked who had been in the house with Sarah but she didn't know. Thinking about it made her feel scared.

'Was it Lewis?' Megan asked.

'Lewis is on Skye. I remember that.'

'I thought he might have come home early and you'd had a row.'

'I can't remember who was there. I'm so tired...' Sarah felt her brain shutting down. She wanted to find out more about Lewis. Had anyone tried to get in touch with him, or with her family? But she couldn't keep her eyes open. Sleep engulfed her.

When she woke, she had no idea how much time had passed. There was a movement beside her bed and she turned her head. It was Catriona, staring at her, with steely eyes.

Sarah gave her a faint smile. She felt relieved to see her though couldn't think why.

Catriona pulled her chair closer to the bed. 'I've been waiting for you to wake up,' she said. 'I wanted to speak to you about our conversation on the phone yesterday.'

'I... I can't remember speaking to you.'

'Come on, Sarah. You might have fooled everyone else but I can tell when someone is lying. I think you remember everything you saw and heard yesterday.' Catriona took Sarah's hand and leant towards her. 'What did you see?'

Sarah stared into Catriona's icy blue eyes then glanced around the ward. It was deserted except for an old lady who was sound asleep in the far corner. Megan was gone. Something about Catriona's stare made her feel uncomfortable and she tried to sit up, but Catriona pushed her back onto the bed.

'I need to go to the toilet,' said Sarah, glancing over Catriona's shoulder towards the door, hoping a nurse would reappear. She didn't want to talk to Catriona when she was glaring at her like that.

'Tell me what you saw and heard yesterday when I was with Alex.'

'I told you! I can't remember.' Sarah tried again to push herself into a sitting position, but Catriona stood up and put a hand on her chest to hold her down.

'Sorry, Sarah, but I can't let you go yet.'

Chapter Twenty-Six
FINELLA

Friday, 20 May 2005, 9.45am

Finella staggered to her feet outside her front door as Vicky drove away. Alex started to get into his car. 'Leave Vicky alone. Don't go after her!' shouted Finella.

But he ignored her, and his car shot out of the drive.

Finella grasped the doorframe and bent forward as pain surged through her lower back. She took deep breaths, feeling furious. How dare he threaten to take her children, push her to the ground, then chase after her friend, someone who had provided Finella with much-needed comfort these last few months. She wasn't going to tolerate it any longer.

Finella fetched her car keys, feeling determined. Alex wasn't going to walk all over her any more. For years she'd put up with him belittling her and she'd noticed him doing it to Judith, too. *I suppose second place is better than nothing... Don't worry, Judith, you'll catch up eventually...* He was doing the opposite to the boys. *If your brother snatched something from you, don't cry like a baby, show him who's boss... We're better than everyone else, lads, and don't forget it.*

As snatches of conversation flitted through her mind, Finella felt rage, with herself as much as with him. What kind of mother put up with that treatment of her children, subduing her daughter and turning her already wild sons into misogynistic brats? She had kept quiet, hoping it would pass, that things would get better. She had tried to influence her children for the good while Alex was out, bolstering Judith's fragile self-esteem and teaching the boys some humility, but her own confidence had been eroded, bit by bit, over the years. It was time to reclaim it.

Finella paused in the hall, one hand on the doorknob, the other on her back, as a fresh spasm gripped her. It was like being in labour. She breathed deeply and chose to ignore it. Alex would be out of sight soon; there was no time to lose.

She raced to her car and accelerated away from the house towards the junction. She looked left and right. There was no sign of him. Where would he have gone?

He was following Vicky and she was most likely to have gone home so Finella turned left and made her way out of the town. She passed the turn-off to Megan's house and caught a glimpse of what looked like Alex's car turning left off the main road onto the single-track road that led past the start of the Ben Calder path and, beyond that, to the upper car park where the gorge walk began. Finella wondered if, instead of following Vicky, Alex was going up the Ben; he was up there so often these days. That would be a relief. Maybe everything that had happened that morning was out of proportion in her head. Perhaps Alex regretted his behaviour and was going for a walk to clear his head. But she had to know.

She put her foot to the floor and misjudged a sharp bend. Too fast for comfort, the momentum pulled her car onto the far side of the road, towards the ditch that ran alongside it.

Advice from someone, her father probably, flashed through her mind. *Accelerate out of a skid.* She slipped into a lower gear, pressed down on the accelerator and forced the car back onto the correct side of the road, just before another bend, which she took much slower, praying not to meet another car on the narrow road. Ahead was the entrance to the lower car park where the Ben path started, and she caught a glimpse of Alex's car disappearing beyond it. Where was he going? She felt determined to follow him but her hands were shaking, not only from the almost-accident but from the increasing agony in her back. She pulled over, gripped the wheel, and took deep breaths, queasy with pain. Her body was drenched in sweat, and she wasn't sure she could drive much further.

She rummaged in her bag and pulled out her phone. Maybe Vicky was at home, in which case there was no need to keep following Alex.

But there was no reply from Vicky's landline and her mobile number connected straight to a familiar message around Glasdrum: *The number you have dialled is unavailable.*

Vicky was somewhere with no phone signal.

Finella recalled Vicky mentioning several times how much she liked to visit the ancient graveyard through the gorge. Her obsession with it was a little odd, frankly, but Vicky had taken Finella's kids there on several occasions for picnics and Finella had been pleased at the time; the kids had loved it. Alex had been furious. 'There's no phone signal up there. What if one of them had an accident? You've seen the "Danger of Death" sign at the start of the path.'

'Alex, we played all over the place when we were kids.'

'It's different now,' he'd grumbled.

Surely Vicky wouldn't have got a sentimental idea about going to the graveyard before she left Glasdrum, despite the deteriorating weather? It seemed unlikely but Finella had decided to continue the couple of miles to the end car park to check, if for no other reason than to find out what Alex was doing. It wouldn't take more than ten minutes and then she'd go to the hospital.

Low mist shrouded the hills, and the upper road was deserted as Finella continued into the barren landscape, her windscreen wipers now on double speed. She tried to shake her sense of impending disaster but it settled like a heavy weight on her shoulders.

The narrow road, with passing places marked by rusting, diamond-shaped signs, snaked beneath rocky crags and between large boulders dumped by glaciers. Finella crossed a wooden bridge over a fast-flowing burn and arrived in the upper car park at the road's end.

Alex's empty car was sitting near the entrance.

Finella drove past it and saw, at the far end, Vicky's old banger. A couple of other cars and a jeep were parked in-between, most likely hill walkers who had set off early to tackle one of the many Munros in the areas. In decent weather the car park would be chock-a-block with vehicles, but with the rain lashing down only the hardiest of walkers would have ventured out.

Finella pulled in beside Vicky's car, her feeling of dread almost overwhelming her. She felt close to hysteria. Was she scared for Vicky? Or was she even scared for Alex? They were both so secretive; Vicky with her mysterious past and her hatred of men, and Alex with his outbursts of anger, the incessant walks up the Ben, a suspected affair with Catriona, and his attempted seduction of Sarah. Finella was tempted to drive away and leave them both to their fate.

The seconds ticked past as she sat in the car trying to decide what to do. She wiped the condensation off the window and spotted the sign at the start of the path: Danger of Death. Locals considered it an exaggeration; it was mostly dangerous to sheep and deer who were chased over the edge by dogs but people had lost their lives, too. During bad weather, streams cascaded down from the mountaintops, eroded the path and sent rocks and mud plummeting down the steep slopes towards the boulder-strewn river.

Finella got out of her car, the pain in both her heart and her back making her immune to the heavy drops of water that flattened her hair against her head. On autopilot and oblivious to the inappropriateness of the court shoes she had slipped her feet into when she'd left the house, she set off along the rough path, stumbling yet compelled to continue, dreading what she was going to find.

The first few hundred metres of the path cut across a gentle incline, trees on either side, the river hidden from view, then the path rose steeply, hugging the side of the mountain as the ground dropped away. A few trees clung at a strange angle to the hillside, while the water thundered far below. Finella had been through the gorge many times when younger but she was now out of shape, in pain and wearing ridiculous shoes; progress was slow as she inched along, her back against the rock face, crossing overflowing burns with careful steps. She thought she heard shouting but it was hard to tell over the noise of the waterfalls that crashed onto the path from above.

When she reached the part of the path that veered outwards around a rocky crag, with wooden walkways bolted to the rock face, she caught sight of Vicky and Alex.

Vicky was on her knees, bending over the edge of the cliff. Beside her, Alex's head and arm were visible. The rest of his body was dangling over the twenty-metre drop. If he fell, he'd have no chance.

Finella stopped, stunned, as the torrential rain continued to hammer down. She was only a few metres from them. What was going on? Had Vicky pushed him over?

Vicky must have sensed her presence and she turned, horror etched on her face when she spotted Finella.

Finella stared back, trying to work out what was going on, but black spots danced in front of her eyes and she clung to the wooden rail as though to stop herself from falling. Vicky shouted something but she couldn't make out what it was as she blinked rainwater out of her eyes and tried to shake the dizziness from her head. She still couldn't tell what was happening. Was Vicky helping Alex or… *trying to kill him*?

Chapter Twenty-Seven
VICKY

Friday, 20 May 2005, 9.45am

The rain was coming down hard as Vicky parked then hurried away from the upper car park and along the rough path. She dodged the rocks and jumped the streams that crossed the path through specially dug trenches.

This is silly, she told herself. She was getting soaked and time was passing. But something drove her on, a sense of family bond and a terrible fear that she might never be able to return to Glasdrum, that she might never again have the chance to see the last resting place of the grandmother who had meant so much to her.

Despite her misgivings, she continued, bent against the rain, lost in her thought. At the highest part of the path, just beyond the series of wooden walkways, she peered over the edge at the gushing white waters that pounded the rocks far below, then lifted her face to the sky to feel the rain against her face and to look at the beauty of the jagged mountain pass above her. She was going to miss this place, its rawness, its sense of escape.

Over the racket from the wind, Vicky heard a crunching noise behind her and spun round: Alex.

She opened her mouth to scream but the wind whipped the sound away. Alex put a hand out and Vicky stepped backwards, closer to the edge. Glancing down, she corrected herself then faced Alex, who took another step towards her.

'What were you doing at my house? I told you to stay away from my wife and my children. We don't know who you are.'

Vicky wanted to run but he was blocking her way.

Alex stood with his hands on his hips, seemingly oblivious to the rain driving against his face. 'There's something about you that really bugs me. I don't trust secretive women. What is it you're hiding, *Vicky*?'

'You have been trying to destroy my life, and my daughter's, just because I refused to have sex with you. I hate you for that.'

He grinned, his teeth white against his tanned face, his foppish hair plastered against his forehead. 'I only wanted to have sex because I was drunk. That's when I go after cheap tarts like you.'

He took a step closer and Vicky stumbled backwards and fell to the ground, wincing when she landed on a sharp rock.

Alex towered over her. 'When I find out who you really are, I'm sure it'll make a fine story for the town gossips.'

'Why are you doing this to me?'

'You ruined my marriage.'

'That wasn't my fault!' Vicky scrambled to her feet and, in a surge of pure rage, shoved him as hard as she could. He stumbled sideways and she pushed him again. This time he lost his footing and fell onto all fours, one leg slipping over the edge. His arm grasped at a young tree that was growing out of the top of the cliff face but his other leg slipped over the side and left him dangling, both hands clinging onto the sapling.

'Help!' Panic was etched on his face.

She leant towards him. 'You're a murderer and a rapist. I hope you die.' She started to walk away.

'Don't leave me! Please!' He was scrambling with his feet to try to swing himself back up onto the path. 'Vicky! I've never murdered or raped anyone.'

Something in his voice made her pause. The surge of anger she'd felt was receding and the situation was sinking in. Could she actually leave him to die? She turned back, and saw relief on his face.

'Why should I help you after what you've done to me and my daughter?'

'I was curious, all right! And I'm sorry. Please help me up.'

'Did the people you killed on the mountain beg forgiveness like this, too? You didn't show them any mercy!'

'What the fuck are you talking about?' he said, struggling to concentrate on what Vicky was saying while keeping his grip on the tree. 'I'm no killer, you stupid woman!'

Vicky panicked as Alex struggled to grip the young tree he was clinging to. She couldn't watch him plunge to his death no matter what he'd done, so she threw herself onto her knees and tried to grab his coat. He had braced his feet against the rocks and now had his arms wrapped around the slender sapling. His weight could uproot it at any moment.

'If you're not the Mist Murderer, then who is?'

With a strangled sob, Alex shouted at Vicky, 'It's Catriona.'

'*Catriona the journalist*?'

'She's not a journalist. She made that up. She made everything up!'

'Why?'

'Vicky, I'm going to fall, I can't hold on much longer.'

Shaking off her astonishment at his accusation of Catriona, Vicky leant out to grab more of Alex's coat. It was impossible to get a grip; he was dropping lower as the tree was slowly uprooted. A vision of Louise flashed through her mind; Vicky couldn't put her life in jeopardy. She sat back on her knees, scared Alex would drag her over the edge with him.

He looked petrified as he suddenly let go of the tree and tried to swing himself up towards the path. One hand made it and he grabbed a handful of bracken. Then he got the other arm up. Vicky tried to brace herself against the ground and take hold of his arms, to hold him in place. But he was slipping back. Their eyes met. 'Why did she do it?' she asked.

Still clutching the bracken, Alex stammered, 'Her father abused her when she was in her teens. When she came back to Glasdrum last year I was up the hill with her when we met him. He was being sickeningly charming, acting as if he was Dad of the Year, telling me how happy he was that Catriona had come home. And the next thing I knew she had walked with him to the edge of the gully then pushed him over. I didn't even blame her; I partly wished I'd done it myself to the evil bastard.'

A yell escaped Alex's lips as some more of the bracken slipped out of his hand.

'And the others?' Vicky asked as she continued trying to pull Alex's arms further onto the path. 'Why did Catriona kill the others?' she shouted, over the crescendo of noise, her arms aching from holding Alex.

'I think she got a taste for it. She said she'd accuse me of killing her father if I told anyone.' Hysteria rose in Alex's voice as some earth and rocks were dislodged by his feet and he scrambled to gain a hold on the cliff. 'I followed her up that hill so many times to stop her but I couldn't be there all the time. I… I didn't know what to do. Catriona was insane and she had it in for me because I didn't help her when she was young.' Alex's eyes suddenly looked beyond Vicky. 'My God, Finella!'

Vicky turned. Finella was standing on the wooden walkway only ten feet away, her face deathly pale. 'Finella! Help us!' Vicky shouted but Finella didn't move.

Vicky felt Alex's arms slither from her grip and she shrieked. She buried her head in her hands, unable to watch as he bounced off the rocks on his final journey.

Chapter Twenty-Eight
MEGAN

Friday, 20 May 2005, 10am

Megan looked at her father in shock. She backed away as Donald came towards her in the hall of their house.

'Dad!' she exclaimed, then repeated it, as a question, 'Dad?' She glanced at Lewis but he had his head down, staring at the floor. What was going on? It was as though Lewis already knew…

She approached her brother, unable to make eye contact with what felt like the ghost of her father. 'How long have you known?'

After glancing uncomfortably at their father, Lewis cast his eyes downwards again and Megan felt a surge of fury. All that grief and worrying! For nothing, it seemed. She turned her attention to her father. 'And you…' She pointed with her left hand. 'You…' she sputtered, speechless for once. She continued stabbing the air in front of her Dad for a few moments before the fight went out of her. She felt light-headed and sat on the bottom step.

'It's been a shock, pet. Come into the kitchen where it's warm.' Donald walked over to her, took her good elbow and guided her to her feet. 'What the hell are you wearing?' he asked, taking in her strange attire. Megan stared at him; it really was her dad, talking to her as though he was just back from a short trip.

'It's a hospital gown.'

'You'll catch your death in this weather. What were you thinking? Come and have a hot drink.'

Megan allowed her father to take her into the kitchen, settle her on a chair beside the ancient Aga, and drape a coat around her shoulders. Lewis slipped into the kitchen and sat at the opposite side of the room to Megan, looking wary, as Donald busied himself making tea.

Being dead had aged him. When Megan had last seen him he had been a hearty-looking sixty-five, but now his darkish grey hair was a shock of white, his once rotund farmer's face was gaunt and he had the mottled look of a serious drinker. There was a deep sadness in his eyes that hadn't been there before.

'Just milk?' he asked and she nodded. An uncomfortable silence had fallen and Megan couldn't bring herself to break it. Part of her wanted to laugh hysterically. A teaspoon chinked against the side of a mug as Donald heaped sugar into his tea, then clattered into the sink when he discarded it, and still none of them spoke. Where would they start?

Megan felt overwhelmed. The ache in her arm and head were worsening; the codeine was wearing off. Out of the blue, the situation hit home like an iron being smashed against her skull and she started to shake. Tea sloshed over the side of her mug and she placed it carefully back onto the table.

'You're looking awful peaky, pet,' said Donald.

Lewis sprang to his feet. 'She looks a fucking mess and it's your bloody fault,' he shouted. Donald stayed where he was and bowed his head as Lewis continued. 'Every goddamn thing that's gone wrong in our lives is your fault and I wish you really had died that night.' Lewis sat back down again. He seemed shocked at his own outburst.

Still trembling, Megan nevertheless felt better. Lewis's outburst had assured her the situation wasn't normal; she wasn't in a parallel universe where murdered people returned to make tea as though nothing had happened.

The three of them sat a while longer, looking cautiously at one another. Donald took a flask from his pocket and poured a dash of something into his tea. Eventually Megan couldn't bear it. 'So who the fuck did I find buried out there? *Wearing your ring!*'

Donald cleared his throat. He took a gulp from his mug, unable to meet Megan's eye.

Lewis spoke up. 'Remember Gregor's stepdad, Callum?'

Megan nodded. She vaguely remembered him. He was one of the many wasters who had hung about the churchyard drinking cheap booze and scaring tourists. 'It was him! Morag said he'd disappeared that night, right enough. Poor bastard; murdered and nobody even noticed.'

Donald lifted his eyes. 'It wasn't murder, pet. And I'm sorry you had to find him. Can't have been easy. Especially if you thought it was me.'

Megan got up and pointed at her dad. 'Actually I didn't give a shit that it was you. You were dead to me a long time ago.' She paced across the kitchen, wincing at the pain in her arm, unaccustomed to the weight of the cast. 'So, how did Callum end up in there? Let me guess, he keeled over dead and you thought it kindest to take care of the burial. Save Morag a few bob paying for a lair?'

'It was an accident.'

'Oh boy, I bet it was. I bet your ring just fell onto his finger *by accident.*'

'Callum found out I was Gregor's dad and he turned up that Hogmanay demanding money to pay for his upbringing. It was half an hour or so after Gregor himself had been to see me, shouting at me about how I'd abandoned his mum, so I wasn't in the best of moods. Lewis had come home and chased Gregor away. But I was left with that drunkard, Callum, shouting at me, then Lewis started giving me grief about having a fling with Morag, and then your mum joined in—'

Megan gasped. 'Mum was there? She knows about this?' Megan felt her world turn upside down. Her mother had kept this secret. Maybe that was what had destroyed her brain. 'What a bloody mess,' muttered Megan.

Donald nodded. 'Aye, it's a shambles, right enough.'

Megan stared at her dad, bemused by his choice of words. A shambles was when the boys got their P.E. kits jumbled up, not people being accidently killed and buried. 'So what happened then?' she asked, weary to her bones.

'I kept telling Callum to piss off home but he wasn't having it. He had a go at me, and Lewis tried to get him off me but I lost my rag and hit him with a shovel. Harder than I meant to.'

'Jesus,' Megan's hand flew to her mouth. 'Just like that?'

'If I could go back and fix it, pet, I would. But I can't. I killed a man and I've had to live with that.'

'So you buried him with your ring so people would think it was you and then you just buggered off?'

'I've been on the Hebrides, living rough mainly. It's been hard, especially in the winter. But I don't deserve anything better after what I did.'

Megan tried to take it all in. 'Why didn't you go to the police if it was an accident?'

'I panicked. Got Lewis to help me dump Callum's body in the hole I'd dug to fix the old tank, then I scarpered. I wasn't thinking about the long term. But once it seemed obvious nobody had missed Callum, I didn't feel I could return. I knew Murdina would never forgive me, and rightly so.'

'Mum knows about it?'

Donald nodded. 'If I'd known what it would do to her...'

'How do you know?'

Donald nodded his head in Lewis's direction. 'He knew where to find me and came to tell me you'd dug up the body. He'd tracked me down before, not long after it happened.'

'That's why you were so depressed after Dad disappeared, Lewis. You knew what he'd done. You'd helped him cover it up!'

Lewis nodded. 'I'm sorry, Megs. I kept quiet to protect Mum. It took me a while but I found him in the Outer Hebrides. I wanted to see if he was all right, I suppose; it was an accident after all. But I could see he wanted to punish himself so I left him to it and went to London. I couldn't face staying in Glasdrum. It was only meeting Sarah that made me want to come back. She's given me the confidence to deal with the past.' Lewis got to his feet. 'I better get up to the hospital to see her.'

'So,' said Megan, 'are you telling me nobody even missed Callum?'

Donald shrugged. 'Nobody reported him missing.'

Megan remembered her conversation with Morag the day she took Gregor's drugs. 'Morag thought Callum had buggered off. That's what the men in her life do.' Megan looked from her dad to her brother and back again. 'Hang on. That's what the men in my life do, too! Who would have thought Morag and I would have so much in common? Plus, of course, she's my half-brother's mother. Maybe we should give her a ring and invite her to this little reunion we're having.' Even as she voiced her venom against men, thoughts of Johnny flickered through her mind. He had not abandoned her; she had pushed him away.

'It's not funny, Megan,' said Lewis.

'And I'm not fucking laughing, am I?' She turned her attention back to Donald. 'So what brought you back? Other than hearing from Lewis that I'd dug you up?'

Donald cleared his throat. 'I read an article in the *Journal* about the Mist Murderer by yon Catriona MacKinnon. I always kept up with local news.'

'That'll be your great sense of community, right?'

Donald ignored Megan's sarcasm and continued. 'Sadly, I've an inkling who is pushing these men off the hill. And if I'm right, they aren't going to stop.'

'Come on, Dad, give us a break. All that Mist Murderer bollocks is just Catriona trying to make herself into a big shot journalist. They were accidents; overconfident morons who didn't look where they're going on a misty mountain cliff.'

'It's Catriona.'

'I know! Her name is plastered over every article. She's trying to make a name for herself.'

'No, Catriona's been killing those hill walkers.'

'*What?*'

'When I read her dad had fallen and died last year, I straight away didn't believe it. I'd known Angus since we were lads and he'd never have made a mistake like that. The only person up there with him was Catriona.'

'Why would she kill her own father?' Megan stared incredulously then muttered, 'Actually that's a stupid question. This morning I can think of at least one good reason for doing your dad in.'

'I think he'd been interfering with her.'

'He was a kiddie-fiddler? A fucking paedo?' Megan sat up straighter. 'How do you know that?'

Donald gave an enormous sigh. 'Just bits and pieces. Stuff he used to say when we were younger. He'd joke about young girls… and a couple of times I saw them together when Catriona was a teenager. There was something in her eyes when she looked at him…'

'And you did nothing?'

Donald hung his head in shame. 'I distanced myself from him. Put it out of my mind. Gave him the benefit of the doubt, I suppose. I didn't have anything concrete to go on and in those days nobody talked about stuff like that. I've regretted not speaking up about Catriona every day of my life.'

'But even if she pushed Angus over the gully, why would she kill the others? They must be horrible coincidences.'

'Maybe… or else once she started killing she couldn't stop.'

'That's a ridiculous idea.'

'Let's hope so, but I can't get it out of my head. And I can't live out there on my own any more. I decided to come back, in case it really is Catriona. Someone needs to stop her. And I need to face what I did, too. I'm finding it harder every day to live with my conscience. Something about living rough all these years; I've had time to think about how I've lived my life and I've not much to be proud of.'

Megan felt her heart squeeze in disappointment. Donald had come back to Glasdrum with an insane notion of stopping a serial killer and a vague sense of guilt. It wasn't to see her or her boys. Megan laughed bitterly and stood up. 'I'll let you get on with your killer-chasing work then.'

Her phone rang and she looked at the caller: Finella. She wasn't in the mood to listen to her moaning about her husband and children so she ignored it. 'I'm going upstairs to change,' she said and left her father and brother in the kitchen.

Her phone rang again, persistent, and she threw it onto her bed. Megan took off the hospital gowns, struggled into her running trousers and a baggy T-shirt, then pulled a zip-up fleece onto one arm, leaving her cast free on the other side. When the phone rang a third time she flipped it open with an exasperated huff. 'Finella?'

'No, it's Vicky. Finella's with me but she's not well. I'm taking her to hospital. We're in the car just now. I've had to phone the police…' Vicky gave a strangled sob.

'The police?'

'Alex is dead. He fell in the gorge.'

'How do you know?'

'I was there. Finella too.'

Megan was thrown. What on earth they all doing through the gorge together in weather like this? Especially

Finella. It was too much to take in. 'Sorry, Vicky, but I've got a bit of a crisis here myself at the moment.' Something made her hesitate to tell Vicky about her dad reappearing; she was still getting to grips with that herself.

'Guess what Alex told me just before he died?' asked Vicky.

'I've got to go, Vicky! I don't care what Alex's dying words were.'

'It's important! He said Catriona was the Mist Murderer. He'd been trying to stop her.'

'Jesus! That's what my dad just said too.'

'Your dad?'

'Yeah, Donald's not dead after all.'

There was silence at the other end of the phone. Megan could almost hear Vicky's brain whirring. 'Donald's alive? Then who—' Vicky was cut off by a loud moaning noise.

'Fuck,' said Vicky, who normally never swore. 'I've got to get Finella to hospital. I've pulled over but she's in a terrible state.'

A frightening thought occurred to Megan. 'Are you sure about Catriona?'

'Alex seemed certain and it makes sense. She started with her dad. He'd been, you know...'

'...abusing her,' Megan finished the sentence, then added, 'Catriona's at the hospital with Sarah.'

'What? I can't hear you properly.'

Megan raised her voice. 'Catriona was sitting with Sarah in hospital when I left. About an hour ago.'

'What if Sarah had found out what Catriona's been doing? Maybe that was what she kept ringing me about yesterday! You have to go back to the hospital, Megan.'

'But you're going there now with Finella.'

'I'm only dropping her off. I can't get involved. I have to get away from this town. Alex had been digging about in my past and I can't risk staying in case he'd told anyone, or even got in touch with Louise's dad. He'll kill me if he finds me, Megan.'

The line went dead before Megan got a chance to respond. A huge wave of exhaustion swept over her. Everything ached, including her heart. She should have been delighted to discover her father was alive; instead she felt numb. And her best friend was being driven out of town because Megan hadn't kept her promise to keep quiet about Sarah and Alex kissing – which had turned out to be of no importance.

Megan wanted to lie down and sleep for a hundred years but she couldn't rest yet. Sarah was in hospital with amnesia and a killer by her bedside. 'Lewis!' she yelled, running to the top of the stairs, hoping she hadn't missed him. 'I'll come with you to the hospital. Vicky's already phoned the police.'

At the top of the stairs her legs wobbled and she grabbed the bannister before she toppled forward. How ironic, she thought, if she fell down the stairs and knocked herself out against the old iron just as Sarah had done. Iron, ironic… Old Megan would have laughed, but new Megan wasn't finding life amusing any more. New Megan was longing for a life of security and stability. She thought about her father, Callum and Morag and had a frightening glimpse of what the future might hold for her if she carried on with her reckless lifestyle. As she went down the stairs as fast as she was able, she decided she'd have a proper talk with Johnny when all this trouble was over and see if he'd have her back. Maybe they could be a proper family again. But first: 'Dad! Lewis!' She tried to shout but her voice was feeble. *What a bloody wreck I am*, she thought. *It's definitely time for some changes.*

Donald was on his way out the front door. 'You should get to bed, pet.'

'I need to get to the hospital, Dad. You're right! Catriona is the Mist Murderer. And she's by herself with Sarah.'

'What?' said Lewis, his voice cracking in panic. 'Shit, let's get over there.'

'Sarah won't be in danger,' said Donald. 'Catriona's targeting men that remind her of her dad.'

'But if Catriona knows Sarah had found out about her...' Megan tailed off. She was starting to feel extremely ill. 'Vicky phoned me to say Alex has died. They had thought Alex was the killer but it turns out he'd been trying to stop Catriona. I think Sarah might have found out.'

'I can't believe this,' said Lewis, heading for the door. 'God, I wish I'd never come back to this bloody town.'

'I'm coming with you,' said Megan, hobbling after him, followed by Donald. 'Let's hope we're not too late.'

Chapter Twenty-Nine
CATRIONA

Friday, 20 May 2005, 10.15am

Catriona had her hand on Sarah's chest as she lay on her hospital bed, holding her down. For a moment she'd been consumed by rage that Sarah might have discovered the truth about her, but faced with Sarah's terrified face as she lay like a child in the bed, Catriona eased off the pressure then sat down. She felt close to tears; everything was getting too much. Life was unbearable.

'I'm sorry, Sarah. I shouldn't have scared you.' Catriona looked down in misery.

'Hey, what's up?'

'Life is shit, you know?'

'Is it because of Alex?'

'What do you know about that?'

Sarah frowned. 'I can't quite remember but I thought he was trying to hurt you last night.'

'You phoned me yesterday and said you saw me and Alex going into his office.'

'Yeah, that's it. I was worried. Alex isn't nice.'

'Men aren't nice.'

'They're not all bad.'

'You'll find out one day they're all rotten to the core.'

Something in Sarah's look of sympathy made Catriona's heart

feel as though it was going to burst. All her life she had needed someone to help her and nobody ever had. 'Alex did hurt me, but not last night. The damage he did was many years ago.'

'What did he do?'

'It's what he *didn't do* that makes me hate him.' Catriona chewed her lower lip, biting back tears. *Keep quiet. Don't tell her anything.* But she couldn't keep it to herself any longer. 'He knew what my father was doing to me but he didn't help me.'

'What did your father do to you?' asked Sarah but Catriona could see understanding and horror spread over her face.

'The worst thing a father could do to his daughter.'

'Oh,' Sarah's eye's flooded with tears. Catriona, too, couldn't stem the flow. When she was younger she hadn't cried but as time had passed she'd felt more, rather than less, upset about what had happened. In the last few years she'd been crying every night and even during the day when something triggered her feelings of disgust and rage. The first time in years she had got to sleep without sobbing was the night after she'd disposed of her dad. The relief she'd felt had been immense. He was gone, and with him some of the terrible memories had started to fade. But it hadn't been enough.

Sarah interrupted her thoughts. 'What did Alex have to do with it?'

'We went out together for a couple of years when we were in our mid-teens. I was in love with him. I thought he was going to marry me and take me away from Glasdrum and... and... *him.*'

'It didn't work out?'

'One night I told Alex what *he* was doing to me. I thought he'd save me.' A harsh laugh escaped Catriona's lips. 'I couldn't have been more wrong.'

'What did he do?'

'He left me. I was damaged goods and Alex wanted perfection. He went off to university and took up with the wholesome Finella. I realise looking back that he had never intended being with me long term; I was an easy lay for a horny teenage boy.'

'God, Catriona, this is awful. No wonder you hate him. You should go to the police about your dad.'

'The police can't give me what I want.'

'What's that?'

'Revenge.'

'But... how?'

'I want to expose him for what he really is.'

'The Mist Murderer?'

Catriona gasped in relief. Sarah still believed Alex might be the killer. All was not lost.

She'd been worried all her hard work to set Alex up as a killer would have come to nothing if Sarah had overheard her and Alex talking the previous evening in the office. Catriona knew there would never be enough evidence for a court to convict Alex of murder but the finger of suspicion was all that was required to ensure his life, with his perfect wife and three perfect children, would be in tatters. That would make Catriona very happy.

What if Sarah was bluffing? Catriona searched her face but couldn't see any signs that she was lying. And surely if Sarah suspected Catriona of being a killer she would have phoned the police, or at least told her boyfriend's sister, that annoying little cow Megan. What trouble she'd caused for Catriona, always up the hill running, like some kind of mountain patrol. But Catriona had been clever; she'd made sure Megan saw Alex but had kept herself hidden, always wearing different jackets, hood up, with men's trousers and boots.

The first real sense of pleasure Catriona remembered feeling in her whole life had been the fear on her father's face when she pushed him over the gully cliff face, closely followed by the horror on Alex's as he watched. 'You could have stopped what he was doing to me all those years ago,' Catriona had shouted at Alex. 'And if you tell anyone what I've just done, I'll say *you* pushed him during an argument. Everyone knows you don't like each other.'

'I never liked him because of what you told me!'

'You *not liking* him didn't help me one bit! You have no idea what I endured at the hands of that man and you were the only person I confided in. You could have saved me, but you left.'

'I'm sorry, Catriona. I really am.'

'You will be.' She had left Alex there on the mountain, traumatised by what he'd witnessed. That evening, Catriona reported her father missing and his body was found the following morning by his shocked Mountain Rescue colleagues.

Over the winter months, Catriona had watched Alex's life with Finella disintegrate as Catriona dreamed of repeating the incident with another man. It had felt so good, and she hated them all. During a couple of short stays in mental health units while in Edinburgh, Catriona had met other women who had suffered abuse in various forms by the men in their lives. Alex, cowardly as ever, had been too scared of repercussions to report what Catriona had done, and he took to tailing her up the hill whenever she phoned him to say she planned to kill again. At first she had only told him that to torment him, to force him to try to stop her and to bring chaos to his orderly life. But one day in April, Catriona found herself alone on the hill in thick mist, a lone male walker ahead of her.

It had been easy to lure him to the edge with her beautiful blue eyes; men were suckers for a pretty face. *Come and see what I found over here, just where the rocks drop away, it's the most wonderful thing…* The man had followed, eager to see what this stunning woman wanted to show him. A rare flower? A fossil? An unexpected view? And when he had stood beside the cliff, looking at her with hungry eyes like her father, Catriona had taken a step towards him. She had reached out and touched his arm, felt the solidness of his body, a slight resistance to her first tentative push. That was what had got her. The man had pushed back against her hand, and the internal mist had clouded her brain and stopped her thinking. Instinct had taken over and a surge of adrenaline had allowed her to push the man off his feet, over the edge, his screams swallowed up by the vastness of the landscape.

Catriona shook the memory out of her mind and looked at Sarah. 'Yes, Alex is my suspect. Well done for working it out.'

She turned at the sound of heavy footsteps approaching from behind. With a start she recognised the man: Donald MacDonald, her dad's childhood friend. Bile rose in her throat at the sight of him and the memories he brought back. Catriona was sure Donald had known what was going on. She'd heard her father joking with him about how much he liked pretty, young girls, and Donald had seen the way Angus touched her, reminding her what was in store for her during the hours of darkness. Hatred raged through her as it did when she saw any man who reminded her of her father.

'Catriona,' said Donald. 'What's going on?'

In that instant she was certain he knew what she'd done. Perhaps everyone did. Donald's son Lewis pushed past his father and went straight to Sarah and they embraced. Behind them, two medics were coming towards the bed. Like a cornered animal, Catriona stared with wide eyes.

Donald spoke to her. 'I've come to help, Catriona. Come with me.'

Catriona looked back and forth between Donald and the bed where Lewis and Sarah had their arms wrapped around one another.

She got to her feet and took Donald's outstretched arm. He nodded courteously at the medical staff as he led Catriona out of the hospital to Lewis's car. 'Where can I take you?' he asked her.

She shrugged. 'I've nowhere to go. Never have done.'

They sat in silence in the car park for a few minutes until Catriona spoke again. 'Why did you come for me?'

'I know why you're doing what you're doing. And I was worried you might think Sarah had found out…'

'Sarah was in no danger from me. I would never harm another girl.'

'Just men like your father.'

A bleak look settled onto Catriona's face as she stared out of the car window into the distance. After another few minutes she asked, 'Want to go for a walk with me? I can show you what

I did to them.'

'If it'll make you feel better, then yes, I'll come with you.'

Donald drove to the church car park. He followed Catriona when she set off up the Ben path, struggling to keep up with her as she forged ahead, her head held high, oblivious to the weather, while Donald hunched forwards trying to shelter his face, stumbling from time to time. They plodded upwards for an hour and were nearing the gully cliff face when Catriona stopped.

'Why have you come up here with me when you know what I've been doing?' she shouted to be heard above the wind that ripped around the side of the mountain.

'So you can make peace with yourself before they come for you. It's important. I've done bad things in my life and I've spent the last five years trying to come to terms with them.'

'What makes you think I'll be caught?'

'Everybody knows what you did. Alex told them before he died...'

'Alex is dead?' Catriona felt cheated. Her plans to make his life miserable would come to nothing.

'He fell to his death in the gorge this morning. He knew about your father, didn't he?'

'Yes, he knew and did nothing, just like you.'

Donald hung his head. 'I could have saved you but I didn't. For that, I'm more sorry than you'll ever know.'

Donald's frankness threw her. Memories crowded into her head; her fear lying in bed, waiting... and the resentment she'd felt that the whole town thought he was a hero. It had felt so good when she'd pushed him away from her forever. There had been nobody to save him, and it had felt like saving herself.

She looked at Donald, her father's friend, the man who, like Alex, had kept quiet. She felt, again, that desire for salvation.

With a primeval roar, Catriona ran at him. She pushed him and was surprised when she met with no resistance. Donald stumbled sideways, teetering at the edge. Another shove and he fell. The wind muffled the thumps as his heavy frame plummeted then disappeared into the misty nether region of the mountain.

Catriona felt her chest tight with elation. Revenge was sweet but she knew it couldn't continue. She couldn't face being locked up in a cell, alone with her thoughts for hours every day.

She stepped forward and followed Donald off the mountain.

Extract from the **Glasdrum Journal,** *Thursday, 26 May 2005*

Special Tribute Edition – In memory of journalist Catriona MacKinnon

The Glasdrum community was united in collective grief this week following the tragic deaths of three local residents in separate but similar circumstances.

Local journalist Catriona MacKinnon, 38, was found at the bottom of Crofter's Gully on the afternoon of Friday, 20 May. A keen hill walker, Catriona is thought to have lost her way in the mist and fallen to her death. Her funeral took place on Tuesday and was well attended by local residents still reeling from the tragic loss, less than a year ago, of Catriona's father, Angus MacKinnon, hero of the local Mountain Rescue Team.

While searching for Catriona, who was reported missing by a colleague, the body of Donald MacDonald, 70, who had been missing from the area since early 2000, was also found at the bottom of the gully. A friend of the family has confirmed they believe Mr MacDonald, who was suffering from dementia, had returned to the area and attempted to climb Ben Calder as he had done regularly as a younger man. Police have appealed for information from anyone who might have witnessed Mr MacDonald on Ben Calder in the days leading up to his death.

In a third tragic but unrelated incident, Mr Alex Campbell, 38, partner at law firm Campbell and Co, fell to his death in a steep gorge near the foot of Ben Calder, also on Friday, 20 May. He is survived by three children and his wife, Finella, who is recovering in hospital after sustaining a serious back injury during an attempt to rescue her husband. Mr Campbell's funeral will take place on Friday, 27 May.

Police have reissued their warning to hill walkers to stay on paths, especially during misty conditions.

Reporter: Sarah Townsend

Extract from the Glasdrum Journal, Thursday, 2 June 2005

Local man Gregor Cameron, 27, is in hospital recovering from injuries sustained during a vicious gang attack. A police source confirmed that the perpetrators were thought to be drug-dealers from the Glasgow area but they have not yet been apprehended. Mr Cameron's home has been thoroughly searched and no trace of drugs found, so it is thought to have been a case of mistaken identity.

Reporter: Sarah Townsend

Extract from the listings section of the Glasdrum Journal, Thursday, 16 June 2005

Two-bedroom detached cottage for sale in spectacular location overlooking Camusmhor beach. The low asking price reflects the seller's desire for a quick sale.

Epilogue

Glasdrum remained shrouded in mist for much of the rest of summer 2005. Locals remarked on what a dreich season it had been, and tourists who would have stayed a week left after two days, with nothing to see but greyness in every direction. Locals and visitors continued to traipse up Ben Calder, regardless of the conditions, but there were no further deaths on the mountain that year; regular warnings had been erected on the path about the steep drops and frequent poor visibility. In the Stag's Head people laughed at the speculation there had been a killer on the loose.

Once Megan had recovered from the shock of her father's death, she and Lewis were surprised to discover a small inheritance from him, which they split three ways with their half-brother, Gregor. Megan used her portion to buy the cottage by the sea she had always loved.

Living at the end of Camusmhor beach made Megan wonder almost every day where Vicky and Louise had gone and whether she would see them again. She hoped life was treating them well after their sudden departure from Glasdrum and she tried not to dwell on the bargain she'd got when she bought the house at a knock-down price due to her friend's misfortune. As the years passed, Megan and Johnny's on-off relationship continued in a haphazard fashion but she got her act together work-wise and found a job at a recently opened women's refuge, which at times felt like penance for her role in making Vicky feel she had to flee from Glasdrum. Escape from domestic violence had brought Vicky to the town, and the unwanted attention of another man had caused her to leave again. Whenever Megan considered quitting her job simply because she didn't like being told what to do or her manner rubbed fellow workers up the wrong way, she thought about Vicky, kept her mouth shut and managed to hold onto the job. Doing good for vulnerable women in the refuge gave her a sense of satisfaction she had never experienced before.

Finella, too, often reflected on what had happened to Vicky. Judith was deeply unhappy after the terrible events of May 2005, although more troubled by the disappearance of Louise, her idolised best friend, than the loss of her distant father. For the twins, the death of their dad initially manifested itself in increasingly wild behaviour, but as Finella adjusted to her new position as grieving single mother, free from the shadow of Alex's put-downs, she found a renewed confidence in her parenting skills and managed to curb some of the boys' most unruly behaviour. She became a local dignitary as the great and good of the community rallied round her, horrified at Alex's tragic accident and supportive of his stoical widow. Finella adapted to the role with finesse, returning to the school's Parent Council and taking up Alex's position on other fundraising committees. By 2007, she was no longer the GP's daughter or the solicitor's wife; she was Finella Campbell, Glasdrum Community Councillor.

Sarah recovered quickly from her bang to the head, and when Lewis explained why Gregor had been in the house looking for his drugs, Sarah willingly told the police she'd tripped on the stairs and was mistaken that there had been someone else in the house. With no reason to suspect foul play, and three gruesome deaths to deal with that same day, no further investigation was undertaken, and it was presumed Megan must have phoned the ambulance before she passed out. The Inverness head office of the Journal asked if Sarah could step into Catriona's shoes on an interim basis and she did so well they soon made it permanent. She embraced small-town life, reporting on rotary club funding of new pontoons for the harbour, the launch of a new lifeboat for the expanding Glasdrum fishing economy and the controversial opening of the women's refuge. She and Lewis stayed in Murdina's house and he recovered some of his equilibrium once his father was laid to rest in a proper grave. He remained haunted by the makeshift burial he had given Callum and regularly walked to the remote wooded area to visit the spot and try to come to terms with what had happened. He felt inordinately sad for Callum, that he had been killed and nobody had missed him. To die unloved and alone was terrifying and Lewis soon asked Sarah to marry him, determined to have a family and lead a decent life to make up for his role in Callum's death.

For many years, Glasdrum thrived. Finella became a member of the Highland Tourism Board and attracted investment into the area to increase the leisure boat facilities, locking horns on several occasions with Councillors trying to increase the use of the harbour by fishing vessels.

The dark events of 2005 faded from memory as Finella and Megan's children progressed through school, with only Judith, a loner throughout high school, retaining a clear memory of her precious childhood friend, Louise.

Louise also kept hold of some recollections of Glasdrum but they were tainted by bitterness passed on to her by her mother, Vicky, as their lives lurched from one disaster to another for the next eleven years. It wasn't until 2016, when she was twenty-two, that Louise returned to Glasdrum to visit the town where she spent her formative years and from where she had been uprooted so abruptly.

But that's another story.

~

Acknowledgments

Thank you to the readers of my first novel, Daughter, Disappeared, whose positive feedback gave me the confidence to self-publish a second book.

I'm grateful to my mum, Mary, for reading and editing the book several times, as well as for endless support with my writing, and with life in general. My daughter, Rhania, has been unwaveringly supportive, and I'm also grateful to my friend and fellow author, Sarah Jane Douglas, for editing the story chapter by chapter as I wrote it.

Thanks to Emergents/Xpo North for funding editorial reports, and to the helpful folk at Reedsy, especially Ricardo and Arielle, as well as the professionals I've worked with through them: Mary-Theresa Hussey, whose developmental edits made me think about the tone and style of the book and where the story was going; DeAndra Lupu, who copy edited the book with a super eye for detail; and designer Mark Thomas, whose creativity and helpfulness is second to none.

About the Author

Fiona grew up in Fort William, graduated from Edinburgh University, then worked in London as a Recruitment Consultant before moving to Tunisia where she ran a watersports base near Sousse with her local husband (more about that at fionamacbain. com). She returned to the UK with her 6-month old daughter in 1999 and has since worked as a Customer Services Trainer, a French Tutor and an Administrator, writing in her spare time. She lives in Inverness with her two younger children.

You can follow her on Facebook @fionamacbainwriter or on Twitter @fionamacbain

Carry on reading for a sneak peak at her next novel... due out in 2018...

Chapter One – LOUISE

Saturday 30 April 2016, 2.30pm

Louise's recollection of Glasdrum was hazy. Eleven years had passed; half her lifetime. But she experienced a sense of familiarity as she stepped off the train and breathed the sea air.

With nowhere in particular to go, she heaved her rucksack onto her back and followed the other passengers out of the station, past an industrial shed circled by gulls attracted by the stench of rotting fish. A couple of young tourists held their noses and laughed.

As they approached the pedestrianised High Street, the scattering of people from the train became caught up in another group making their way along the road. Louise found herself in the centre of the melee, walking beside a couple women in long dresses, their heads covered by scarves, and she heard one of them chastise a young child in a foreign language that sounded like Arabic. A man with dark hair and shabby clothes caught up with the woman and child. He spoke brusquely, and she cast her eyes downward, pulling the scarf over her lower face.

The group swelled in size as it gathered outside a 1970s office block near the pier in the centre of the town. Distant memories of playing on that pier came back to Louise as the whiff of vinegar hit her nose from the chippy on the corner. On the steps outside the decrepit building that was perched between the road and the harbour, stood an older man in a ceremonial purple gown with heavy gold chains lying across his shoulders. He was waving in a regal fashion at the growing number of bystanders.

A sudden noise, like a giant dying seagull, started up behind the procession, and Louise turned, startled. Her laden backpack bashed against the foreign man who was now right beside her.

'I'm sorry,' she said.

'Is no problem,' said the man, with a dazzling smile. She turned away as the single, loud drone was joined by others; a pipe band, in full Highland outfit, had assembled and soon drowned out the crowd's murmurings. The tune was barely discernible but the bass drum boomed and on the steps of the offices, a plump woman of around fifty, with a smart bob and a pale blue dress, stood beside the man with the gold chain clapping her hands and stamping her high-heeled shoes. She nodded at another woman beside her, smaller, with short hair and scruffy jeans, obviously trying to get her to join in, but without success. Beside them, an Arabic man in a suit smiled but appeared uncomfortable, as though not sure if he was also being encouraged to clap and stamp.

The racket stopped and someone coughed into a megaphone.

'People of Glasdrum, please be upstanding for Provost Roseburn!'

'Aye, we're on our feet already,' said voice from the crowd.

The Provost took the megaphone but instead of using it, he addressed the crowd in a strident voice. 'If you can hear me at the back without this thing, give me a wave.'

Heads turned towards the back of the crowd and various arms flapped about.

'Excellent!' he thundered. 'Now, people of this fine town, let's get on with the business of the day: welcoming our Syrian friends to their new homes in the heart of our community.'

The Provost approached the Arabic man, shook his hand and passed him a silver key with a purple ribbon tied to it. 'This key symbolises your welcome to our community. We look forward to many years of living and working side by side, of learning about your culture and teaching you about ours.'

The Provost waited for the applause to die down before speaking again. 'Before we finish, I must urge all of you to vote on Thursday in the District Council elections. This will be the second term since we broke free from the Regional Council, something I consider to have been a resounding success! What we have achieved for our own community in the past three years without being tied to the tyranny of Inverness rule is remarkable. My daughter Finella here...' he pointed to the woman in the blue dress beside him '...worked tirelessly to negotiate funds from the windfarm company to construct new houses for locals and refugees, and once she's elected to the Council she plans to turn her attention to our rapidly declining waterfront -'

'Oi! No politics the now,' said a voice in the crowd.

Undeterred the Provost continued. '... Our town needs tourists and we need to smarten up the harbour area to secure employment for everyone, including our new residents.'

Provost Roseburn beamed at the Arabic man and started clapping. The crowd joined in and after a moment's hesitation, so did the Syrian representative, a bemused look on his face.

As the celebratory noises quietened, screams were heard. People turned towards the pier where a blonde woman with a pram was shrieking and pointing into the water.

The crowd surged towards the edge of the quay and Louise followed. A man in a business suit was floating face down in the scummy water in the corner of the harbour.

~